D0365344

No Holiday for Crime

No Holiday
for Crime

DELL SHANNON

WILLIAM MORROW & COMPANY, INC.
NEW YORK 1973

Printed in the United States of America.

Linington, Elizabeth
    No holiday for crime.

    I. Title.
PZ4.L756Np   [PS3562.I515]   813'.5'4   72-13048
ISBN 0-688-00145-9

But human bodies are sic fools
For a' their colleges and schools,
That when nae real ills perplex them
They make enow themselves to vex them.
                    —Robert Burns

Let a bear robbed of her whelps meet a man,
rather than a fool in his folly.
                    —Proverbs 17:12

1

"I CAN JUST HEAR the whole force laughing at me," said Lieutenant Goldberg, formerly of Central Robbery and Theft LAPD. He squinted up dolorously from the hospital bed.

"Don't be such an egotist," said Lieutenant Mendoza, formerly of Central Homicide. "We're too busy to think about you, and you're nearly over it anyway."

Lieutenant Goldberg's last investigation for Robbery and Theft had been a case involving stolen goods smuggled across the Mexican border. The stolen goods had been a dozen cagefuls of exotic tropical parrots, and Goldberg and one of the San Diego detectives had subsequently succumbed to parrot fever.

"It's a judgment on me," he said gloomily, "for laughing at you when you caught the measles from the twins. Have you caught up to that burglar yet?"

Mendoza's grin gave way to a scowl. He stabbed his cigarette out in the ashtray on the bedside table. "Set me chasing burglars—I might as well be riding a black-and-white again," he said. "No, we haven't."

"They say it's a sign of age," said Goldberg, "when a man can't adjust to change." He sneezed and reached for Kleenex.

"*¡Vaya al diablo!*" said Mendoza amiably. "I'm not the old dog learning new tricks—that'll be you, and I wish you joy of working under Pat."

"Don't be petty, Luis," said Goldberg. "The Jews and

the Irish always get on fine. So what about that houseman —has he pulled any more jobs?"

Mendoza stood up and yanked his cuffs down automatically, straightened his tie. As usual he was dapper in gray Italian silk, snowy shirt, discreet tie, his hairline moustache neat. "That nurse said ten minutes. Well, if it's the same boy, yes, he has, but I'm not sure of that, and we've got no leads at all. Don't remind me. And don't offer any suggestions—it's not your job any longer."

"Oh, well," said Goldberg philosophically, "you can't win 'em all. At least I'm getting out of this damned place tomorrow. Thanks for dropping in, Luis—say hello to the gang, hah?"

"You'll be adjusting to change in no time," said Mendoza. "Merry Christmas, Saul."

"And a happy Hanukkah to you, Luis."

Waiting for the elevator, Mendoza thought about the burglar and frowned. Change be damned, he thought. Doubtless they'd settle down to it, but to be dealing with housebreakers like any team in a squad car— "*¡Por mi vida!*" he muttered.

Change had come to Central Headquarters LAPD in the name of greater efficiency after the powers that be had discussed and decided. Los Angeles might boast the top force anywhere, but it was also the smallest police force any city of size possessed. Keeping it at top performance, the changes sometimes came. Robbery and Theft had been dissolved as a separate department, last month, and the new bureau of Robbery-Homicide created; that was the major change, but there'd been a few others. Captain Medina had got shot up by a hood a couple of months back, and retired a year early, so Pat Callaghan had got his step in rank and Goldberg was transferred up to an expanded Narco bureau, with most of the men from his old office. Mendoza had inherited Robbery's policewoman, Wanda Larsen—he couldn't imagine why, there wasn't much for her to do—and a couple of men, Detectives Rich Conway and Emil Shogart. With that small addition to staff, Robbery-Homicide now covered all theft and death on the Central beat, and these days that could be quite a job; as usual, they were busy.

Getting into the big black Ferrari downstairs, Mendoza glanced at his watch. Two-fifteen; he'd stopped to see Goldberg after lunch. In another six hours it would be officially Christmas Eve: a mild, clear December Sunday: one time, like a few others in the year, when police officers got reminded that the hoods and crooks didn't take holidays off. Alone of all the men in the office, Sergeant John Palliser would be off tomorrow: to the others it would be just another day, hopefully a quiet one. But there were always cases to work; Mendoza reviewed what they had on hand at the moment, heading back toward Parker Center.

The hijacker. Inside information there?—not necessarily. In the last three weeks three trucks ferrying expensive cargoes of liquor from warehouses to retail stores had been hijacked. It was a job difficult to get leads on: there were a lot of restaurants and bars in L.A. whose owners might jump at getting a few cases of liquor at a cut rate.

The burglar and/or burglars. That case—if it was a single case—had got underway back in November before the departmental changes. It looked (said Goldberg's records) like the same M.O., in a vague sort of way. Six hits, four apartments and two single houses, entry made through windows, and the places picked clean of all possible loot: at one place he'd even taken an obsolete set of encyclopedias, at another a cheap cigarette-making machine. Otherwise, a run-of-the-mill burglar, working evenings, and no lead on him at all.

The latest teen-age body full of the acid, found in an alley along Main, not yet identified.

The hit-run along Wilshire four days ago: a vague make on the car, the first two letters of the plate-number. The victim had been an elderly pensioner on the way home from a Christmas shopping trip.

A couple of service station heists, no leads on those either. The rate on that kind of thing always rose in December, people needing money for Christmas shopping. He could only return thanks that the hordes of shoplifters were dealt with on a lower level as a rule.

And, of course, the new one just reported this morning . . . Parking the Ferrari, Mendoza grinned to himself. That one ought to belong to Bunco—the victims having only themselves to blame.

Upstairs, he found Sergeant Lake studying a new paperback on dieting. At least the powers that be hadn't asked them to move: they'd given Robbery-Homicide another corridor of interrogation rooms and a second communal detectives' office across the hall: four more desks and typewriters. The new sign pointed the way just beyond the elevators.

"Anything new, Jimmy?"

"Nope," said Lake. "Not much. Art found that Elphick, where Dakin said he'd be, at work. He's talking to him now. John and George are out on that gas station heist, and Jase just came back from somewhere—"

As if conjured up by his name, Detective Jason Grace rushed out of the old sergeants' office. "Hey," he said excitedly, "hey, we did it! We've got her! Ginny just called— the agency just called her to—we can have her right now, today! Oh, by God, but that's the best Christmas present we'll ever—" His chocolate-colored face wore a broad grin. Matt Piggott and Henry Glasser, just coming in, heard that and they all beamed back at him.

"That's great news, Jase—congratulations," said Lake, swiveling around from the switchboard. The Graces had been sorting through the red tape with the County Adoption Agency since August, trying to get little Celia Ann Harlow, so unexpectedly orphaned by that wanton killer.

"Say, look—if I can take off now—Ginny says they say we can *take* her right now, this afternoon—just some more papers to sign, and—" Grace was excited.

"Go, go," said Mendoza. "Merry Christmas, Jase."

"It surely will be!" said Grace, and vanished precipitately toward the elevators. They looked after him, smiling.

"And for the baby too," said Piggott, his long dark face serious. "Cute little thing. At least some good news to brighten the day. Listen, I'm not sure it's the same boy pulling all these break-ins now. The one on Friday night, he didn't find some cash this Moon had stashed away, and everywhere else, the place was picked but clean."

"¿Qué?" said Mendoza absently. "Well, as Saul reminds me, we can't win 'em all." He went across the hall to the new office, where Sergeant Hackett sat at his desk talking to a nervous citizen.

"Mr. Elphick," he said to Mendoza. "Lieutenant Mendoza." He shifted his bulk in the desk chair and sighed. A recent bout with flu had, happily, reduced him by thirteen pounds and he was trying to stay there by skipping lunch.

"Listen, I dunno why Al hadda go and tell you guys about that. He dint have no call," said Elphick aggrievedly. "Look, it was only about four bucks, and hell, you guys make me go in court, evidence, that bit, my wife'll give me hell—listen, can't we forget it, huh?" Mr. Elphick was about forty, shabbily dressed, and needed a shave.

"Not necessarily court, Mr. Elphick," said Hackett. "We'd just like a description to add to Mr. Dakin's. Come on, just tell us what happened and where."

"Oh, hell," said Elphick unwillingly. "It was only about four bucks, I let it go—I wasn't hurt any. I make good money, you know construction pays good now—and my wife—Al dint have no call drag me in on it—he was just tellin' me what happened to him and I said I bet was the same lousy pair conned me, and when—"

"Yes, yes," said Hackett. "From the beginning, please."

"Well, hell," said Elphick. "My wife— Well, I know Al just casual, see, we worked on a couple jobs together, and we both drop into this place sometimes, see, this Irish Bar. He was tellin' me about it yesterday, this dame give him the eye and he, well, like makes a deal with her, and she leads him down this alley, says it's a way to her back door, and this guy strongarms him and picks him clean. He was mad—"

[13]

Al Dakin had been mad enough, on thinking it over, to come in this morning and tell his story to cops. Al Dakin, however, was a bachelor.

"So, let's hear a description," said Hackett.

"My wife'd go straight up in the air," muttered Elphick. "Oh, hell. Well—well—the dame was kind of medium, not tall or short—she's got a lot of black hair, and one o' these little real short skirts—I never got a look at the guy, he jumped me from behind, I guess he was hidin' behind a trash-can or some place—he's kind of big, all I could say— And look, if you expect me to go in court, just forget it, I'm not about to—"

"All right," said Hackett. "Any guess at the woman's age?"

"How'd I know that? She's young, I guess—looks maybe twenny-five—" He shrugged. "Dames, all the makeup and all, I wouldn't say—"

"Any further on?" said Mendoza when they'd let Elphick go. "And any guess how many victims haven't reported it?"

"Oh, don't be silly," said Hackett. "A Mrs. Stone came in awhile back and wanted to look at that body, said it might be her nephew by the description of his clothes. Shogart took her down to the morgue—"

"And is now," said Mendoza, "bringing her back, I would guess." A wailing female voice came nearer up the corridor.

"But why did it have to be Johnny? Why—all this awful dope—those fiends who make the kids use this awful—" A burst of sobs, and Shogart's deep phlegmatic voice.

"If you'll just sit down, Mrs. Stone, and try to—I know you're upset—"

Policewoman Larsen hurriedly crossed the hall from her desk. This was the kind of thing Policewoman Larsen was there for, presumably, but it didn't happen often.

"Merry Christmas," said Hackett tiredly.

"Nothing new, Arturo. *Se comprende.* Anything more on the hijacker?"

"*Nada.* I had that last driver down looking at mug shots, but what can he tell us? The fellow had a ski-mask on, same as the other jobs. People!" said Hackett. "And we haven't even got the tree up yet, with this damn flu going through the whole family—"

"*¡Tenga paciencia!*" said Mendoza cheerfully. "We could be busier. And you haven't heard about Jase—" Hearing about that, Hackett looked a little happier; Palliser and Higgins came in to hear that, and smiled.

"Good news, all right. Say, Luis, come to think I haven't had a chance to show you the latest snapshots—" Inevitably Higgins reached for his breast pocket and Hackett uttered a mock groan.

"Dangers of late marriages—at least I will say, Luis, you never foisted all the snapshots on us—"

But Higgins was busy passing them out, his craggy face fond. "Isn't she a doll? And smart as they come too—even at just three months she—"

They grinned covertly at Higgins, looking at the latest snapshots of Margaret Emily. Higgins the longtime bachelor, so unexpectedly falling for Bert Dwyer's widow, had been pleased enough with his secondhand family, Bert's kids Steve and Laura; now he was still a little incredulous that he and Mary had a firsthand daughter. Well, she was a cute baby.

"You just wait till April," said Palliser. "We'll outproduce you, George." And he was still feeling amused at the joke Fate had played on his Robin, starting a baby when she'd planned to be a working wife. "It's a handful of nothing on that heist, by the way. Stanton couldn't give us any description."

"Helpful," said Mendoza. "Burglars and heist-men—*¡condenación!*" But he had had to admit that the change had been, in a way, a logical one; on a beat like Central's, the robbery and homicide were so often connected.

"It was just one man, and that ties it in loosely with that one last week," Palliser went on. "But even that isn't sure, because—"

"Lieutenant—" Lake poked his head in the doorway, looking resigned. "A new body. Of all places, over by the museum in Exposition Park. One of the maintenance crew just found it and called in."

"*¿Y cómo no?*" said Mendoza. "All right, Jimmy. Come on and do some legwork, Art."

Higgins went along too, while Palliser started a follow-up report on the heist of last night.

Exposition Park was a complex of buildings out on Exposition Boulevard, a generous tract squared by Figueroa Street, Santa Barbara Avenue, and Vermont. There were the famous every-variety-known rose gardens: the Armory, the great Coliseum, the Sports Arena, the L.A. County Museum of Natural History, and in a separate building, the Science and Industry Museum. Turning in the narrow avenue from Figueroa, the Ferrari nosed up past the Science Museum where a little knot of men gathered. The ambulance hadn't come yet.

They showed their badges. "One of you called?" asked Hackett.

"Yessir, I did—I spotted it first. Ben Bates is my name, Officer, I'm head o' the maintenance crew here, and one thing I tell you right off, she can't've been here long, not more'n a few minutes. We been cleanin' floors today— look, Sunday, usual we'd be open, but day before Christmas, a holiday, it ain't. Open, I mean. We been doin' the floors, this building and over in the other museum—and I only got over here about half an hour ago, figured start on the top floor anyways before we knock off for dinner—I come in the front way with my key, right up there, and she wasn't there then—" He was a big stocky man, excited and upset.

Mendoza and Higgins had parted the little crowd and were looking at the corpse.

"And then about twenty minutes later, I come back out to go help Bill fetch over that heavy polisher—and there she was! And I figured—"

It wasn't a very big corpse: a slight girl with blonde hair, sprawled limp just at the curb where the walk led to the building steps. Mendoza squatted over it.

"No handbag," said Higgins, fingering his prominent jaw. There was no cover for twenty feet around: just pavement. "Poor girl. Seems—well, I don't know. Christmas Eve." She was lying on one side, and from what they could see she'd been middling pretty: small pert features, fair skin. The short well-shaped nails of the hand outflung from the body were carefully manicured, painted pale peach. "Not raped?"

Mendoza shook his head. "*No sé*, but it doesn't look like it. Strangled at a guess." There were marks on the girl's throat. He picked up the hand. "Did she fight him at all? Her nails are too short to have a guess. She's still warm, she can't be an hour dead."

"But right here in broad daylight—" Bates was still shaken. "Poor young lady—who coulda done such a— Not half an hour ago I come right by here and she wasn't— It was when I come out after I'd unlocked the other door for—"

The ambulance came purring up, and the attendants came to look. "You want photographs, Lieutenant, or shall we take her?"

Mendoza stood up and lit a cigarette. "What for? There's just the corpse. I don't need a crystal ball to guess what happened. She was shoved out of a car, already dead. But let's have a good look all through the grounds for her hand-bag." He surveyed the scene. "He couldn't turn around here, not even if he was driving a Honda. He'd have to go up to the Coliseum before he'd have space to turn. None of you heard a car?"

"Heard a car? In the grounds like? With all that traffic out there a block off?" Bates shook his head. "How'd any-body notice the difference? No, I didn't see a car nowhere in the grounds, all day, except our own cars over there behind the other building." It developed that the other five men had been occupied with the floors at the Natural History Museum during the short time the corpse could have arrived on the scene.

"All right," said Mendoza. "Let's try up by the Coliseum first." Hackett and Higgins started up there in silence, each taking one side of the narrow drive, peering at the ground. "You can take her," said Mendoza. And everybody knew that Luis Rodolfo Vicente Mendoza was a cynic from the word go, but as the ambulance men lifted the small body to a stretcher, he thought, Christmas Eve. She couldn't be older than the early twenties. Her clothes were good, a brown tailored suit, lemon-colored blouse, rumpled now; he noticed that the skirt was a modest length for these days, just covering her knees. One low-heeled brown shoe had come off. "I'll want her jewelry." There was a ring on one hand, a necklace.

The ambulance left, and he drove the Ferrari up to the Coliseum gates. "Any luck?"

"Not so far, and there's not much cover. You think he just drove in the handiest spot empty of people and dumped her?"

"That's what it looks like. So he may have dumped her handbag too." There wasn't much cover here, or back there where the corpse had been: what shrubbery there was, formal and low-growing. Hackett was pacing up to the left where a walk led around the Coliseum to the various gates, Higgins up to the right. "I don't think," said Mendoza, "if he did dump it here, he'd have got out of the car—it probably wouldn't be—" But Hackett had suddenly pounced.

"He didn't bother to turn around, Luis. He came round the Coliseum and drove out on Hoover. Dumping the handbag as he went." Mendoza and Higgins had hurried up.

"And just the shapeless kind of thing that's a real bastard to work," said Higgins.

It was almost certainly the corpse's handbag; it matched her suit, a capacious dark brown leather bag with several compartments. Hackett lifted it delicately by thrusting his pen under the double straps. "Any bets on prints?"

That, of course, was the first thing to look for. Mendoza used the phone in the Ferrari to call up a mobile lab truck, and when it arrived Scarne dusted the entire outside of the bag. Latent prints always offered them a shortcut, but only if there were any liftable ones present. This time, as so often happened, there weren't.

"Smudges," said Scarne sadly. "Sorry."

"Way the cards fall," said Higgins. "It's still going to help." Then they could open the bag. They took it back to the office, to look at the contents; as usual with any female handbag, there were quite a few. They spread them out methodically on Mendoza's desk.

A blue billfold with a change pocket; there was forty-seven dollars and fifty-eight cents in it. In the plastic slots for cards and photos, an I.D. card: Lila May Askell, an address in Santa Barbara. In case of accident notify Mr. Edward Askell, an address in Salt Lake City. Snapshots of, probably, family groups: a couple of girls in their late teens or early twenties, an older couple, a young man. A library card for the Santa Barbara public library. A California driver's license good for another two years. A gasoline credit card.

One used and two clean handkerchiefs. A large gold compact full of loose powder. A clean powder puff. Three lipsticks, two nearly new: Coral Glow, Peach Glow, and Cherry Frost: different brands. A bunch of keys on a ring. A paperback novel, *Neither Five nor Three* by Helen MacInnes, with a paperclip probably marking her place about midway through. A small bottle of aspirin. A two-page letter signed *Mother*. A small unopened package of Kleenex. A ballpoint pen.

And in the zippered center compartment, they found a Greyhound Bus line ticket from Santa Barbara to Salt Lake City, with changes indicated at Los Angeles and Las Vegas.

"She was on her way home for Christmas," said Hackett. "We'll ask, but she probably had a layover for her bus here."

"Let's go and see," said Higgins. There was still part of a working day left: it was five-fifteen. The night watch would come on at six—right now, Tom Landers, Rich Conway, Bob Schenke and Nick Galeano, an expanded night watch as their job had been expanded. Any indicated legwork that could be accomplished they could take over: not much, tonight.

And now somebody had to call Mr. Edward Askell of Salt Lake City, to tell him that without much doubt his daughter was dead here. Murdered here. Why and how? Echo answers, thought Mendoza; he pulled the phone toward him, lighting a new cigarette, and told Lake to get him headquarters at Salt Lake.

A captain of Homicide there took what information Mendoza could give him, said they'd be in touch with Askell. "You'll want an identification, I suppose. Soon as possible. Shame, on Christmas. Well, I'll take care of it. You might give me your office number—he'll probably want to call."

Outside, the sudden dark of tropical places had descended. It was officially Christmas Eve. Mendoza went out and across the hall. "I understand you got that teen-ager identified," he said to Shogart.

Shogart looked up from his typewriter. He had been a fixture in Goldberg's office for years, and phlegmatically accepted the change to a new superior: a heavy-shouldered dark man in his forties, another plodder like Piggott. He detested his Christian name and was known by his initials to anybody he called friend. "Poor damned female," he said. "Just another fool of a kid getting hooked on the dope. By the time the aunt found out, too late to do anything. Boy's parents are dead, she'd raised him. Seemed like a reasonably respectable female—widow. Shame she had to find out on Christmas Eve. Though any time—" He shrugged and went back to the typewriter.

Mendoza scratched and yawned. "Unions," he said.

"So what about them?"

"Not for cops any more than the pros. No holidays—just the routine going on forever."

Shogart grinned. "We need our heads examined, all right."

"But I am now going home," said Mendoza.

He went home, to the big Spanish house on Rayo Grande Avenue in Hollywood, to his late-acquired hostages to fortune. Redhaired Alison was supervising the twins' supper while their jewel, Mrs. MacTaggart, put the finishing touches to dinner. Alison, hearing him come in the back door, flew to greet him.

"Thank heaven you weren't late—we'll get them to bed early and start on the tree, I've smuggled everything into the hall closet—"

The twins erupted at him. "Daddy, *Mamacíta* reads a new *cuento* all about *La Navidad—y San Nicolás—*"

"—With *el ciervo* that come when it rains—*la lluvia,* an'—"

Mendoza burst out laughing. This was going to be the first Christmas that the twins, three in August, would really take deep interest in; but Alison's attempts to impress them with traditional Yule stories had evidently met an obstacle in that the twins were still oblivious to any difference between Spanish and English.

"No, Johnny—*El Reno,* I told you," said Alison. "Go and finish your supper now, *querido*—your father'll read to you later—"

"Johnny is silly," said Miss Teresa solemnly. "*I* know 'bout *El Reno. El santo* come in a *trineo*—Mama says—"

"Now, my lambs," said Mrs. MacTaggart briskly, "you come and finish your nice suppers." Their accidentally-come-by sheepdog Cedric ambled up to offer Mendoza a polite paw; the four cats, Bast, Sheba, Nefertite and El Señor, had hardly looked up from their plates in the service porch. "Let your father catch his breath now. You'll be wanting a dram before dinner—" El Señor understood English and abandoned his haddock to demand his share of rye whiskey. But Mendoza shook his head.

"*Nada,* Mairí. It seems I'll be too busy." He kissed Alison again and she cocked her head at him.

"Tough day, *amante?*"

"The usual. I must be getting sentimental in my old age." Luis Mendoza, for his sins, had put in twenty-four years as an LAPD officer. "*Feliz Navidad, mi corazón.* I'm just feeling sorry for Lila Askell, who didn't make it home for Christmas—and I wonder why. I think I'll have that drink after all, Mairí."

El Señor floated up to the drainboard and received his half-ounce in a saucer.

"Oh, and the Graces have got the Harlow baby—the County relented finally this afternoon."

"How wonderful—the nicest Christmas present anybody could—Luis, you haven't brought the office home with you?"

[21]

"Not really," said Mendoza. "We'll get the tree up after—"

"Shh! It's going to be a surprise, they were too little last year—"

Hackett found Angel in their bedroom frantically wrapping Christmas presents. "That damned flu—I got all behind, and I meant to get these fruitcakes ready weeks ago—"

"The County gave Jase a Christmas present," said Hackett. "They've got the Harlow baby."

"Oh, Art, how wonderful! I'm so glad—yes, the baby's fine, all cured, thank goodness, and— For heaven's sake," said Angel suddenly, "get *out* of here, I've got all your presents to wrap—"

And four-year-old Mark and twenty-month-old Sheila came shouting about Santa Claus; Hackett laughed and went to pick one up in each arm.

Matt Piggott and his Prudence had just been married in September; they had an apartment on Rosewood Avenue, but Prudence was house-hunting. Prices now—but a police officer was reckoned a good risk, and that, reflected Piggott, was just plain crazy. As the devout fundamentalist Christian he was, he thought the craziness was just more of the devil's handiwork.

But as he drove home he looked forward to telling Prudence that the Graces had at last got the Harlow baby. As a kind of unexpected Christmas present.

And when Higgins came home, to the house on Silver Lake Boulevard, Steve Dwyer had a new set of snapshots to show him, just picked up at the drugstore. Steve had definitely decided to be a professional photographer since Higgins had got the Instamatic to take pictures of the baby.

Mary said resignedly, "Between you and Steve, George, it's going to take all my time to keep her from being a well-spoiled brat, you know that."

"Now, Mary." Higgins picked Margaret Emily up from her crib.

"And she *was* asleep—"

"I think she's awful photogenic, George," said Steve seriously.

"Let me hold her, George," pleaded Laura.

Margaret Emily, awakened, began emitting regular loud bellows. "Honestly, George! I'd just got her settled down—"

"Oh, the Graces got the Harlow baby. The County called this afternoon—"

"Wonderful," said Mary, necessarily raising her voice over the bellows.

The tree had been up, shiningly decorated, for a week, and a multitude of wrapped presents waited under it.

"The County just called this afternoon," said Palliser, "and Jase took off—never saw a happier man—"

"What a nice Christmas present." Roberta smiled at him. "I'm fine, don't fuss, John—since I got past the morning sickness, I'm fine."

There was a tree up at the Pallisers' too, in the living room of the forty-thousand-dollar house on Hillside Avenue, and presents under it in gay foil. Of all the men of Robbery-Homicide, Palliser would spend Christmas Day at home.

Theoretically, the boss could too; but he probably wouldn't.

Tom Landers came into the office a little late, on night watch, and found Rich Conway there alone reading a paperback. He and Conway had taken to each other at once; they were the same age and shared interests. Landers was still in pursuit of Policewoman Phil O'Neill down in R. and I., and Conway had recently been dating one of their girls too, Margot Swain who was stationed at Wilcox Street in Hollywood. They'd set up a double date for a week from next Tuesday; they were both off on Tuesdays.

"Bob and Nick went out on a head-on, down by the Stack. More routine. Shame, Christmas Eve—two D.O.A.'s."

Conway put his book down. He was a wiry dark fellow, lacking Landers' slim height; he had a long straight nose and a mobile wide mouth and the most cynical gray eyes Landers had ever seen. "Day watch didn't leave any loose ends, except this new body. Nothing to do on it, but Jimmy left a note—we might get a call from Salt Lake."

They did, about an hour later: a shocked and saddened citizen asking questions, where, how, why. They didn't know too much about the corpse; Landers explained about the need for identification. Edward Askell said, in fading tones, that he would come over at once, and hung up suddenly.

"Pity. Christmas," said Conway. Landers echoed him. It would be nice to be home for Christmas—up in Fresno with the family—but to cops, Christmas was just another day. He had a date to take Phil to Christmas dinner tomorrow; she hadn't any family here either.

Nothing showed to give them any work; they sat talking desultorily, until ten past nine when a couple of calls came in at once. Schenke and Galeano had come back by then, and finished a report on the head-on collision. The first call was from a citizen over on Alcazar Street, something about an assault, by what Landers could gather. The other was a body in a parking lot on Wilshire.

Landers and Conway drove over to Alcazar Street in Landers' Corvair.

"I don't know what it's all about," said the citizen, one Alfredo Ramirez. "The lady's all upset, looks like somebody's beat her up, I don't know, she comes ringing the doorbell, says please call cops—my wife tries to help her, she's bleeding— Look, lady, here are the cops, so you tell what happened—"

She was crouched on the sagging couch in the living room of this old frame house; she looked up at Landers and Conway slowly, and ordinarily she'd have been a nice-looking middle-aged woman, still a good figure, neat clothes, well-dressed; she was clutching an expensive mink stole, and her torn black lace dress looked expensive too, and her now-ravaged face had been made up. Incongruously, her quantity of mousy brown hair straggled about her face wildly, a stout hair-net still attached by one pin; and she raised a hand to her head and said suddenly, "My—my wig —my best wig—oh, I must look— But *Stanley*, what's happened to—"

Landers had his badge out. "If you'll just tell us what this is all about, ma'am."

There was a Christmas tree here, a small green tree on a table in front of a window, brave with gold tinsel and lights; and a few presents waiting under it.

"Oh, yes," she gasped, "Yes—he held us up—I fought him, I tried to—but he pulled me into the car—*our* car— there was a shot, and Stanley—my husband—we'd gone out for dinner, Roberti's on Wilshire—we'd just come out—"

Landers and Conway exchanged a glance. The state of her clothes, probably an examination for rape was in order. "Can you tell us your name, ma'am?"

"I'm Mrs. Stanley Macauley," she said mechanically. "Christmas Eve—we're having all the family for dinner tomorrow, it was easier to go out tonight—we'd just come back to the car, and this man—he had a gun—*Stanley*—"

"Did he attack you, Mrs. Macauley?" asked Conway gently.

She began to cry. "Yes—in the back of the car—I tried to fight him, but—when he let me out I just—the first house I saw—"

They called an ambulance. The doctor at Central Receiving said she'd been raped and mauled. She'd also been robbed; there had been about seven dollars in her purse.

When they got back to the office they heard from Schenke and Galeano about the other one: part of the same thing. A Stanley Macauley, plenty of I.D. on him, shot dead in the parking lot behind Roberti's restaurant on Wilshire.

"It looked like a small caliber," said Schenke.

Landers looked at the clock; it was eight minutes to midnight. "Merry Christmas," he said with a crooked smile.

2

CHRISTMAS DAY was sunnier than the day before, one of
the mild blue-and-gold days southern California can produce in midwinter. The family men on day watch drifted
into Parker Center late—just another day or not, it was
necessary to watch the kids, big and little, open presents
under the tree. Mendoza came in at a few minutes past
nine and met Hackett and Higgins in the lobby. Upstairs,
Shogart hadn't come in yet, but he had a long family
ranging from a baby to a teen-ager; Piggott was in, reading
a report, and Glasser was on the phone.

There wouldn't be much they could accomplish today
anyway, except for reports and the most urgent witnesses;
they couldn't chase down statements from witnesses or do
any legwork today. Mendoza had told Wanda to stay home.
They wouldn't need her. He wondered again why she'd
been assigned to them.

Jason Grace came in in a hurry. "I'm late, sorry—we were
pretty sure we would get her, but at that we didn't have
everything—the crib, and enough blankets, and—we were
out shopping to the last minute—we're having a party tonight— Say, what's that camera you got?" he asked Higgins.
"I don't know much about it but we'll want pictures—"

Mendoza sat down at Palliser's empty desk and lit a
cigarette, a report signed by Landers in his hand. "These
Macauleys. Jimmy, get me Bainbridge's office."

Bainbridge wasn't in, but one of his bright young men,

[26]

Dr. Amherst, had had a look at both bodies. "What about the girl?" asked Mendoza.

"Not raped, for ninety-nine percent sure—no interference. Knocked around and manually strangled, best I can do pending autopsy. Have you got her identified?"

"Yes, Doctor. We'll probably get identification on both the latest ones today—"

"Both?" said Amherst sardonically. "There are a couple more here, well mangled, and what looks like a wino from the Strip."

Mendoza hadn't got to the report of the head-on at the Stack. "Well, this Macauley."

"Never knew what hit him," said Amherst. "He looks like a healthy specimen, around fifty. All his own teeth and hair. The bullet got him square over the heart, and my guess is that's where we'll find it. There's no exit wound so it's still inside somewhere. Small caliber, but I'll tell you better after autopsy."

"You'll let us know about that? . . . Yes, Doctor, thanks very much." Mendoza asked for Central Receiving and asked about Mrs. Macauley.

"You want to talk to her, of course," said the doctor there. "Not yet, I'm afraid, Lieutenant. She's only just awake —she was rather heavily sedated. Say about one o'clock, she'll be able to talk to you. The family's rallied around, I understand—with her now. What happened to her husband? We just heard her story."

"He was shot dead," said Mendoza. "One o'clock, Doctor, thanks . . . That restaurant. Roberti's. Where is it, Art?"

Hackett picked up Schenke's report. "Just past the Ambassador Hotel. String of restaurants along there—"

"Not the kind of restaurants, *obvio*," said Mendoza, "that have uniformed attendants in their parking lots."

"No. Or we'd have at least another witness. Seems funny to be writing reports on burglars, doesn't it?"

"Saul tells me it shows you're aging when you can't adjust to change. *Como sí.* Here's a note from Tom"—he'd just found it—"that Askell should be here sometime today. Anything else new in, Jimmy?"

[27]

"Not so far. There will be," said Lake prophetically. "On a holiday, with all the liquor flowing."

Mendoza looked round to hear Piggott say something about the devil. "Where'd Matt vanish to?"

"Somebody else's Christmas spoiled," said Lake. "Bob left a note on it—that head-on on the freeway. A fellow just came in to identify the bodies, Matt took him down."

Glasser had wandered down the hall after coffee.

"Seems funny, writing reports on burglars," he said, sipping.

"The resistance to change around here—" said Mendoza.

"Now, Mrs. Macauley, do you feel well enough to answer some questions?" Mendoza sat down in the plastic chair facing her. She looked at him for a moment in silence. She'd be a nice-looking woman at a different time and place: now she'd been crying and her eyes were red and puffy and she hadn't any makeup on and looked her full age.

"At a time like this, I don't see why the police have to—" Young Mrs. Linda Swift looked at him angrily.

"Now, honey," said her young husband, Bill Swift. The rallying-around family consisted of the Macauley's married daughter, and Florence Macauley's sister and brother-in-law, a Mr. and Mrs. Hendry. "They want a description of this guy if she can give one, and as soon as possible—you can see that."

"Oh," said Linda.

"I'm all right," Florence Macauley said to Mendoza tiredly. "I see that, Bill. Of course. I just don't understand —why he had to shoot Stanley. He'd given him all his money. I don't understand why he had to kill him—just for no reason. No *reason*. Stanley saw the gun, he didn't try to put up a fight and maybe get us both—hurt. He gave him the money—"

"Just a minute, Mrs. Macauley. We'd like to have it from the beginning, just what happened. We've got the doctor's report, it doesn't matter about that part. When you came out of the restaurant—"

"I'm all right. Linda and Bill are going to take me home in a little while, the doctor said—" They were in one of the patients' lounges at the end of this corridor, a neat sterile place of plastic furniture and metal tables and few ashtrays. Mrs. Macauley was dressed; probably her daughter had brought her fresh clothes, for the ones she'd been wearing had been sent to the lab by now. She sat on a plastic couch and looked at Mendoza and Hackett wearily, and her daughter sat beside her and looked at them a little doubtfully.

"What time did you get to the restaurant?" asked Mendoza, to start her off.

"About eight, a little before, I think. Maybe a quarter to. We'd expected it to be crowded—we were late, but I'd been—getting things ready for—for today. The family dinner, you know." She swallowed and suddenly Linda sobbed once, and pressed a handkerchief to her mouth. "The tree's been up for a week, all the decorations, but all the last-minute things—I'd got the gelatin salad all made and the turkey ready for the stuff—I'm all *right*, Linda. I must tell them—all I can, so they can—try to find the man. Well, we'd expected a crowd there, but there wasn't. Not at all. But then Christmas Eve's—a sort of family time as well as Christmas Day, isn't it? So we were waited on right away, and Stanley had a drink—bourbon and soda—and he said I should too because I'd been working so—I had a martini —and then we had dinner. I don't know what time we came out to go home—" They knew by then that the Macauleys owned their own home up in Hollywood, had driven down to Roberti's because they both liked it, it was a nice place with good food. "It wasn't late, we didn't sit over dinner—maybe ten to nine."

"Yes. The parking lot's at the side and behind the restaurant." Mendoza had been there to look. "Now think about the lighting—where your car was." There was an A.P.B. out on the car, a four-year-old Buick sedan. "There are just a few arc-lights in the lot, it's not altogether dark. Did you—"

"He came from behind the cars," she said. "Stanley'd parked in the first line, nearest the building. He—he came out from behind the cars, there were about ten or twelve other cars there but nobody else—just Stanley and I—"

"You mean he'd been in front of the cars?" asked Hackett. "They were parked facing in?"

"Yes, of course. That's what I meant. It all happened so fast, I—I hadn't time to be frightened until— We both saw the gun in his hand right away. What? I don't know anything about guns. I don't think it was very big. He said to give him all our money—no, he said that to Stanley—and Stanley did. He gave him his billfold, and—"

"Can you describe the man at all, Mrs. Macauley?"

"I'll try. He was a Negro, but I don't think very black. Shabby clothes—dirty old clothes, like overalls. He was taller than Stanley—Stanley's five-foot-nine—and awfully thin. What? Oh, he was young—I'd say in the twenties, that's the best I—"

"Any accent?"

She shook her head. "Just, he spoke—you know, awfully rough, and he swore. Stanley gave him his billfold and I was frightened then, I tried to give him my handbag, but he threw it into the car and took hold of my arm and pulled me into the car with him—or started to, and Stanley said something like, what was he doing, and there was a shot, and he just—shoved me down across the seat and the next thing I knew we were driving away—"

"All right, Mrs. Macauley," said Mendoza. "That's all we'll ask you right now—"

"Oh," she said suddenly. "And he smelled—I just remembered that—he smelled like a—a gas station. All oily, you know, his clothes and—when he, I mean later when he—"

"Mmh," said Mendoza. "All right, thanks very much. If you think of anything to add to that description—" She was blinking away tears. Mendoza caught Hendry's eye and moved away to the window. "You understand, Mr. Hendry, we have to get a formal identification of the body. Could you do that for us now?"

Hendry's lips tightened; he was a big stocky man, nearly as dapper-neat as Mendoza if a good deal fatter. "I see. Yes, sure, I can do that. The kids can take Florence home."

They took him down to the morgue and he made the formal identification. "Poor devil," he said above the corpse. "Stanley—the best fellow you'd want to meet. Only fifty. Just for—he wouldn't have had more than twenty-five dollars on him. And an animal like that—where the hell do they come from, Lieutenant? And damn what color they are—there was that gang over in West Hollywood beating that pensioner the other day—just *animals*—"

"I wouldn't dignify them by the word, Mr. Hendry," said Mendoza. "Even wild animals never kill wantonly. Only by necessity. Do you think your sister-in-law might be up to looking at some photographs in a day or two?"

"Mug shots," said Hendry, nodding. "In case you've got him on file. I think so. I'll ask her. She's a pretty level-headed woman, and after she's over the first shock—I expect she will be."

"We'd appreciate it very much."

Landers, in his newest suit and a tie even Mendoza would have approved, picked up Phil O'Neill at her apartment at four o'clock. "The captain said I could take off early, I did some overtime last night," she told him, shutting the door after them. Landers looked at her pleasedly. Everything was just right about Phil, that was all. Phillipa Rosemary—only not, as she said, for a lady cop. If she just wasn't so damned sensible about not having known each other long enough—

"You promised to be good," she reminded him.

"Oh, I am—I am," said Landers. "You just look good enough to eat." Her flaxen curls just reached his chest, despite her medium-high heels; she had on a plain navy dress with a big gold pin on one shoulder, and a bright crimson wool stole: it was really very mild for Christmas Day.

"Where are we going?"

"New place—new to us, anyway. Is it too early for dinner?"

"You get all out of routine on a holiday. Can't be, any-way—you go on watch at six. I'll be ready for food when we get there, I skipped lunch."

"I won't get the axe if I'm half an hour late," said Landers comfortably.

Inexplicably, their favorite restaurants, all the six Frascatis', had closed. It was rumored that they'd been merged with a big chain. The new place was out in the valley, high in the hills above Burbank; it was called The Castaways. In a quiet and nearly empty dining room, they sat beside an enormous picture window that gave them a view right across Hollywood, the ocean-range of foothills, into the beach towns, on this clear a day. The light was rapidly fading in the sky.

"And on a really clear day you could see the ocean," said Phil, sipping her drink. And a moment later, "Oh, Tom, watch! It's just like jewels!" The sudden dark of midwinter was coming down almost within seconds, and all across that range of city and hill spread before them, the lights were flashing on, diamond-winking and colored.

"That's pretty good." Landers was fascinated too. They watched in silence until nearly total dark had fallen and the panorama of the city's sprawl of lights was complete. "It's clear enough now, on a night just after it'd rained that would be something."

"I hope to goodness," said Phil, sitting back, "it stays clear for New Year's. And as warm as this. Those poor girls on the floats—some years it's a wonder they don't all get pneumonia."

"Hey, don't remind me of that," said Landers in alarm. "The list won't be posted until tomorrow."

"Oh—" said Phil. "Have you ever got picked out of the hat?"

"Once—when I was a rookie. Just hold kind thoughts it doesn't happen again."

Phil's navy-blue eyes smiled. "I've heard rumors that the special rest rooms have meters that take a quarter."

"That's only one damn thing about it," said Landers, and turned to the waiter.

To the rest of the nation, New Year's Day may mean this

or that; to L.A. County it means the Rose Parade and the big game in the Rose Bowl. An average New Year will attract the out-of-state visitors and bravest local residents to make a crowd of half a million for the parade; and for the hotelkeepers and mechants it means gratifying profit, but to the police only a large headache. It had been the practice for some time now that long lists of names from the Pasadena force, the LAPD, and the sheriff's department, were fed into a mechanized lottery-like machine to turn out a temporary force of men to police the parade and game. The unlucky ones whose names were chosen started the day at 2 A.M. at Pasadena headquarters for briefing; the plainclothesmen had to don uniform again, and they'd be lucky to stagger home by mid-evening. To complicate the traffic problems, there are only two main roads leading in or out of Pasadena.

"I'm just keeping my fingers crossed," said Landers.

"I'll hold the good thoughts." But Phil was entranced again by the view. "Tom, let's come here for that double date next week. Am I going to like this Conway—and the girl?"

"Conway is no business of yours," said Landers. "Not having met the girl, I couldn't say."

About five o'clock a fattish man of middle age came slowly out of the elevator and looked at the sign that said *Robbery-Homicide*. He stopped at Lake's desk. "Lieutenant Mendoza? I was told to ask—"

"Yes, sir." Lake buzzed Mendoza.

"I'm Edward Askell," said the man.

Taken into Mendoza's office and given a chair, offered a cigarette, he said, "Thank you, I don't smoke. I don't understand it. At all. It's a hard thing to say, God's will, and try to believe it. I can't. I can't understand how it could happen."

"We don't know much about it either, Mr. Askell. If you'd answer some questions about your daughter—we'll try to find out. But—you know I have to ask you to identify her body."

"So the captain said—a Captain Shearling—he came to

tell us. All right. She was our oldest, you know. Three girls and a boy—and Lila was our first. She was a good girl—bright, quick, we raised her—the right way. In the church—"

Mendoza listened to more of that on the way to the morgue, with half an ear. Families didn't always know everything about pretty young girls.

Askell, it seemed, was a construction engineer; it wasn't a poor family background in any sense. And he identified the body without breaking down. He just kept asking, "Why? How could anything like this have happened to Lila?"

Mendoza would like to know too, for his own satisfaction. He took Askell back to his office. "If you don't mind some questions—"

"Anything," said Askell. "Anything I can do to help you. Her mother's—" He shook his head. "It's a hard thing to think, God's will. She was twenty-three, Lieutenant. I can't understand how a thing like this could happen to Lila. Some girls—wild, not brought up right—but Lila—" Dully, without being asked, he told Mendoza about Lila: Hackett came in, with Higgins behind him, to listen in silence. And it all sounded depressingly, from their viewpoint, as if Lila had been the nice modest Christian young woman he claimed.

The family belonged to the LDS Church, attended services regularly. Lila had never had a steady boyfriend, in high school or later. She'd gone out with several young men, but she'd never been serious about anybody, except for—but that was awhile ago. She'd taken a course in therapy at a local hospital, she was an accredited hospital therapist, and that's what she'd been doing in Santa Barbara, working at a hospital there. She and another girl, a girl she'd known in school who'd taken the course too—Monica Fletcher—they'd seen the ad in some hospital newspaper, the job in Santa Barbara, and they'd thought it might be interesting, California and all. They'd been rooming together in Santa Barbara, Monica could tell them all about Lila and what she'd been doing recently, who she'd

[34]

known. But so could the Askells, because she wrote home every week. She hadn't had a regular boyfriend here either, she'd been working hard at the hospital. She'd been homesick. She liked the job all right, she liked the money, but she didn't like being so far from the family.

"She'd just decided, you see," said Askell. "She called us on the twenty-third, in the morning. She said she'd decided to come home, it was the idea of being away from home at Christmas made her decide. She'd given up the job, it meant losing a week's salary but— She was all excited, and bound to get home for Christmas if she could." He stopped a moment, collecting himself. "She told us—she'd sent all our presents by mail already—they'd already been delivered— and she'd send most of her things on by United Parcel, so she wouldn't have much to carry with her. She said the first bus she could get was the morning of the twenty-fourth, it'd get her into Los Angeles about noon and she'd have to wait over a bit for the next bus to Las Vegas, but if she couldn't make it home for Christmas Day it'd surely be the day after." He stopped again.

"Was Miss Fletcher coming with her?"

"No. She said Monica liked Santa Barbara fine, but I guess—well, maybe her family isn't so, what they call close, as ours is. Lila was homesick."

"Do you think—" Mendoza wondered what to ask him. "She wouldn't have—mmh—picked up with any—"

"Of course not!" said Askell, not so much indignant as bewildered. "Lila was particular—choosy her mother calls it—about people. She was a—a serious girl, she took her job and her religion all serious. You mean, would she have walked off with some fly-by-night—well, of course not. What do you think happened?"

"Well, all we know is," said Hackett, "by what it looks like, she was thrown out of a car after she'd been strangled. But—"

"Lila'd never get into a car with some man she didn't know," said Askell. "That's just plain silly. It couldn't happen."

They exchanged glances. "Maybe it was somebody she

thought she knew," said Hackett. "After all, it was broad daylight, Luis."

"She wouldn't have," insisted Askell. He looked at them anxiously. "Are the papers going to say that? Her mother—her sisters—"

"We don't give everything we know to the press," said Mendoza absently. "We'll do some poking around and see what turns up. You understand there has to be an autopsy?"

Askell nodded dumbly. "We don't hold with—but if it's the law, I suppose— When—when could I have her?"

"Probably tomorrow or next day."

"Well, I'll stay over. I'd best call home. I'll take her back with me, of course. But I just don't understand how it could have happened."

Even knowing that she had got here by Greyhound Bus, they hadn't been able to do any legwork on that yet. There had been only three buses due to arrive or leave from the station at Sixth and Spring today; the single ticket-seller on holiday duty was not the regular one. Tomorrow, try to find the driver of that bus, ask around the station. The Salt Lake City captain was on the ball; he had suggested to Askell that the LAPD might want a good photograph of Lila, and Askell had brought one with him: "She still wears her hair that way. Wore, I mean." Get some copies, ask all around that area.

And quite possibly, of course, they never would find out anything more about what had happened to Lila Askell. That nice modest moral girl.

"It's about time that burglar hit again," said Hackett, standing up and stretching.

Mendoza yawned. "I'm going home," he said.

But as usual, the little mystery, the slightly offbeat thing he couldn't see through, worried him. Essentially, he thought, his egotism: the notion that Mendoza couldn't figure a thing out bothered him. Lila bothered him. A nice modest religious girl, who wouldn't have got into a stranger's car: so she ended up getting strangled and dumped out

[36]

of a stranger's car. Askell said she hadn't known a soul in L.A.

A stranger?

His mind slid back to those child rape-murders. He had said it then, the familiar stranger. Somebody placed, somebody known, but still a stranger. Even these days, the essentially honest citizen had a terrible trust in life, in his fellow citizens: that they would not suddenly strip off masks to be revealed as—the animals, he thought, and grimaced. Not the word. Animals lived by rules and did not kill without reason. To distract his mind from Lila he snapped on the police-frequency radio, halted for a light at Sunset and Vine.

"—A 211, in progress now, code three," it said suddenly. "K492, see the man at Woodman and Spencer, a 240PC." Robbery and assault of the person, Mendoza translated automatically. The radio was silent for a block and then spoke again. "K541, see the resident, 3120 Manning, a 390—415." A drunk disturbing the peace . . . "K943, at corner Hollywood and Highland, a 390W." A drunken female, probably also disturbing the peace. "K980, the drugstore corner Sunset and Fairfax, a 484." Purse snatching. As the Ferrari turned on to Rayo Grande Avenue, the radio crackled again. "K411, see the woman northeast corner Hollywood and Vermont, a 311." How nice, thought Mendoza. Indecent exposure.

And it was full dark of another Christmas Day, the electric lights making day again of the city: the city where, whatever its name or place, crime never paused for holidays. As he turned up the drive he muttered to himself, "Progress? *Claro que esto es según se mire*—it all depends how you look at it."

He went in the back door to be greeted solely by Cedric the Old English sheepdog, who offered a paw and shook his hairy face-veil to show his walleye. "Well, *bufón*, where is everybody?" Sounds of revelry led him to the living room, where the twins were still engaged with Christmas presents, Johnny getting the hang of a new tricycle with triumphant yells and Terry attempting to fit a doll's hat to an indignant Bast. Alison turned from rescuing Bast to exclaim, "Good Lord, are you home already? I'm sorry, Luis, but where time went today—"

"A very wifely welcome." He bent to kiss her. "But what are you doing here, Mairí? It's supposed to be a day for family joy, and you've got your sister—"

"Ach," said Mrs. MacTaggart, "we're not so much for the Christmas at home, it's Hogmanay is the great day— that is, the New Year—and this pair enough to wear out their puir mother. I'll get you a dram. There's a roast of beef near done, and I'll be getting the twins' supper."

"Luis," said Alison.

"¿Querida?"

"We don't spoil them, do we? Give them too much?"

Mendoza laughed. "I don't suppose a happy childhood can do anybody any harm, cara." Thinking of his own somewhat less than happy one, he added absently, "Progress. Yes, indeed." The twins suddenly discovered he was home and made a beeline for him, shouting. The cats fled to take shelter.

"Oh, well," said Alison, starting for the kitchen after Mrs. MacTaggart, "I suppose it's all right if they're *disciplined*—" All the money: the money the miserly old man had concealed all those years, and Luis running the slum streets. She shouldn't feel guilty about spending the money, but she supposed they both always would, having grown up without any . . .

"At least," said Mendoza as he sat down to carve the roast beef, "you seem to have got them away from all the bloody horrors of Grimm. The new fairy tales—I like this fellow—"

"Andersen," nodded Alison. "A special edition, and nice illustrations. You're worried about something."

"*Un poco*," said Mendoza. "The state of the world, cara. As well as Lila."

But after dinner, with the twins asleep and Alison busy over letters, he sat at his desk in the den and absently handled the cards, practicing the crooked deals. He thought better with the cards in his hands, though the domesticities had ruined his poker game.

It was funny about Lila. . . .

"You don't usually bring the office home," said Mary. "Something offbeat?"

"In a sort of way," said Higgins. "After listening to that Askell, I just wonder what could have happened." He buttoned his pajama jacket slowly. The house was very quiet; the family, first- and secondhand, was asleep; and Mary looked very fetching in a new blue nylon gown, sitting up in bed over a book, her gray eyes smiling at him. "What Art was saying back awhile, you know—what we mostly see, the stupidity and cupidity. But once in a while you get a thing that—doesn't fit. The pattern, I guess I mean. This Askell girl—"

"So I'll be a good listener," said Mary.

"Well, that wasn't quite what I had in mind."

"—Always providing the baby doesn't wake up and start howling—"

Hackett was wondering about Lila too, but sensibly he reflected, wait and see what showed with a little legwork on it.

Grace wasn't thinking about anything except the baby. Their very own baby, at last, legally theirs.

Landers was wishing that Phil O'Neill wasn't quite such a sensible woman.

The Pallisers were discussing names. Roberta had settled on David Andrew or Elizabeth Margaret. Palliser objected to the latter. "It gets nicknamed," he said, "Liz. And Betty. And—"

"I rather like Betsy."

"It's too cute, damn it. The other way round, I'm agreeable. But—" They bent over the Dictionary of Common Christian Names, arguing amiably.

At eleven-twenty the night watch had a call: another burglary.

"We just got home, we went to the movies," said Dan Purdy angrily. "Locked up same as always—I been tellin' the manager here, these old apartments aren't safe! My God, Officer, near ever'thing we got—ever'thing we *had*— all our clothes and the radio and the little old TV, just a black and white, I work for a livin' honest, those bums on Welfare all got color TV but we don't—didn't—and Millie's garnet ring and necklace belonged to her ma—and my dad's old watch, the case was solid gold, he was a railroad man—"

Landers wrote up the report, yawning and thinking about Phil O'Neill.

3

When Mendoza came into the office, late, on Tuesday morning, Hackett was sitting in his desk-chair reading Landers' report on the burglary. "Here's our boy again, Luis. He sort of stands out. I mean, we inherited a lot of break-ins, we've had more since we took over, but this bird is just a little different. I've been thinking of a word for him. Diffident."

"*Maravilloso,*" said Mendoza, hanging up the perennial black homburg. "Get out of my chair. Why?"

"The M.O.—all the same. Private residences, mostly apartments And I've been looking at addresses—it's roughly the same territory. He's never hit west of Virgil, east of Alvarado, above Third or below Olympic."

Mendoza considered that, taking the report. They had indeed inherited this and that from Goldberg's unfinished business. The hijacking. On Central's beat, there was hardly a night went by without a mugging, but that too was anonymous: and not all of them got reported. The break-in at a big pharmacy out on Third had been earmarked for Pending when Mendoza's team took over. The two gas station heists from ten days and a week ago scarcely tied up to the burglar.

"The loot," said Hackett, "not big. I wondered if maybe he hasn't got access to a car?"

"Now that is a far-out idea, Arturo," said Mendoza. "And I'd remind you we've got other things to think about than that burglar. You and George, or somebody, will do some solid legwork around the Greyhound station." He went across the hall to see who was in. It was Grace's day off; they were probably out buying more equipment for the baby. Piggott and Glasser were both typing reports: they'd been following up a couple of cases due to be tossed in Pending. Palliser wandered up with a paper cup of coffee, and Shogart sidestepped him, coming out.

"Where are you off to?" asked Mendoza.

"Got a witness coming in to look at some mug shots, that mugging in MacArthur Park last week."

"And so what job do I get?" asked Palliser.

Before Mendoza could tell him, Higgins marched in with a long sheet of mimeographed paper dangling from one hand. "Here's the bad news, boys. I stopped off at Communications to see if they had copies yet. Parkinson said he didn't think any ranking officers out of Central got on it, but I want to check."

"Oh-oh," said Hackett. "It isn't *likely*, but you never do know." Higgins thumbtacked the sheet onto the bulletin board: the list of unlucky ones, fingered at random to police the Pasadena streets and the Rose Bowl, on New Year's Day. They scrutinized it in silence for several minutes, automatically following the alphabet down from C to G to H to L to M to P and S. Nobody from this office had been fingered. "Small mercies," said Higgins. A copy of this list would be up in every precinct house and every sheriff's station, and the chosen ones cussing their luck. It was another of the thankless jobs reserved for cops, a thing that had to be done.

And Sergeant Lake was answering a call. "Seventy-seventh," he said tersely to Mendoza. "They've got the Macauley car."

"So have it towed in. Where?"

"Rammed into a service station pump out on Manchester. They say, inoperable."

"Fancy words. Have it towed in, and I'll see it when it arrives. Art, the—"

[42]

"Greyhound Bus station, all right. But somebody ought to look at that burglary, it does belong to us."

"John can take a lab truck and poke around. A waste of time, but we have to go through the motions."

"I've got Callaghan now," said Sergeant Lake. "He wants to see you."

"Well, he knows where my office is."

"He says it's about a hired dropper supposed to be in town—"

"*¡Dios me libre!*" said Mendoza.

Palliser went to look at the scene of the burglary. The Purdys, a couple in middle age and not looking exactly prosperous, were still furious. They'd been asked not to clear up after the burglar; they said they hadn't, and Duke started dusting all possible surfaces for latents while the Purdys unburdened themselves to Palliser.

"Just out to the movies, come home and find this—the few little pieces of good jewelry I had, my mother's ring and—the radio and the TV—it's not right—"

"It's not that we blame you, did you say Sergeant?" Dan Purdy was a smallish man with false teeth that clicked. He was a salesclerk in the men's department at Robinsons'. "You guys do a good job when you're let, the damn judges letting these thieves out as soon as you catch 'em. And you can't be everywhere at once. If I told that damn Morrison once I been at him a hundred times, the locks on this place are no damn good at all! All he says is, he's just the manager, don't own the place, it isn't up to him install new locks—some big company owns this place, and the rents like they are you'd think they'd give you something for it, but catch them! I don't say we got much, Sergeant, but what we've got we'd like to keep if you get me. I went so far to get a locksmith up here, ask how much to put good locks on, and he tells me seventy bucks, windows and all. Now who's got that kind of money loose, I ask you! I just ask you!"

Purdy had, thought Palliser, a valid complaint. It was a

middle-aged apartment, about twenty units on three floors, and the Purdys' apartment was on the ground floor at the back. It would have been easy enough for anyone to come through the front door, whose lock lacked a deadbolt; the burglar had just as easily pried up the bedroom window, an old double-hung one with a rusty bolt offering little resistance.

"And Morrison says, we don't like it, we can move. You know what it costs to move these days? Even the little stuff we got? Even six or eight blocks? I don't make the biggest salary in the world, Sergeant. What do they expect us to do, anyways?"

Palliser couldn't tell him. Duke said presently that he'd come up with nothing but partial latents, all useless. He went away in the lab truck, and Palliser went to see Morrison, the building manager, who lived in a third-floor apartment. Morrison growled at his diplomatic suggestions. "Look, I don't own the place. If the owner don't want to lay out for new locks, it's not up to me." Mr. Morrison, however, Palliser noticed, had a stout chain on his front door and a lock with a deadbolt.

He went back to the office to get a report out, and like Hackett, read over the back reports on the burglar with some interest. In the welter of muggings and heist jobs over the past couple of months, the rather modest burglar stood out curiously. An amateur? Picking places easy to break in? Palliser read lists and added estimates. There was nothing reported stolen valuable enough, or identifiable enough, to go on the hot list to pawnbrokers. The average loot from one of those jobs might yield twenty, thirty dollars. It really added to petty theft. Anonymous loot: grandmother's garnet ring, the transistor radio, the old tape recorder. The burglar needn't even know a fence.

It was just a little offbeat. And it seemed funny to be chasing a burglar.

"All I know is," said newly promoted Captain Patrick Callaghan, "I get the short end of the stick." He looked at Mendoza querulously: in the absence of Hackett and

Higgins he dwarfed the office, wide-shouldered and looming, with a crest of hair redder than Alison's. "So, the big shake-up, greater efficiency, and what happens to me? Half my men get transferred away from me because Seventy-seventh and Harbor need beefing up—damn it, I know that, but Central isn't exactly about to shut down for lack of business, Luis. So they hand me a whole office of plain-clothes dicks who've been dealing with these nice genteel burglars and heist-men for years and wouldn't know a deck of H from headache powders—"

"Oh, I wouldn't say that. A lot of heist-men on the job to support a habit these—"

"And the new lieutenant they give me hasn't reported in yet, for God's—"

"Now, Saul was pretty sick, Pat. Psittacosis can be—"

"All right, all right. Ten-dollar words. Parrot fever, for God's sweet sake! He's supposed to be in after New Year's. Oh, Goldberg's a good man, but all these burglar chasers of his— Ah, I blow off steam, it's just that we've got quite a little business on hand. And now this thing. This Harry Singer."

"So what about him?"

Callaghan lit a cigarette and sighed. "Convictions the D.A.'s office has to sweat for, with the damn judges and courts. But we've got this one nailed but good—a supplier, a big supplier, with a pusher ready and willing to sing loud and clear on him, dates and facts and names and all. The pusher, if you'll believe me, never was hooked on the stuff himself—in business strictly for profit—and, if you'll believe me further, he's now got religion."

"¡Qué mono!" said Mendoza. "What's it got to do with me?"

"If we nail this one," said Callaghan seriously, "we'll put a lot of pushers out of business, Luis—at least temporarily. Anyway, dry up one big supply. We'll get him. But I've got a lot of dope from a couple of pigeons that there's a dropper in town hired to get my pusher so he can't sing. This Harry Singer. He's done time back east, I got a package on him from the Feds. I just thought you'd better know he's around. He's wanted for P.A. violation from Leaven-worth."

"Thanks so much. Who is your pious canary and where to be found?"

"Oh, you don't need to worry about him," said Callaghan. "I was feeling a little nervous about him anyway, and I've got him in protective custody. Nice private cell of his own, all the Bibles and hymnbooks he wants. I just thought you'd better hear about Harry. If you should come across him—here's the package on him."

"I'll bear it in mind," said Mendoza.

The ticket agent at the Greyhound Bus station was co-operative, but not very helpful. Yes, he'd been here on the twenty-fourth. "But I wouldn't be noticing the passengers off a bus unless somebody asked me about something or—" He looked at the photograph of Lila Askell; copies had been made up by the S.I.D. overnight. He shook his head. He was an alert-looking man in his forties with friendly eyes. "Nope, doesn't ring a bell, sorry."

But he could tell them about buses. There'd been a bus in from Santa Barbara at 11:50 A.M. that day. A bus out for San Francisco at twelve noon. A bus in from San Diego at—

"How about one heading for Vegas?" asked Hackett. "On the way to Utah?"

He had the schedule out to show them. "Yes, Sergeant. Due to leave for Vegas at three-fifteen that day."

"She had a three-hour wait," said Higgins. They didn't ask because they knew that no records were kept of passengers' names; the tickets just handed over as they boarded the bus. The baggage would be carried on the same bus; Lila's, tagged properly at Santa Barbara, had probably reached the station in Salt Lake by now. "She wouldn't have stayed here." The station was bare and not very big: a pair of rest rooms, a few dusty benches, a cigarette-machine. The agent didn't remember her, but— "Do you remember if that bus was very crowded?"

"Well—day before Christmas. It was pretty full, yes. I do recall there were four or five servicemen, they'd be on

Christmas leave, maybe near enough to go home for Christmas."

"Army, Marines?"

He shook his head. "I didn't notice—uniforms much the same now. Just uniforms, I noticed. They all got off the bus, the passengers, out in back there, and came through the station. I don't recall that anybody hung around— maybe a couple used the rest rooms. Sorry I can't tell you any more. This girl—er—missing or something?"

"Or something," said Higgins. They went to the door and looked out into the street. "A three-hour layover, Art. Where would she go, not knowing anybody here? She'd have time to get some way off and still make it back by three-fifteen."

She had got some way off, Hackett pointed out. "It was noon. She'd been on that bus for a couple of hours or more —call it a hundred miles from Santa Barbara. I think she'd have wanted some lunch."

Sixth and Spring Streets was not the best area of Los Angeles, and Lila Askell, according to her father, hadn't known the city at all, only passed through it once before. But to the east down Sixth, she would have seen the tall shabby buildings, no greenery, while in the other direction she'd have caught a glimpse of the greenery of Pershing Square, the cleaner-looking red brick of the Biltmore Hotel up there. She might have guessed that better streets lay that way—with, presumably, more attractive coffee shops and restaurants.

They started up Sixth. Just past Broadway there was a big cafeteria on this side of the street; from outside it looked clean if rather bare. "It would be a cafeteria," said Hackett: but they went in and asked. Yes, the same cashier had been on duty on the twenty-fourth. No, she couldn't say she remembered this girl coming in. She couldn't say she hadn't; they had a lot of people coming in, some regulars and some just casuals.

They went on to the drugstore on the next corner; it had no fountain. The next square block, of course, was taken up by Pershing Square with the tri-level parking lot under it; and on all sides of that, there were drugstores, two small coffee shops, another cafeteria: but most prominent, across on the corner of Olive, was a big chain-name restaurant under a flashing neon sign. They waited for the light and crossed to it.

"This is a waste of time," said Hackett. "We've skipped a dozen places. We ought to split up and cover every place where you can buy a sandwich, four blocks around the station."

"We might get lucky."

Palliser had got switched onto the Macauley case when he got back to the office; the Buick had just been towed in to the headquarters garage, and he went down with Mendoza to look at it. Scarne and Fisher from the lab had been alerted and met them there.

"What a mess," said Scarne. The Buick—Mrs. Macauley, called and asked, had said there hadn't been a dent in it anywhere, Stanley was very careful with a car, a careful driver—was a wreck. Its nose was stove in, the right fender crumpled, all four tires flat. They peered inside without touching it; the driver's window was down all the way.

"What the hell's that?" asked Fisher. "An animal of some—"

Mendoza said interestedly, "Mrs. Macauley's best wig. Well, well. Pulled off in the struggle. And I think her handbag. Well, you boys can start dusting, and hope you come up with something useful."

"Just an educated guess," said the man from Seventy-seventh Street precinct who'd brought it in. "It could've been drag-raced, you know these wild punk kids. Or the driver could've been drunk, of course. Anyway, the tank's nearly dry. Its front end got rammed in when it was left in that gas station, just rammed up against one of the pumps."

"Mmh," said Mendoza. He had sent Wanda Larsen down to R. and I. with the description Mrs. Macauley had given them: the computers should turn up a few names and faces to match it, and then they could haul those men in for questioning, for Florence Macauley to look at. If the lab turned some latents to match one of the names and faces, that would be a useful shortcut. They watched them work for a while without picking up anything, and Mendoza said, "Well, let us know."

Macauley's body had been found, and reported, by another couple coming out of the restaurant. They hadn't seen or heard anything before coming on the body, very likely within a very short time since it had become a body; but a small-caliber handgun doesn't make much noise. They had nothing else to offer: useless to ask them any questions.

Upstairs, Wanda was back, neat and blonde and efficient. "Six turned up in Records, sir. The computer—I got the packages for you."

"A starting-point," said Mendoza. "Could be he's right here." Records, the inevitable routine and piled-up filed-away case histories, did quite often clear up the new ones coming along.

The six men turned up by the computer, fed information by Phil O'Neill, were not the most respectable of citizens. All were Negro; they ranged from light to medium dark. They varied from five-ten to six-one, a hundred and thirty to a hundred and seventy, nineteen to twenty-seven. Five had previous convictions of rape, one of attempted rape. Three had records of armed robbery, two records of assault, one count of manslaughter. Mendoza sighed at the dispositions of these cases. One-to-three, three-to-five and P.A. after a year, probation, Sheriff's Farm one year, one-to-three and P.A. after six months—

"*Lo que no se puede remediár, se ha de aguantar*—what can't be cured," he muttered, "but I sometimes wonder why we work so hard catching up to them. So we go look for these louts to start with, ask for alibis and so on, and most of them won't be able to prove where they were when and it'll stay up in the air.'" He looked at his watch. "I wondered why I was hungry—after lunch, John."

Mike Donlevy was the fifth truck driver to have his cargo

hijacked; that had been a week ago. What with the fractured skull, he hadn't made a statement at the time; they hadn't been able to question him at all.

He turned up at headquarters at eleven o'clock, just as Hackett got back. "You're not the guy talked to my wife before. A middleweight like, she said, and talking about the devil bein' behind it. You ever do any pro fighting?" He glanced Hackett over professionally.

"Only in the course of the job," said Hackett. "I hope you're feeling all right now, Mr. Donlevy. Come in and sit down." They were alone in the sergeants' office.

"Sure. I'm O.K., only I'm still Goddamn mad," said Donlevy. "You didn't? You got the build, I just wondered. I was in the ring twelve years, see. Which is one reason I'm still Goddamn mad."

"Is that so?"

"I am telling you, it is so," said Donlevy. He raised a fist the size of a ham and contemplated it. "Me," he said. "Me! Basher Donlevy! I never been knocked right out all the time I'm in the ring. I won a few, so I did. I had a right cross nobody could see comin', Sergeant. Acourse I been out of training, I got to admit that. But *me*, jumped and laid out without I put a finger on him! Whoever it was. I was mad then and by God I'm still mad. Me, with a fractured skull! I hit the canvas a few times but I never took no kind of real hurt, even from that Spanish guy outweighed me twenty pounds." Mr. Donlevy was looking belligerent and dangerous. He exactly matched Hackett's six-three-and-a-half and weighed in perhaps at two thirty. Some of it would be beer and starch and apple pie, but not all of it by any means, thought Hackett.

"Well, I can see that," he said, grinning. "The doctor said there was a weapon used, something like a lead pipe. He got you from behind, we figured. Just like—"

"Even *so!*" said Donlevy. He had a large flat bulldog face, very bright blue eyes, large ears, and tightly curling black hair. His wife had given his age to the doctor as forty; he didn't look that.

"Well, the M.O. was the same on all of them. He waited

in the back of the truck for the driver to come back—none of you expecting it, even after the first couple of times it happened and got into the papers." There were a lot of trucks driving around everywhere in the city, making routine deliveries of liquor to retail liquor stores, markets, restaurants. The hijackings had been fairly crude. They had wondered after the first couple about inside information, but the subsequent ones showed a pattern. The trucks, all leaving from central warehouses down here, had been hijacked after making only one or two deliveries. Quite naturally the drivers would make deliveries to the nearest consignees first, which was why all the hijackings so far had occurred on Central's beat. In the two cases where the hijacker had waited for a second delivery to be made, the first deliveries had been to places minus any parking lot off the street. Canny, thought Hackett: a truck parked on the street, it was more likely that someone would see the driver attacked, and he'd be found much sooner. In every case, the driver had been left unconscious in the parking lot, not to be found for five or ten minutes.

And there were all too many owners of restaurants and bars who would jump at the cut-rate stuff. There'd be nothing about it to say it hadn't come from a legitimate source; by the time it was loaded by cases onto warehouse trucks, it was all labeled and sealed.

The trucks, of course, had been abandoned later in places which offered no clue at all as to where they'd been. Boyle Heights, Montebello, Rancho Park, Alhambra—even one down in Santa Monica. Park a truck on the street, walk away, who would remember?

"I can't give you any kind of description," said Donlevy regretfully. "That's what I can't get over, Sergeant. Back I come to the rig—I been driving for Smart and Final since I left the ring, ten years back—back I come, climb up to the seat, and bang! That's it."

"Even if you'd seen him you probably couldn't give a description. The two drivers who got a glimpse at him said he was wearing a ski-mask."

"Well, I'm no help to you," said Donlevy. "I'm sorry.

The wife said they told her I should come make a statement when I could, so I come. But that's all I can tell you. When I think what these damn bastards are getting away with! I'd only made one delivery, a couple o' cases o' beer to a joint on Spring doesn't even have a hard-liquor license. There must've been ten thousand bucks' worth of stuff in that rig. Bourbon, Scotch, vodka, gin—by God! And Smart and Final standin' the loss. It isn't right, Sergeant."

"Well, I'm sorry you can't help us," said Hackett.

"So am I," said Donlevy. "I'm damn *mad* I can't help you, Sergeant. But I'll tell you this, Sergeant." He looked at his balled right fist. "These bastards, whoever, I just hope to God they'll pick my rig to knock over again. Because if they do, I'll be ready for 'em. Me, knocked clean out before I even made a fist! I tell you, from now on—Goddamn lead pipe or whatever—they want to play dirty, Mike Donlevy can play just as dirty any day! Every time I come back to the rig from now on, I'm gonna be wearing a set of brass knuckles, and I'm climbin' in the rig face first, you can bet. With both eyes peeled, Sergeant."

"And I'll wish you luck. But they say lightning never—"

"Don't take any bets," said Donlevy. "I'll be ready for 'em if they *do*."

The afternoon papers had made minor headlines of the Macauley killing; he had been a prominent realtor, a former city councilman.

Palliser, Piggott and Glasser had gone out looking for the six men out of Records. They hadn't found any of them by three-thirty.

At three-forty Higgins came to an Orange Julius bar just past the corner of Hill on Seventh Street. Doing the tedious routine, he had started back at the bus station and hit every place that dispensed food of any variety between there and here. At one o'clock he had taken twenty minutes for lunch at the chain-name restaurant. He was wondering now what use it might be to find a waitress who could say, yes, that girl was here, she had a sandwich and left a quarter tip.

Who could not say, she went on up Broadway, or wherever.

But the routine had to be done.

The Orange Julius bar was a hole-in-the-wall, like all of them. It offered the standard hot dogs, hamburgers, malts, besides its famous fizzy orange froth. At this hour, even along a busy block, there wasn't a customer in the little place: he counted six empty stools before the clean white counter. There was a girl, slim in a white uniform-dress, a dark-brown girl with straightened black hair piled on her head in a topknot, very neat. Higgins got out the photograph of Lila, and his badge.

"Oh!" she said to the badge. She smiled at Higgins, and said respectfully, "Sergeant. You'll be out of the detective office. My brother's just a rookie yet."

"That so?" Higgins smiled at her.

"Out of Seventy-seventh," she said. "Can I help you, Sergeant? You like something—"

"No thanks. This girl—have you ever seen her in here?" And what a hope that was.

She studied the photograph. "She's pretty. You know, I did, Sergeant. I surely did."

"What?" Higgins was startled. "Are you sure?"

"I'm sure. I've got a good memory for faces, but I had a reason, too." She raised suddenly troubled dark eyes to him. "I should've done something. I don't know what I could've done, but I— But, you know, it was getting toward Christmas Eve, and I was off at two—I was watching the time—and I still had Mama's biggest present to pick up, and—I let it go. I let it be." She looked at the picture.

"Tell me about it," said Higgins gently. "If you're sure it was this girl."

"It was this one." She spoke in a low voice. "They came in about twelve-thirty. Like I say I was going off at two—"

"On Sunday?"

"That's right. Getting to Christmas Eve. She was dressed nice, kind of plain. A brown suit and a yellow blouse. And they had hamburgers—he had an orange and she had a vanilla malt to go with them."

[53]

"A man. Can you describe him? I'd better have your name, Miss—"

"Louise Chaffee, Sergeant. Yes, a young man, and—I don't know if I can make it plain to you, how it was. Why I noticed particular. She was—she was nervous with him. I could tell. Like—well, like that time I let Maggie set up a blind date—not *knowing* a fellow, you're nervous, kind of. Not knowing what he's like. It was like that. It wasn't anything I heard her or him say exactly, he laughed a lot, but— Oh, a woman'd know what I mean! Just, she was shy of him, sort of. I had some other customers in too, but I noticed. They were only here about twenty minutes."

"The man? Young? I think we'll want a statement from you—"

"Well, there wasn't anything—anything really, I could suspect anything wrong about it—you know? I couldn't have done anything, no reason. It was just a *feeling*. I hadn't thought about it again till you showed me the picture. Well, he was just a fellow. I don't know I could describe him—I guess he had sort of light hair. He laughed a lot. He had on a gray jacket, and no tie. Did—did something happen to her, Sergeant?"

"Yes," said Higgins. "We'll want you to make a statement. If you're sure."

"I had a feeling about it," she said wretchedly. "She was —shy of him. I—but it was Christmas Eve, I had Mama's present to—and it was broad daylight, Sergeant. Patrolman Kaplan right at the corner out there. If she was that leery of him she could just go off— And I'd clean forgot about it till you showed me the picture. But whatever I can do to help—"

Palliser came back to the office at five o'clock, after an abortive hunt for one Thomas Waffer, still on P.A. for armed robbery, and was handed a new complaint: attempted break-in. He went out to see what it looked like, feeling sour and tired. They hadn't anything to show for a long day's work; but that was nothing new.

It was an address out on Third Street, and turned out to be a market wearing a well-known chain name. The manager, Raymond Osney, apologized to him.

"Bring you out here for nothing, Sergeant. I'm sorry, just thought I ought to report it. I didn't notice it until just awhile ago when I was out in the stockroom, when the Smart and Final truck came in. We've been held up six times in the last two years and had four break-ins and four attempts the last year, you know? My God, the crime rate." He showed Palliser the jimmy-marks on the door of the big stockroom behind the market. "Obviously, they didn't get in. Probably Christmas Eve—possibly last night, we were closed yesterday, of course. I've wondered about dogs, you know."

"Dogs?" said Palliser.

"The guard dogs. Why the company doesn't use them. Very efficient, by all I've heard. And the losses from burglaries alone—let alone the holdups. This market alone, the holdup men got away with over ten grand all told, but the burglaries are worse. It's the liquor and cigarettes they're after, mostly, and you'd think the company would invest in some adequate protection. Our burglar-alarm system here, in my opinion, is useless. An old installation, and the last time I tested it, it wasn't working properly. I called the head office, but—"

It would be a waste of time to turn out a lab man on those pry-marks, thought Palliser.

"Considering the crime rate, especially in this area, I suggested the dogs. To the head office. I understand you can rent them. From places specializing in the trained guard-dogs, that is. Well, I suppose I've wasted your time, but I thought I ought to report it—"

Higgins had just finished briefing Mendoza on Louise Chaffee, who would be off duty at five o'clock and come in to make a statement, when a uniformed man brought in a manila folder.

"Autopsy reports," said Mendoza. "Now let's see what

[55]

showed. Stomach contents should tell us if Louise's girl was Lila Askell, at any rate." But he hadn't slit the flap when Sergeant Lake looked in.

"I've got a call from Central Receiving, Emergency. They've just had a man brought in, beaten up, possible skull fracture, says he was attacked by a man and a woman posing as a prostitute—"

"*¡Condenación!*" said Mendoza. "That pair of cons—I said we'd hear about them again." And just how to mount a hunt for them—and for all the good it would do to catch up to them, human nature being what it was— But it was another job to work.

4

SHOGART WAS IN: all of Goldberg's old files had been brought up here, and as the only man familiar with them Shogart was weeding out the dead wood. Mendoza chased him over to Central Receiving to get that story, and came back to find Higgins telling Hackett about Louise.

"So she did pick up with a stranger after all. Funny," said Hackett thoughtfully.

"No," said Mendoza. "Or, the familiar stranger. I've got a little idea there— Well, let's see what the autopsy says."

The autopsy report confirmed that Lila Askell was the girl Louise Chaffee had noticed. Contents of stomach, ingredients of a hamburger—bread, cheese, mayonnaise, tomato, mustard, ground beef—milk, ice cream, french fries. Digestion just started, estimated time of death a scant hour after eating. "One-thirty," said Mendoza. She had died a virgin. Healthy young woman, no indicated diseases, no vestiges of alcohol or narcotics. She had been beaten, not severely—a precise list of contusions, right eye, mouth, left cheekbone, various places on the body—and manually strangled. "Yes," said Mendoza, passing it on to Hackett, "and that doesn't take long. Somebody in a temper, maybe because she was going to walk out on him—"

"But when did she pick him up and who was he?"

"She didn't. I had a little idea there. She wouldn't, by her past history, have picked up anybody. But she'd been on that bus for two hours or more, and we heard it was crowded. Any bets she didn't have a seat-mate?"

"My God, of course," said Hackett. "That feels right, Luis, for what this Louise says."

"And just maybe," said Higgins, "it was one of our fine upstanding young servicemen on Christmas leave."

"*Pues sí.* Or said he was. Not in uniform, Louise would have noticed that." Mendoza was swiveled around looking out the high window at the line of Hollywood hills on the horizon. "Mmh, mitigating circumstances can we say? It was Christmas, and if the fellow was polite, friendly, she wouldn't want to be rude to a fine upstanding young serviceman—or anyone else. He says, let's go to lunch together, what can she say? Not that it was much of a lunch, and a funny place to go—"

"But he paid. Louise was definite on that."

"Mmh," said Mendoza again. "You can see how it might have happened. After all, it was—"

"To take the words out of your mouth, broad daylight," said Hackett. "If he started to get fresh, threw a pass, she could just walk off. Or yell for cops. Why—"

"We don't know where they were when and if that happened, Arturo. He wouldn't throw a pass on the street."

"But she wouldn't have gone anywhere—private—with him."

"We're arguing ahead of evidence," said Mendoza. "The lab's got her clothes, they may turn up something." He was still frowning as he took up the other autopsy report.

Stanley Macauley had probably never felt the bullet that killed him; he had died instantly. The bullet had been lodged in his heart. Bainbridge estimated it was a .22, had sent it to S.I.D. Macauley had been a healthy specimen for his age, only slight indications of beginning arteriosclerosis. Stomach contents, with digestion barely started, small amount of alcohol, salad greens, salad dressing, beefsteak, potato, cream pie. "Condemned man ate a hearty meal," said Mendoza to himself, passing the report on to Higgins. The only way to work that one was by the routine, look for and then at the men in Records conforming to the description with an appropriate background for that kind of assault: that was a place to start. Unless Mrs. Macauley could pick a face out of the mug shots. And she might pick one, and be wrong.

Sergeant Lake looked in. "There's a Miss Chaffee here."

Mendoza was waiting for the elevator, hat in hand, when Shogart emerged from the next one. "So the report can wait till morning," he said. "To brief you, it sounds like the same pair. Woman with black hair, medium-sized, medium good figure, the same old routine—alley a shortcut to her back door, bingo, the guy jumped from behind, wallet gone. He wasn't seriously hurt. Lost about fifteen bucks. He's feeling like a damned fool, which he is."

"Yes," said Mendoza, "and that's a shapeless sort of thing too, E.M. How do we go looking? Are they worth setting up a decoy?"

"Well, they could end up killing somebody," said Shogart. "All accidental like. I'll do the report in the morning."

When Hackett got home, coming in the back door, he found Angel frosting a cake. "Nice," he said, bending to kiss her, and as she dropped the spatula in the dishwater, rescued it in midair to lick it off. "Mmh, almond. Very nice."

"Not for you," said Angel. "Calories." But her mountain-pool eyes smiled at him. "Have you found out any more about that poor Mormon girl? It seemed so odd—"

"Well, I'll try this on you for size, see what a female thinks of it," and he outlined Mendoza's idea about the fellow bus passenger.

"Y—es," said Angel. "Yes, I can see that, Art. She wouldn't want to be rude, and there'd be no reason to, well, be afraid of him. In broad daylight. If they'd been talking on the bus, sitting together—people do, and on a holiday too, the day before Christmas. I can see her going to lunch with him—and what a funny place—but I can't see her going anywhere private, where he might have the chance to throw a pass. And besides"—she set the cake-plate on the drainboard—"you said she'd been thrown out of a car. If it was another passenger on the bus, just passing through, where'd he get a car?"

Hackett stared at her. "My God, I never thought of— my God, yes! Only—"

Mark came shouting, discovering that Daddy was home, and the great silver Persian shot past fleeing a pursuing Sheila, these days less tottery on her fat legs. "Mustn't chase the kitty," and Hackett bent hastily to pick her up. "You know, Angel, that is a thought. Luis just talking off the top of his mind—"

"Belatedly I'm improving my education," said Mendoza, coming into the living-room at seven-thirty. "All the fairy tales I never had read to me. I like this Andersen fellow." He looked around at this part of his household, all serene: the cats settled in a pile on the sectional, Cedric dutifully at Alison's feet. Alison was wearing a favorite topaz hostess gown, and her copper hair caught gleams from the shining ornaments on the great Christmas tree across the room.

"Um. The Ugly Duckling," she said vaguely, looking up from her book. "Which reminds me, you know if it stays as sunny and warm as this for long, that mockingbird's going to be back to nest early."

"¡Dios me libre! Our little feathered friends—"

"Luis, I've been thinking about that girl." She put down her book. "You're woolgathering, you know. The nice story about the other bus passenger. But she was thrown out of a car. In Exposition Park, of all places. So where did the other passenger acquire a car all of a sudden?"

"¡Vaya!" said Mendoza, struck. "My God, I didn't—" he stopped. "My God, you're right. My maundering wits—"

"And I know it sounds farfetched," said Alison meditatively, "but they do say Los Angeles is getting to be quite a crossroads. Like that place in Egypt. What I thought was —it *is* farfetched, but I wondered if she ran into somebody she knew? From Santa Barbara? Well, look, it's only a hundred miles up the coast. How long had she been working there?"

"Since last February. But—"

"Well, there you are. She'd have met all sorts of people in eleven months. And she was working at a hospital," said Alison, suddenly further inspired. "A patient—"

"If you're going to say a mental patient, I don't think it was that kind of hospital," said Mendoza. "That's reaching, *cara*."

"Well, it was just an idea. With just what you've got on her now, I don't see that you've got any leads to work at all. The Louise girl said she couldn't be sure she'd recognize the man—even if he is in your records, and nothing says he is."

"Let me relax in peace, woman. Put some more brains on it tomorrow. Of course it's possible the other passenger's destination was L.A. because he lives here, so he'd have a car—"

"Talk about reaching," said Alison.

When Mendoza came into the office on Wednesday morning Grace was there—"He was waiting for me when I got here," said Lake—with a sheaf of snapshots. Of, of course, Celia Ann. "We took these at the party last night—" He began passing them around eagerly. "Isn't she a doll?"

"How'd you get snapshots so quick?" asked Higgins, coming in on the heels of Palliser and Hackett. "Let's see. She surely is cute, Jase. Of course she's older than Margaret—I've got some new shots in the camera now, finish up the film tonight if Steve doesn't get hold of it first—"

"Oh, I got one of these Polaroid outfits, you get the picture right away, you know. Here's one I got of her eating ice cream— get those big eyes—"

"Say, the film-pack for that really costs," said Higgins. "You'll be sorry about that. I looked at it too, the camera isn't bad, it's the upkeep—"

"Well, when you get the pictures right off it's worth it. Here she is with Dad—and in this little pink dress Ginny got—"

They looked at the snapshots, smiling at his eager pride, and they thought back, inevitably, to that day last August, the quiet professional office, with the shocking, bloody corpses, and the sudden discovery of three-month-old Celia Ann, brown and plump and smiling, hidden in the shower where her mother had left her before the wanton bullets were fired. At least Celia Ann was one orphan who'd found a good home—shoe on the other foot at that maybe, the way the Graces had been moving heaven and earth to get her legally adopted.

"She is a honey, Jase," said Hackett, handing back the snapshots. "Don't let George be a wet blanket."

"I just say, you take many pictures, that thing'll keep you broke buying film," said Higgins. "You wait and see. Did I show you the ones I got of Margaret in the bath—"

"Yes," said everybody. Grace put the pictures away reluctantly. He'd be having more to show tomorrow, all too likely. But little Celia Ann was special to the Graces.

"By the way," said Hackett, following Mendoza into his office, "Angel's a smarter detective than you are. I tried the other passenger on her, and she said so where'd he get a car? I—"

"Yes, so did Alison. Me maundering away ahead of any solid evidence—the car we're sure about. Nobody could have brought her there on foot."

"So where do we go on that now?"

Mendoza shook his head, looking frustrated. "A forlorn hope—get the press to run a story, please will any passenger on that bus trip come and see us? Over a holiday? With the bus full? Who might have noticed anything? Or would see the story in the paper?"

"Likely those passengers are scattered to the winds now," agreed Higgins.

"The lab may come up with something on her clothes," said Mendoza.

"And they may not too. There's no solid lead at all."

"I think I'd like to talk to that girl she's been living with," said Mendoza. "Once in a while my Scots-Irish wife uses a little ESP. Just once in a while. Meanwhile—" He put out his cigarette in the brass tray. As usual he was smartly dressed, the gray Italian silk, a dark tie with a severely plain gold tie-bar. "What we do have is a lead on Macauley. I'm going to get Mrs. Macauley down here sometime today to look at some faces. But we've got these names out of Records to look at, so let's get with it. I take no bets we don't get handed something new today. The holiday's over—nice quiet Christmas."

"Nice and quiet," said Hackett. There'd been another body last night, a natural death, just an old fellow slipping away in his sleep, but there'd be paperwork on it. The paper this morning had spoken of sudden death on the freeways and surface streets, the expectable drunk drivers. There were, as always in this week of the year, many out-of-staters around town, many with cars, crowding the hotels and motels, attracted by the parade and game. A lot of them were unfamiliar with California traffic laws. Every cop in the county would heave a sigh of relief next Tuesday, with the new year officially underway and traffic getting back to normal.

Lake thrust his head in. "There's been another hijacking. Retail liquor store out on Wilshire."

"Not Mr. Donlevy," said Hackett regretfully. "I hope sometime they do try him again. I'll go."

The driver wasn't much hurt, only banged on the head and shaken up. His name was Herman Keller, and he kept saying, "I was so surprised, and I seen the stories in the papers too, but you just never think it can happen to you— I was so surprised—" It had been his first delivery of the day, and the liquor store had its own small parking lot at one side. He'd only had one case to take in, and when he came back, the waiting hijacker knocked him over the head from behind, pushed him out of the cab, and made off with the truck within thirty seconds. The keys had been in it— "You don't bother, every stop—it's not like a private car, God's sake, I'm only gone three-four minutes—" And by the time Keller came to and got back to the store to phone, the truck was long gone.

The highjackings were fairly crude. The trucks carrying the liquor practically always bore advertising to mark them, not like the ones ferrying ordinary groceries to markets.

Hackett called the warehouse—not Smart and Final this time—and got the plate-number of the truck, and after some delay, some idea of the manifest. Looking at his hasty notes, he groaned mentally. At today's prices, ten G's easily, all the cases of liquor; and also, doubtless intended for some of the fancy liquor stores in the suburbs, a good deal of gourmet foods, teas, imported candies, choice olives.

He went back to the office and put out an A.P.B. on the truck. They were on it early; but they'd been on a couple of others early too without picking up the truck before it was abandoned.

Grace, Higgins and Palliser were out hunting the men Records had turned. Mendoza reported Mrs. Macauley to be on her way down to look at mug shots. "That's another little something, Art. She said he smelled oily, 'like a gas station.' Well, it's a job men like that can get—not much education needed."

"What are we doing about these hijackings, anyway?" asked Hackett. "Writing up reports, for God's sake. Wait for the next one."

Mendoza was reading a report; he shrugged. "¿Qué?" he said. "It's nothing new in crime, but it's only lately there's been a rash of it again all over the country. With good reason—inflation, black markets, barter. Almost any kind of hood, damn what his record says, might go off on that kick. Where do we look? The drivers ought to be alerted by now."

"That's not a very constructive attitude."

"If you have any suggestions—"

"I've brought in one of these boys," said Palliser from the door. "Thomas Waffer. Anybody like to sit in?"

"I've got this damn report to write," said Hackett. "Isn't there anybody else in?"

"Sure. Just asking," said Palliser amiably. He passed Sergeant Lake in the doorway.

"Mrs. Macauley's here. Mr. Hendry's with her."

Mendoza got up.

It was Piggott who escorted them down to one of the little private cubbyholes in R. and I., and got a couple of books of mug shots to start Mrs. Macauley off. Phil O'Neill brought them in, her flaxen curls shining, her uniform crisp. Mrs. Macauley looked at her with faint interest.

"Say," said Piggott, "is Tom minding his manners, Miss O'Neill?"

She smiled at him. "You can trust me for that. These do to start?"

"Fine. Now, Mrs. Macauley, if you'll just take your time and look at the photographs carefully. I know it's hard to be sure sometimes, and if the fellow who attacked you is in here, the picture won't look exactly like he did when you saw him. But if you find one that might be, just speak up." He'd stay here awhile to get her settled down; it was confusing to anybody, set down before a book of hundreds of photographs. Hendry beside her was looking curious and interested.

"There are such a lot," she said doubtfully. "Well, I'll try." She was in black, but not dowdy; pearl earrings and pin. Outside of crisis, a sensible woman; and she'd want this X found and punished.

Well, they might find him, thought Piggott.

"Interesting plant you've got here," said Hendry. "All the latest scientific gadgets, eh?"

"Well, sir, we need every bit of help we can get to keep on top of it nowadays. The devil getting around pretty fast and furious."

Hendry looked surprised. "Well, I guess some of the things you fellows run into seem pretty satanic all right. This thing right here—just no reason—"

"No reason except the devil's prodding," said Piggott, still thinking about the judges and courts. "The smartest thing the devil ever did, Mr. Hendry, was to convince people he doesn't exist." However, it was Wednesday: choir-practice tonight. Both he and Prudence were in the choir, and they were rehearsing some of the good old rousing ones that had a swing to them, "When the Roll is Called," and "Onward

Christian Soldiers"— "You just take your time," he said, "and if you think you spot the right man, you tell Miss O'Neill out there."

Thomas Waffer had a rap sheet of some length, but the most serious listing on it was for armed robbery, five years back. The rest read, possession of narcotics, petty theft, attempted assault, D. and D., auto theft. He was a native of Los Angeles, a dropout from sixth grade, probably illiterate. He didn't like cops, and he eyed Palliser and Glasser sullenly.

"I ain't done nothin'. Why you bring me in? I ain't—"

It always started like that with this kind; it got tiresome, but it was part of the job. They prodded at him patiently. Where had he been last Sunday night, the twenty-fourth, at nine o'clock? Was he with anybody who could back him up?

"Sund'y," he said. "Las' Sund'y? At night? Whyfor you guys wanta know? None o' your business—I'm clean, I ain't—" They went on prodding, and he finally said, "Well, I was just home. Sure, I was home—say, that was Christmas Eve, so sure I remember—I was home with my wife, an' she—"

"Which one?" asked Glasser. By his record, he had lived with several women on and off. There was no record of a formal marriage.

"Which—why, Gloria, acourse. My wife. Well, it's a name I don't recollect, the Welfare lady said, somethin' law—"

"What's the address, Waffer?" asked Palliser. "Where?"

He gave them an address on Forty-second; it wasn't in his recent records, but he was off P.A. and that didn't matter. "You have a job?" asked Glasser.

"What? Nossir, I ain't workin' reg'lar right now, but I been lookin' for a job—"

"Has Gloria got a job? What are you living on?" A fool question, Palliser thought.

"Well, she get the Welfare for the young 'uns, see— gonna get 'nother seventy, eighty, time she have the baby nex' month. But I ain't been doin' nothin', we get along, you got no call to—"

"Will you tell me why we waste time like this?" said Glasser outside in the corridor. "So we go see Gloria, was he there, and she says, oh, yessir, he was. So what do we have? An alibi?"

"I suppose," said Palliser, scratching his handsome straight nose, "that we get too cynical, Henry. There must be a few people living on Welfare who really need it, handicapped people, and old people, and so on, who'd starve without it."

"Damn few," said Glasser.

Just after noon, Phil O'Neill called from R. and I. "Your witness has turned up two shots she likes. I suppose you want her back with the packages on both."

"I suppose we do," said Sergeant Lake, who was feeling slightly bilious after an unappetizing lunch of celery sticks and raw carrot. He caught Mendoza just leaving for what would be a more substantial meal—Mendoza's metabolism did not threaten the extra poundage.

When Mrs. Macauley came in, Mendoza took the manila folders from Lake and without looking at them asked, "How sure are you of these? Any preference?"

She looked at Hendry. Her eyes were red again, because she'd been crying yesterday and then this morning used them hard on pages and pages of not-very-big photographs. "I—after a while they all look alike. I thought I could be absolutely sure—I'd never forget that man's face—it was dark but there was some light, you know. But—I tried to be careful. I found that one first, he looked *almost* like— I was *almost* sure—and I looked at some more and went back to that one, his name's Hibbs—and then I found the other one, and I could be almost sure about him too. They're alike, I know. I—if I had to say, I'd say the second one's more like him. What I remember."

"Mmh." Mendoza sat down again and offered cigarettes; she declined, and Hendry got out a cigar. Mendoza opened the folders.

Jasper Hibbs. An interesting record. Petty theft, auto theft, shoplifting, D. and D., armed robbery three counts, statutory rape. Suspended sentences, probation, thirty days in the County jail, one-to-three, three-to-five. He was twenty-eight now and had served exactly two years and eight months inside. He was Negro, light-medium, five-eleven, a hundred and fifty, knife scar on one arm. He was on P.A. now from the latest armed robbery count; the address was Sixtieth Place.

The second one was the same general type, but the face was tougher, even stupider-looking. A mean one in drink, Mendoza could guess. The rap sheet was longer too: j.d. counts of assault, weapons possession, narco possession, mugging; as an adult, attempted rape, rape, armed robbery. He had done a little more time. He was Chester Gosling, Negro, medium, twenty-seven, five-ten, one-forty, a user when he could get anything—Mary Jane, bennies, speed, H.

"Thanks very much, Mrs. Macauley. We'll see if we can turn these two up. We appreciate your taking the time—"

"And then what?" asked Hendry. "I mean, so you find 'em. What then?"

"We'd like to arrange a show-up. That is, if Mrs.Macauley will come in and look at them, in a line of other men, and see if she can positively identify one of them."

"I see. And suppose she can't? To be positive."

Mendoza shrugged. "We like a positive identification. Barring any more solid evidence. The lab is still going over the car, and if they come across any latents—fingerprints—that can be tied to either of these men, that'd be nice solid evidence. But we can't arrest people on suspicion."

"I suppose not," said Hendry. He was eyeing Mendoza's beautifully-tailored Italian silk with a mixture of surprise, small hostility and curiosity. By his own tailoring, he would guess accurately at its price tag; and honest cops weren't supposed to make that kind of money. Mendoza supposed that in the interests of upholding the integrity of the LAPD, he ought to explain about the miserly grandfather; he let it go.

"What—what about our car?" she asked hesitantly. "We heard you found it—"

"Rather a total loss," said Mendoza, "I'm afraid. You'd better get your insurance firm on it. We'll let you know when S. I.—when the lab's finished with it."

"Well, I see. Thanks," said Hendry. "I don't know what for."

"We try to do the job, Mr. Hendry."

"Now, Walter. We've got to help them any way we can. With Stanley—Stanley dead for just no reason at all."

Mendoza sat down at his desk again and brought out the cards to practice crooked deals. He thought about Lila Askell. An Orange Julius bar, for God's sake. Funny place to take a girl to lunch. How long had they been around? Forty years. At first, just the sweet orange froth—advertisement for the Golden State, tourist attraction, everybody who drank orange juice lived to be a hundred. These days, the sandwiches, the snacks. And Broadway—Seventh Street—those crowded busy streets, even more hectic than usual the day before Christmas, crowds at the last-minute shopping—who'd have noticed that anonymous couple?

Where, in fact, to look, to find out just what had happened to Lila Askell? Who the young man was—more fair than dark, a man who laughed a lot?

"Are you going out to lunch at all?" asked Lake.

Hackett had just come back to the office at two-fifteen, to check in; he and Palliser and Grace were still running down names from Records. Lake gave him the two new ones, the ones Mrs. Macauley had fingered, and those would take priority now. But before he started out on that, a call came in from a sheriff's station out in Belvedere. They'd just found the hijacked truck.

All according to pattern, thought Hackett; and Luis might say what he liked, they ought to try to do something constructive about it. Almost anybody might go in for that, so all right, the pigeons had the word and were supposed to be looking around—but that was a slow way to do it.

He went out to look at the truck. They had always been turned up the same day: the hijackers knew the plate-numbers would be out on the air very soon. Take it some-where private, a big commercial garage would be ideal, and strip it, drive it off and leave it.

This one had been left parked along a main drag, Mednik Avenue. It was a busy street; nobody had noticed when it had been left or by whom. Just, there it was.

As if in contempt, all the fancy gourmet foods had been left in it; only the liquor was gone. The cases and cases of bourbon, Scotch, rye, vodka, gin—

"I suppose you'll tow it in and go over it," said the sheriff's detective. "Never left any latents yet, I understand, but we have to go by the book."

"That is a fact," said Hackett. "As if we hadn't enough else to do." As plain Homicide: and now, all the stealing to deal with too. Well, supposedly the computers made it easier. As if anything to do with human nature was ever easy, or uncomplex.

He called the lab to come and tow the truck in. It was five to three. He went back to the Central beat and started looking for Jasper Hibbs.

There was another incident of what Higgins called L.A.'s own invention in slaughter: the rocks thrown off freeway overpasses. This one produced a D.O.A. There was, in the middle of the afternoon, a heist-job at a small market over on Virgil. A good deal of new construction was going on in L.A. now, the new high-rise buildings on Wilshire and all over— "Everybody," said Piggott, "rejoicing because they didn't fall down in the quake, hah! It didn't hit anywhere near—just wait for the next one!"—and an accident at a site on Beverly Boulevard came along a little later, an earth-slide with two men suffocated. So at four-fifteen Mendoza was alone in the Robbery-Homicide office, practicing the crooked deals and thinking about Lila Askell, when Lake buzzed him.

"Call from Traffic. Assault with intent, sounds like, at the Biltmore Hotel."

"¿Y depués?" said Mendoza. "Woman's work, Jimmy." He reached for his hat.

At the Biltmore, the badge brought him a twittering manager, concerned for the hotel's reputation but also humanly shaken. "A nice old fellow," he told Mendoza in the express elevator. "The ambulance just came, thank God, I hope he'll be all right. A nice fellow, old Mr. Pound. I like him—we all like him. I shouldn't say mister. A terrible thing—here in October, you know, a vacation he said, and then he decided to move to California—he'd been living in Chicago—it's down here, seven-fourteen—" He led the way. "The men from the squad car were very good, they—"

Two men with a stretcher passed them, moving fast. One attendant recognized Mendoza and said, "We've got to get him in fast, he's lost a lot of blood—he's past talking now anyway."

"Oh, dear, oh, dear," said the manager. "Old Mr.—I shouldn't say that—decided to move out here, he said, no family at all, he's a widower, and he came back just before Christmas, but he hadn't—"

The room was the ordinary Biltmore Hotel room, well and quietly appointed, a double bed made up, white-tiled bath off to one side, closet the other. There had been a struggle of some kind here: the desk was lying on its side, inkwell spilled in a dark splotch on the beige carpet, Gideon Bible upside down beyond, a pen, a notebook scattered. Two water glasses lay nearby, apparently empty. There were other, darker stains nearer the door, one great puddle with clusters of clots visible.

"We think it happened awhile ago," said one of the uniformed men. "The ambulance men said—"

"He didn't come to the dining room," gabbled the manager. "For his Christmas dinner. Yesterday. He said—you see, he hadn't decided exactly where to settle down—he liked Santa Monica—he'd rented a car, you see—but he liked the valley too—and when the maitre d' came and told me—Gustav noticed he hadn't come down—not a young man, and I thought I ought to investigate—"

Mendoza raised his brows at the Traffic men. "He found

him and called in. Looked like assault all right, he was beat up but good. Poor old fellow. Looks as if the room's been ransacked too."

"All alone in the world—" The manager passed a handkerchief across a wet brow— "Such a nice old man. Retired Army officer, did I tell you that? Lieutenant colonel, a career Army man, and he was only staying here till he decided—"

"It looked," said the other Traffic man thoughtfully, "touch and go, whether he makes it."

5

MENDOZA SENT the Traffic men back on tour and called the office; Higgins was in, and would get the lab on it. Waiting for that, Mendoza heard more from the manager, Carlos Di Silva. Lieutenant Colonel (ret.) Archer Pound had been at the hotel since the twentieth, this last time; he came and went every day, an active man, but had always had dinner in the hotel dining room; Di Silva did recall him saying that he hadn't any friends in Los Angeles, adding cheerfully that doubtless he'd soon make some. "He's such a nice old fellow," said the manager agitatedly. "I'd been afraid—a heart attack or—but this! Whatever could have happened—"

The men from the lab, Duke and Fisher, arrived with Higgins behind them; they looked around the room, Di Silva hovering in the background. The closet door was open. "Not many clothes," pointed out Higgins. "Only one suitcase." It was aged scuffed brown leather.

Di Silva said, "Excuse me, but the lieutenant colonel has several suits. Good suits. And three suitcases when he came. He has a light gray suit, I know, and I've seen him in a navy—"

Mendoza inspected the dresser top. "Wallet, empty—don't yelp at me, Duke, it'd never take prints, it's new deerskin, and"—he looked—"not much in the rest of it." In the little plastic slots, an Illinois driver's license, membership card for a veterans' organization, a library card for the Chicago Public Library. "Do you know if he used any credit cards?"

Di Silva shook his head. "I don't know, he paid the hotel in travelers' checks, sir, but a lot of people—"

"Well, if he had any, they're gone. And," added Mendoza, "I don't see a watch. Check with the hospital, see what was on him—"

"He always wears a ring," volunteered Di Silva, "I noticed that, it's a West Point class ring, and he's got a gold wristwatch—I told you he rented a car from—"

"So we'd better check that too," said Higgins. Duke had just dusted the phone and pronounced it clean. The garage said the rented car was still there. With the keys in it: a Plymouth Valiant. Pound had left it there—they had a record—at 5 P.M. on the twenty-fourth, hadn't been back since.

"*Así, así*," said Mendoza. "So what do we deduce? The good officer made the wrong kind of new friend?"

"What it looks like," said Higgins. Fisher beckoned from the bathroom and they went to look. A bottle of bourbon, half empty, sat on the back of the toilet, with a dispenser soda bottle beside it. "Um. They were having a friendly drink, witness the glasses out there, when—what? They got to arguing politics, or the new friend turned out to be a fag and propositioned him—"

"Oh, I'm sure the lieutenant colonel—quite the gentleman, and—"

Mendoza went back to the office and called Central Receiving Hospital. The night watch was just coming on; he flipped a hand at Landers and Conway passing his open door.

"Oh, the assault," said the intern he finally got. "Well, he's in serious condition. Lost a good deal of blood. I take it he'd been in a fight? On the elderly side for that, but his knuckles are skinned raw and he's got a broken thumb, as well as the usual contusions—possible skull fracture, but the most serious thing is a stab wound just under the heart. He was damn lucky it wasn't a fraction of an inch deeper, he'd be dead hours ago. As it was, it nicked a vein, and he's been slowly bleeding internally— What?"

"Any idea when it might have happened?"

"That's why I said he was lucky. That it just barely nicked that vein. I'd estimate that he got these wounds at least twenty-four hours ago. Why on earth wasn't he found sooner? Well, obviously I can't tell you whether he'll make it. He seems to have a very sound constitution for a man of his age, but—"

Mendoza thanked him and picked up his hat. He started home through heavy traffic; nearly rammed into a Buick wearing New Jersey plates which made an illegal left turn in front of him, and was nearly rammed by a Cadillac wearing Illinois plates which tried to change lanes too fast. He got to Rayo Grande Avenue, possibly with the help of guardian angels, and was told he was late.

"And you look fagged to death, man—I'll pour you a dram," said Mrs. MacTaggart. El Señor heard the bottle taken down and came floating up to the drainboard like a fat black bird, his smudged face with its blonde Siamese-in-reverse markings expectant.

"Alcoholic cats," said Mendoza, kissing Alison and reaching for the shot-glass. "It's a wonder to me—*¡Válgame Dios!* —that there aren't even more accidents than we usually get, this one damned week of the year. Are the monsters in bed, *amante?*"

"All ready to be read to."

"*¡Ay de mí!* Why did I ever get domesticated?"

"Well, it took you a while," said Alison.

Hackett, Higgins and Shogart were off on Thursdays. When Mendoza came into the office Grace and Piggott were just coming in. He gave them a rundown on Pound.

"We've also got these two Mrs. Macauley fingered—Hibbs and Gosling. I've put out an A.P.B. on both of them, but that kind can fade into the woodwork and some kind pigeons will probably let them know they're hot. But go looking—we've got an address for Hibbs at least. And the Askell thing—*¡Caray!* Of course if Pound does come to he can tell us who attacked him." Sergeant Lake was unaccountably late; Mendoza, who had experienced most phases of police work, manipulated the switchboard and got an outside line, then the hospital.

"Well, he's holding his own," said the intern. "We've been pumping blood into him and he's rallied slightly. No, not conscious yet—I doubt whether he will be today, but we'll let you know."

"So we can't question him yet. If he does come through he can tell us all about it, so don't break your necks at it today, with all the rest we've got on hand. Ask around the hotel, was he seen with anybody, who did he talk to. He was robbed of money and clothes at least. But, priority on Hibbs and Gosling— *¡Vamos!*"

"Aye, aye, sir," said Grace. They passed Sergeant Lake coming in; he said apologetically that they'd been up most of the night with the eight-year-old.

"Gastric upset. Caroline said, just too much rich food and candy over Christmas."

Mendoza went into his office, and found Policewoman Wanda Larsen efficiently polishing his desk. The blotter was neatly aligned and the ashtray spanking clean. One use for a policewoman; he said genially, "I always thought we needed a housekeeper around here."

"There doesn't seem to be any work for me, everything rearranged, Lieutenant." She smiled at him uneasily. "I'm so used to Lieutenant Goldberg's way—well, it made work, taking the men's reports for typing up and I always—"

"*¡Caramba!*" Mendoza looked at her in awe. "Taking reports— Do you mean to tell me those lazy louts of—of thief-takers dictated reports to you? For typing? Your typing? Well, I will be damned! For two weeks I've been wondering just what jobs I'm supposed to give you. They dictated— *¡Dios!*"

"Why, don't—didn't you have a girl to do that, sir? In Homicide? I thought—"

Mendoza sat down and lit a cigarette. "*Esto no me huele bien*—if you ask me, something fishy about this. A private secretary, those privileged sons dictating reports! Well, I will say," and he smiled slowly, "they won't be doing that up in Pat's office, which is gratifying to contemplate."

"I did wonder," said Wanda. "There hasn't been anything for me to do, really—I kept waiting and none of the men asked me—I thought you, well, maybe were sorry I was left—"

"*¡Santa María!* Just wait till the boys find out they've got a private secretary! And a housekeeper! All of a sudden, I approve our shaking up and rearrangements." He grinned at her. "But I'd like to know how in hell Saul rated such a thing all this time—Homicide never got offered any secretaries—"

"Well, it was on the schedule, at least one policewoman attached to Robbery, on account of searching female witnesses sometimes, I think," said Wanda. Suddenly she laughed. "Oh, my goodness, Lieutenant—you not knowing! Any of you! Here I've been hanging around this place, nobody giving me any jobs, and thinking you didn't *want* me—didn't like me being here—"

Mendoza burst out laughing. "And I've been eyeing you nervously wondering what in God's name I was supposed to do with you! Comedy of errors—but wait till the boys find out! *¡Gracias a Dios!* They'll be all over you, young woman—"

"Well, that isn't part of the job, Lieutenant," she said demurely.

"I can't get over it, a private secretary—"

"And I speak Spanish too."

"Talk about dark horses," said Mendoza. "That Saul, never saying a word—"

"Well, it never occurred to me either. I thought maybe your policewoman had got transferred too, maybe up to Narco—and you didn't like having me instead." She laughed.

"*¡Pobre hija!* Now I know what you're here for, you'll be kept busy! My God, all my years out of uniform I never heard of such a thing—I've worked the wrong departments."

"I'll try to do everything just the way you want, Lieutenant." She looked at his neat clean desk. "But, oh, dear—"

"¿*Como?*"

"It looks," she said, "so *empty* without all the boxes of Kleenex."

Mendoza was still laughing when Sergeant Lake came in. "Mr. Askell's here. Says he doesn't want to bother you, but—"

"Let him in." Mendoza looked at Wanda. "You're going to be like Old Man Kangaroo, my girl. As per Mr. Kipling. Very truly sought after. Most popular female at Headquarters." She grinned a little self-consciously back at him as she went out.

"I know you're busy, Lieutenant," said Edward Askell apologetically. "But—have you found out anything yet?"

Mendoza wondered what further questions to ask him. And would he know the answers to some of the questions? Lila Askell had been away from home for nearly a year: but, her father said, she wrote home. . . . "Not much, I'm afraid. Did your daughter write home about any of the men she dated?"

"Once in a while. She didn't go out much, to put it like that, dated. Lila was a—a serious girl. She was interested in her work. She never dated much even when she was in high school and later on at college—it was a two-year course she had to take in this therapy, operating machines and so on. So many new things they have now. She was—a quiet girl. The only fellow she went out with a good deal—that was when she was in college, eighteen months, two years back—was Paul Mencken. Oh, they weren't engaged, but Lila went steady with Paul for six months or so, and that was—"

"Do you know where Mencken is now?"

Askell nodded, looking at the floor. "He joined the Army. He was killed in Vietnam last year. That was one reason, I think, that Lila took this job over here. She—minded about Paul, she wanted to get away from—from places they'd been together."

Mendoza was feeling frustrated again. "What about men she dated in Santa Barbara?"

"She didn't, much. She used to write about patients some-times, people the therapy helped—I don't recall she ever said about going out on dates, except two or three times Monica asked her to go on a double date— Oh, there was one of the interns at the hospital asked her to go out with him, but she wasn't interested. His name was—let me think—Wormser. Henry or something. But, Lieutenant—it didn't happen up in Santa Barbara. It happened here—Lila getting killed that way—and I can't understand it. She didn't know anybody in Los Angeles, and—I hope you'll believe me, I know my own daughter—she'd never have let a stranger—pick her up, or—"

The familiar stranger? thought Mendoza. But there she had been, at the Orange Julius bar, with the stranger. The fair young man who laughed a lot. And if he told Edward Askell about that, Askell would just say that Louise Chaffee was wrong, that couldn't have been Lila.

The driver of that bus was due back in town today. Any good to talk to him? Put out a plea in the press, anybody riding that bus on that trip, please come forward? Again he wondered, vaguely, if she had been on that bus. She had said she would be: they knew now from Salt Lake that her baggage had been checked straight through. And she'd been seen at the Orange Julius bar within forty minutes of the bus's arrival. But—

"I'm taking her home," said Askell. "They told me last night I could have her—her body today. I've got all the arrangements made—" His face worked a little. Mendoza said the indicated things mechanically. "Well, thank you, I know—I hope you'll find out who—did this terrible thing. That is—well, we know vengeance belongs to the Lord, but—and when someone did that to Lila, some other girl—"

"Yes. You know we'll work it—we want to find out too, Mr. Askell."

Askell got up. "You've been very—" he said, and stopped, and said, "kind." And then he said, after silence, to nobody in particular, "She was only twenty-three." He went out quietly.

*　　*　　*

Steve Dwyer, who at twelve years old had a more agile and spongelike mind than Higgins', and could now quote amply from the *Guide for Beginning Photographers* about f-stops and filters and light-meter readings, had got hold of the camera before Higgins got home last night, and finished the film.

"I got a good one of Margaret with Brucie, I know it's good," he boasted. "I took the roll in, George, but it was after four and so it won't go out till today, and we can't get the prints back till *Tuesday* on account of Monday being a holiday—" He patted Brucie the Scottie mournfully. "But I got another twelve-exposure, I hadn't enough left out of my allowance for a twenty—"

Higgins felt a little annoyed about the intervening holiday too. He'd got a few shots on that film he was anxious to see—one of Mary with the baby, and one of Steve and Laura with the baby. "Say, Steve," he said. "I wonder if we could learn to do the developing and all. It'd save some money, and it might be interesting—"

When Mary came to ask if he needed cigarettes or razor blades, she was just off to the market, oblivious to Laura's piano practicing he and Steve were absorbed in the illustrations of developing tanks and enlargers in the *Camera Guide.*

The lab called and reported that the hijacked truck had yielded no latents at all except a number belonging to its legitimate driver. Mendoza asked if they'd turned up anything useful from the Askell girl's clothes. "I think Scarne's on that," said Fisher. "I suppose you'll hear sometime."

Frustrated, Mendoza took down his hat and went out to look for the driver of that bus. He was now, the Greyhound stationed informed him, off for two days before making the same run again, up to San Francisco, back down the coast and over to Vegas. He lived in South Pasadena. Mendoza called, explained, and drove over to talk to him. He was an amiable middle-aged man named Soames, and he told Mendoza that he had his back to the passengers mostly.

"If somebody comes to ask me something, or there's a disturbance any kind, is the only times I notice the passengers. You drive a bus, the passengers"—he shrugged—"they get to have no faces. Just people in the bus. You get a drunk once in a while, or the yelling baby, it's a nuisance, other people complaining, but otherwise I got no call and no time to notice passengers." He looked at the photograph of Lila Askell and shook his head. "She could've rode in my bus that day—I couldn't say. Usually by the time I get on to start the haul, the passengers are all in. I drive the bus, that's all."

What with the holiday traffic, it took a little time to get there and back. And what other result had he expected?

He stepped out of the elevator, almost under the new sign, *Robbery-Homicide*, and came in past Lake and the switchboard. It was five minutes to eleven by the white-faced wall-clock. Wanda Larsen's desk was just inside the original sergeants' office, facing the open door; she looked up and smiled at him, and he laughed.

"I just thought, to get everybody straightened out—"

"*¡Seguramente que sí!*" said Mendoza. She had lettered a large sign on mimeograph paper and propped it on her desk facing outwards. *Private Secretary for Typing Reports,* it said. "Oh, brother. Wait until the boys—and I cannot get over Saul. And I can just hear what Pat said, if they expected to find your duplicate waiting their commands up in Narco—" He went on into his office and got out the cards, thinking about Lila Askell.

Ten minutes later he jumped as an inarticulate shout sounded past the open door. He went out in anticipation. Detectives Jason Grace and Matthew Piggott were staring at Wanda Larsen incredulously.

"You mean *that's* what you're *here* for?" asked Grace. "Type *our* reports? Instead of us? By God, Matt—"

Piggott was looking almost reverent. "A private secretary? Now to tell you the gospel truth, Miss Larsen, we didn't know just what job you were supposed to be here for—we didn't like to—"

"Wanda," she said, smiling at them. "Just a sort of mis-understanding. The lieutenant was surprised too. I thought you didn't like me, not giving me any work."

"Didn't *like*—" said Grace. "Oh, lady! I did take touch typing in high school but it's not a job I take to."

"Is that what you did in Goldberg's office?" asked Piggott. "For all the Robbery boys? All their reports? Well, I will be—" Piggott was not a swearing man, but they saw words trembling on his lips.

"I just now decided," said Grace, "I approve of all the changes around here."

"I thought you'd all like it," said Mendoza. "You'll make it up to the poor girl, thinking she wasn't wanted, all of us ignoring her and wondering why the powers that be attached her to us."

"I'm pretty fast at dictation. Er—Mr. Grace, *I* didn't get to see those snapshots of your new baby."

Grace pulled them out, beaming. "Oh, by the way," he said to Mendoza, "we found that Hibbs. He's parked in the first interrogation room to the left."

Hibbs was annoyed at being picked up, and said he was real clean. He was only just off P.A. last month, and his parole officer had said he'd been a good boy the whole eighteen months. Now he was off P.A., very possibly he'd be less careful: that was a pattern too. But if there was any consciousness of guilt in him, it didn't show; they were necessarily experts at assessing that.

They asked him about last Sunday night, and he said he'd been at work. "Mr. Taddo can say. I come at four, business was slow but Mr. Taddo can say I'm here till we shut at nine."

He had a job at a bowling alley on Wilshire, minding the automatic setting-up mechanism, cleaning up, checking equipment. Grace went out to find Taddo, who managed the bowling alley. He came back at twelve-fifty to find Palliser and Glasser standing transfixed before Wanda Larsen's desk.

"Are you telling me," said Palliser, "that all this while those—those—never had to type their own reports? Dictating— Well, I will be damned! We wondered why you were assigned to—I mean, we never had a policewoman before, no real job—I will be *damned!*"

"I don't believe it," said Glasser. "So now we know. I wasn't sure I liked all this changing around, but now I do. In spades."

"Nice to be pampered, isn't it?" said Grace, and found Mendoza on the phone.

"Do you think he'll make it? . . . Doubletalk! . . . So he's slightly improved, *bueno.* You'll let us know if he does come to? Thanks so much."

"The alibi checks," said Grace. "Taddo says Hibbs was there all right, four to nine. He's a good type. I'd say that definitely clears Hibbs. Whatever he might get up to next week or next month."

"*¿Qué más?*" said Mendoza. He brushed his moustache the wrong way and back again, which meant he was annoyed. "So let him loose."

"I think so. And then lunch."

Sometimes they all foregathered at the big table at Federico's, happening to knock off from the office at once; sometimes only a couple of them. Today, with their two senior sergeants off, the newest bureau of the LAPD occupied the big table. Mendoza was brooding. The tall Jamaican waiter brought him a shot-glass of rye without being told.

"Gosling has a likelier record for Macauley," said Grace. "What are you fussing over, Henry?" Glasser had a ballpoint pen, figuring on the back of an envelope.

"Damn car payments. Act of God, hell. What God had against my car—" Glasser's Ford had been demolished by the quake last August.

"And there was that article by the Chief," said Mendoza, "in that true-detective magazine last month. And isn't he right. The miniskirts and hot pants—mindless silly females

and most of them respectable too, just following fashion—
but inviting the assault, the rape. Looking like easy females,
asking to be taken for such."

"And isn't that the truth," said Piggott. "Prudence says
she can't buy a ready-made dress with the skirt a decent
length."

"But not," said Mendoza, "Lila. No. Her skirt covered
her knees." He finished his rye.

"Which says?" Palliser swallowed Scotch-and-water and
looked at the steak sandwich set before him.

"*No sé,*" said Mendoza. "But everything doesn't always
get into letters written home." He took up his knife and
fork, looking at the small steak (very well done). "Even
if she was a nice moral Mormon girl. I wonder—"

There was a little silence while food was consumed. "I
think," said Mendoza, "you'd better take an airplane ride,
John."

"What? Where?"

"Santa Barbara. To talk to Monica Fletcher. I think I'd
like to hear what Monica has to tell us about Lila—and any
double dates—and that intern Askell mentioned—and any
other men Lila knew there—"

"Well," said Palliser, slightly surprised, "all right. But
whatever happened to her, it happened here—"

"It's only," said Mendoza, "a hundred miles up the coast."

The formal lab report on the bullet out of Macauley had
come in. A Colt .22, could be any of several models, old
or new. Mendoza was inclined to agree, of the two men Mrs.
Macauley had picked, Gosling had the likelier record. Piggott and Glasser were out looking for him.

Lieutenant Colonel Pound was still unconscious. Grace
had gone over to the Biltmore to ask questions on that.

Wanda Larsen was happily transcribing Grace's notes on
Hibbs into a formal report.

There would be an inquest on Lila Askell tomorrow morning; an inquest on Stanley Macauley tomorrow afternoon.
Other inquests: those construction workers, the D.O.A.'s
from the freeway accidents.

The inside phone burred at him and he picked it up. "Mendoza, Hom—Robbery-Homicide."

"Well, it's just a funny thing," said Scarne. "I'll be sending up a report, but I thought you'd like to know right off. These clothes—the Askell girl. Wool-nylon suit, cotton blouse, nylon underpants and bra, garter-belt and stockings. I've been going over 'em. The underwear's just ordinary stuff, looks as if she put 'em on clean that day. But—"

"Well?"

"On both the skirt and jacket of the suit, there are traces of grass and dead leaves—not enough to analyze for type. On one shoe, the sole that is, bird-droppings, a very small amount, embedded in cotoneaster leaves—"

"¿Cómo?" said Mendoza. "What the hell—"

"I'll send up a formal report."

Cotoneaster leaves? Grass? At Broadway and Seventh?

"*Diez millones de demonios desde el infierno!*" said Mendoza.

6

THEY HAD HAD an address for Chester Gosling from his recent P.A. officer—a housing project on Fifty-second down in Vernon. Palliser and Piggott had started there that morning with no luck: no answer to knocking, and a neighbor across the hall told them Gosling had moved out a couple of weeks ago. Mrs. Gosling was still there; she might know something about him, so they'd try there again.

He had had a job at a service station on Florence Avenue. That was their next stop. The owner, a paunchy oil-stained fellow named Cutts, said, "I like to oblige Mr. Talmadge—" that was the P.A. officer—"but I don't think I'd take another ex-con. It's always the same story, see, they stay and do the job O.K. so long as they're on parole—then the day they're off, that's it, they goof off so you have to fire 'em. Most of 'em just lazy bums can't be bothered to work, easier to steal." Gosling had been fired two weeks ago.

Now, with Palliser deflected elsewhere, Piggott and Glasser went back to the housing project to see if the wife was home.

"A gas station," said Piggott. "And Mrs. Macauley said—"

"Yeah, I think he's hot for it. Wonder if the lab came up with anything on the Macauley car."

In the narrow dirty hall of the apartment building, which offered ample evidence of the habits of the residents, they knocked on the door and waited. After a moment a woman opened to them, stared at the badges, and said, "That snotty li'l Sonny Weaver tole me you was after Chester again. He ain't here."

"Would you have any idea where he's living, Mrs. Gosling? You are—"

"Yeah, that's me. What you want him for?" She was a tall, deep-bosomed woman with a defiant slattern air: her pink cotton slacks were wrinkled and stained, the tentlike white T-shirt dirty.

"Just to ask him a few questions."

"Huh!" she said, and cackled with laughter. "I hope you get him 'n' work him over real good! Bassard run out on me an' take up with that high-yaller girl— You ain't heard about her, huh? Well, I tell you, he's prolly hidin' out her place, time he hear you after him."

"And would you know where that is?" asked Piggott.

"Name o' Ruby Jewel she call herself—got a job dancin' nekkid, some bar down Slauson. You fin' her, you likely fin' that bassard, or she know where he is. An' you work him over good!" She stared at them a moment and shut the door with a bang.

"Well, a lead of sorts," said Glasser, as they walked back down the odorous hall. "There are a lot of bars featuring topless dancers on Slauson Avenue, Matt."

"What with Sodom and Gomorrah getting rejuvenated," agreed Piggott. "But it just occurs to me, Henry, that Ruby Jewel might be in our records."

"And you might have something there. Let's go look."

They went back to Parker Center, down to R. and I., and asked. The computer turned up Jewel, Ruby, as an alias of one Ruthene Lincoln, who had a modest rap-sheet for shoplifting, petty theft, prostitution. She'd been picked up last for soliciting a couple of months ago, and at that time her address was listed as Denker Avenue.

They drove down there; it was a shabby side-street off Florence, lined with tired old apartment buildings. A fat brown woman was in the front yard of the one they wanted, watering a bed of rose bushes against the building. They walked up and Piggott showed her the badge. "Do you live here, ma'am?"

"Yes, that's right. I own this place, that is, my husband and me. You're policemen? Can I help you some way? I'm Mis' Towner."

"We're looking for a Miss Ruthene Lincoln—sometimes she calls herself Ruby J—"

"*Her!*" said Mrs. Towner. "A bad lot that one is, all right. She wasn't here long, Officers. Less 'n three months. I suspicioned what she was, but I didn't have no proof till you arrested her that time. We tole her to get out—we don't want no trash like that in our place, we got decent people livin' here."

"I see. I don't suppose you know where she moved?"

"Nor I don't care. Trash like that—it's hard enough to keep up the place, look halfway nice, ever'thing so high nowadays—"

"Do you know where she was working then, if she was?"

"Yessir, at least I know where she *say* when she move in. Said she was a waitress at a place down on Slauson, place named the Cool Cat or such-like. Waitress!" Mrs. Towner snorted. "I can guess what she's doin' in a place like that! You're after her again, huh? Well, I wish you fellows luck, find her. But that's all I could tell you."

They thanked her and went back to Piggott's Chevy. "Nearest public phone," said Glasser. They found one three blocks up; Piggott pulled into a red zone and Glasser got out to consult the Central book. "Just this side of Figueroa," he said, getting back in.

It was the kind of tedious routine that they were used to doing; but it occupied time. When they got to the Cool Cat Bar it was four-thirty. Los Angeles sprawls far out; they had put more than fifty miles on the speedometer, through city traffic, always heaviest this one week of the year.

The Cool Cat was open for business: a sign proclaimed that it was open twenty-four hours a day, and also promised topless dancers, three shows nightly, a hot piano-player and a combo on weekends.

They went into near darkness, only a few wall lights burning, a brighter light down by a center platform that formed an impromptu stage. There was a rich effluvium of old dirt, perspiration, whiskey, beer, cheap perfume and an elusive hint of marijuana. Past the narrow entrance they felt the room widen out, but it was too dark to see corners. A bulky something came up to them; as their eyes adjusted to the little light, it resolved itself into a large, very black man in dark pants and a light shirt. "We don't serve whites here," he said abruptly in a grating voice.

Glasser flicked his cigarette lighter with one hand and displayed the badge in the other. "We're looking for Ruby Jewel."

The man swore, expressively if not elegantly. "That girl in more trouble? Bring the pigs down—"

"We're not after her, just her address. We want one of her boyfriends," said Glasser.

The man relaxed. "Man, you pick him up, she never gonna know he's gone from the crowd!" He laughed, with a gleam of white teeth. "Thass a load off my mind. I don' want no trouble here. Ruby, she's got a pad over on Nadeau Street—" He added the house number and Glasser took it down.

When they came out to the street again, dark had shut down; the light fading for the last twenty minutes, and now gone entirely. Street lights were on, and the neon flashing.

"This Gosling, Matt. If he is there, he's big and mean. We don't want to lose him. Go back to base and see if Jase is there to come along?"

"There's less than an hour of the day left," Piggott pointed out. "I'm tired of driving in traffic, Henry. Another ten miles and then down here again? Come on, let's go see if he's there."

It was another aged apartment building. There was, in this one, a row of locked mailboxes in the slit of a lobby, and *Jewel* was listed as Apartment Fourteen, upstairs. They trudged up in silence, Glasser reaching to loosen the Police Positive .38 in its shoulder holster. Piggott pushed the bell.

"Hey, man, you early— Oh!" She faced them, disconcerted by strange white faces. She was something, all right; a smooth light tan all over, a spectacular figure in pink and gold hostess pajamas just barely there, not-very-opaque nylon, midriff bare, and gold mules on bare feet. She had a wild mop of black hair, frosted purple lipstick, and a heady aura of perfume surrounded her. "Now who the hell are you and what do you want?" she demanded.

Glasser brought out the badge. "Is Chester Gosling here?"

"Chester?" She looked them over thoroughly, thoughtfully. "You want him? I thought he was clean these days."

"Just for some questions," said Piggott. It had been a long day, and it was going to be good to get home to Prudence.

"Oh," she said. She leaned one elbow on the door, displaying a long-fingered hand tipped with purple-frost nail polish. "Well, he's been here, sure. He oughta be back just a few minutes, he went out for cigarettes. You can come in and wait, you want." She stepped back, and they went in to a gaudy overfurnished room with an expensive stereo in one corner, too many pictures, and a heavy pall of incense. There was marijuana under the incense.

"You fellows like a li'l drink while you wait?" She smiled slowly at them, and they both stepped back a little, farther into the room, as she came forward.

Glasser started to say, "No, thanks," but she had them away from the door now, and shouted Gosling's name. The inner bedroom door burst open and he came out in one lunge, running for the open front door. Glasser went for his gun as he saw the gun in Gosling's hand, and he and Piggott dived flat as shots spurted. The girl screamed. Glasser tripped over her, making for the door. In the hall, they heard Gosling's feet clatter on the stairs, and plunged after him.

"Gosling—stop! Gosling!" Glasser fired once over his head as they burst into the street, Gosling twenty feet ahead. It was dark in the street, but they heard as they ran the slam of a car door, an engine gunned. The car came bucketing past them, a small dark shape with no lights, and Glasser fired at it. "Goddamn the luck to hell" he said bitterly. "Goddamn that—"

"Why, that Goddamn bastard!" said Ruby Jewel from the top of the apartment steps. "That ever-lovin' bastard's gone off with my car! I never said he could take my car—now how in hell am I gonna get to work?"

"Well, the luck runs that way sometimes," said Grace. But Mendoza was not so complacent. He said this and that.

"I said we ought to pick up Jase or somebody to help take him," said Glasser. "And damn it, now I'll have to sit through another board hearing, did I have a legit excuse to fire the gun! Of all the damned luck—"

"Now, Henry," said Piggott. "Temporary setback, like they say. She was mad enough at his taking her car, she gave us the plate-number right off—she wants it back. It's a dark-blue VW, I told Jimmy to get the number on the air."

"Grateful for small favors," grumbled Mendoza.

He got up resignedly, massaging the back of his neck. "Maybe I'm feeling my years, boys. But tomorrow is also a day. Better brief the night men on Gosling, and hope that VW gets spotted."

"It's just an idea," said Piggott. "I think one of those bullets hit the wall in Ruby's pad. We might dig it out and see if the lab can match it up to the one out of Macauley."

"I am getting old. I'd have thought of it thirty seconds from now," said Mendoza. "First little job for the night watch. And I wonder what John's getting up there . . ."

None of the regular commercial flights of the big airlines deigned to land at Santa Barbara that day. Palliser had called Burbank Airport and been referred to a local company, Intercoastal Flights, which said they could drop him off there from a scheduled flight to San Luis, leaving at three o'clock. He drove home to tell Robin, put a second shirt and a razor in a briefcase in case he had to stay over.

"I'll probably be back tonight, depends what turns up."

"You'll call if you won't be? Don't fuss, John, I know enough to lock doors, after all. But I have been thinking, now we have the house, nice to have a dog."

"Well," said Palliser.

"After the baby's here, so the dog won't get jealous. A Sheltie or something."

[91]

"We'll think about it, Robin."

The plane dropped him at Santa Barbara Airport at three-forty. The hospital where Lila Askell had worked was across town, a small private hospital very Spanish-colonial, with a red tile roof. He was received with curiosity, exclamations and questions; evidently Monica had spread the news about Lila far better than the local press. Just an awful thing, you could hardly believe it, the crime rate these days—and inevitably, he was told what a nice girl Lila had been.

Monica Fletcher appeared in the bare little waiting room in five minutes. She was a tall thin dark girl with prominent light-brown eyes and a rather foolish slack mouth outlined in pale pink lipstick. She was quite willing to answer questions, after all the exclamations— "Her poor family! She was so happy about getting home—I couldn't believe it when I heard—" But she didn't understand what he wanted from her, and Palliser wasn't too sure himself. Mendoza seemed to have some idea that Lila, away from home, had unbuckled her rigid morality, so he started asking about boyfriends.

"Oh, she didn't have any, Mr. Palliser, excuse me, you said Sergeant. She didn't date hardly any at all. Really. She was awfully serious, she went to church and all. She was more interested in the job than anything else. But nothing happened to her *here*. And she wouldn't *know* anybody like whoever it was did that to her—I just can't stand thinking about it!" She blew her nose dolefully. She was in the plain white uniform-dress of a nurse, white flat-soled shoes, but he suspected that when she was dressed in her own choice, it would include ruffles, dangly bracelets and spike heels.

"But she did go out with men?"

"Well, only a few times. I used to sort of worry about it—it wasn't natural, her not wanting to go out—she liked to *read*," said Monica. "Just sit and read books. Well, a girl ought to go out sometimes. I know Dr. Wormser'd asked her for a date, he's sort of pompous and stiff, you know, but—but Lila wasn't interested. My boyfriend got her dates a couple of times, we double-dated—"

"Who's that, Miss Fletcher?"

"Ronald Stettin, he's a teacher at the college, his first year. We went—"

"All right, who did Lila go out with?"

"It was only about four times. There was Gene Stover, he was a friend of Ron's and I think he really liked Lila, but she only went out with him twice, on a date with Ron and me. There's a nice place outside town, a roadhouse, with a good combo and dancing, but Lila just didn't go for it. Or this Gene. He called her a few times, but she turned him down. But why're you asking about that? I don't see—"

"Well, we have to ask all sorts of questions," said Palliser vaguely.

"Oh, I suppose so, I just—"

"Did she go out with anyone else?"

"Well, Ron set up another one, one of the postgrad students, Bill Saxon. He was nice, but Lila said he was a smart-aleck, he made fun of her going to church and she didn't like that. And then the next time Ron suggested— well, it was me really—she said she wasn't interested. She was already thinking about going home, you know. I like it here but Lila didn't. Except the job, and she said she could get one at the hospital back home and it's a lot bigger and had more equipment and all. Oh, it's just terrible to think—one of those dope-fiends or something, when Mr. Askell called I—"

"So far as you know, she'd only dated these two men here, Gene Stover and Bill Saxon?"

"And Dr. Wormser had asked her to go out, but she—"

"All right. Did either of them seem—oh, angry when she turned them down for dates?"

"Well, I don't think so. It wasn't anything—anything big, you know, I guess she was just another girl to them. What? Well, sure we got along O.K., sharing the apartment, except she was a lot fussier than I am, at housekeeping and all—" Monica uttered a little half sob. "I've been sorry, think about the little spats we had about my not hanging things up, and the dishes— A person's made the way they're made, you know."

"Yes. This Saxon still at the college? And Mr. Stettin?"

She nodded. "Do you want to see them? But I don't see why—"

"What about Stover?"

Monica blew her nose again. "Oh, Ron said he moved down to Los Angeles awhile back."

Schenke and Galeano had gone to dig the bullet out of Ruby Jewel's apartment wall, and delivered it to S.I.D. They sat around waiting for the first call of the evening, and they didn't wait long; at eight-ten there was a call, a break-in out on Third. Landers and Conway went out on it.

It was a chain market. The manager was waiting for them; the Traffic men had wanted to call an ambulance, but he said he was all right. His name was Raymond Osney, and he said balefully, "I just hope the district manager will listen to me now! And I'll just bet it was the same punks who tried to break in the other night! I had one of you fellows out here looking at the marks—a Sergeant Palliser, very nice fellow. Six holdups and four break-ins we've had, the last— And the burglar alarm system no damn good. *I* keep saying about the dogs. Trained guard dogs. You can rent them, you know. I just hope the district manager—"

"Well, what happened here, sir?"

"The crime rate— Well, I stayed late. I'm usually the last one out, we close at seven-thirty on Thursdays. Everybody else was gone, the butcher'd just driven off, I know his car, needs a lube-job—and I'd locked up and started out the back door, when they jumped me. Knocked me out and tied me up with all this damned adhesive tape, where they learned that one—all the crime on TV—and when I came to, they were busy as packrats carting stuff out—cigarettes and liquor, of course—"

"Did you get a look at them? How many?"

"Three. Three big louts with the long hair and sideburns and boots—Mex," said Osney. "Not that it signifies. You get all sorts. They didn't know I'd come to. I got a pretty good look, they'd put on the stockroom lights so as to see what they were doing. I can give you descriptions, all right. I think I'd seen one of them in here before—probably casing the joint."

"Do you feel up to that now, sir? Could you come in tomorrow to look at some mug shots?"

"You're damn right," said Osney. "I will. I'll do that. Now if we'd had a trained guard dog here—" he sounded wistful. "I've seen articles. Much more efficient than burglar alarms—"

They got back to the office at nine-fifty, and Landers had just sat down and lit a cigarette when a new call came in, from a Traffic unit. Robbery, possible rape, possible shooting, meet the Traffic men at Central Receiving.

"What the hell?" said Galeano. "Business picking up." He and Schenke started out on that. Five minutes later the phone rang on Schenke's desk; Landers picked it up.

"Who's this? Oh, Tom. I'm stuck up here," said Palliser, "overnight. Something showed, and I've got to see this Stettin but of course the college is closed for vacation and he's out on a date, nobody knows where. I'll catch him in the morning. I've called Robin, but you might tell the boss."

"Will do. Something showed on Askell?"

"Just maybe. I'll just pass on a name. Gene Stover. Said to be male, Caucasian, very general description could fit the fellow at the Orange Julius bar. Nothing solid. You might look for him in the phone-book."

"What's he got to do with Lila?"

"I don't know," said Palliser. "It's just the first faint smell of a lead we've had. I'll probably be back sometime tomorrow."

"O.K.," said Landers. He put the phone down and turned to face Bill Moss and his rookie partner, with a large prosperous-looking male citizen wearing a broad red welt on one temple and an indignant expression.

"Mr. Joseph Lambert," said Moss. "This is Detective Landers, Detective Conway. Mr. Lambert wants to lay a complaint." He was grinning.

Lambert came up to Landers' desk and sat down with a thump in the chair beside it. The Traffic men went out;

Landers and Conway stared after them. Lambert was about fifty, bald as an egg, a big heavy man with china-blue eyes and a petulant mouth. He was wearing what had been an impeccably tailored suit, Oxford gray Dacron, white shirt and a gaudy tie; but the suit was smeared with dirt and oil all down one side and the tie was torn.

"Say, what kind of burg is this anyway?" he demanded aggrievedly.

"Are you all right, sir? Your head—"

"I'm all right. Bang on the head. But what kind of burg—I've never been here before. Came to our convention—Association of Rural Employers of America. We're at that big hotel—Ambassador. What the hell, I'm away from home, not that I'm married, not me, boys—I slip a sawbuck to the bellhop, fetch a dame, and he looks at me like a damn deacon! Says it's against the law! My God, any city I ever been in—any hotel—"

"We tend to be kind of puritanical here," said Landers gravely. He exchanged a glance with Conway. L.A. tried to be: they weren't about to tell Lambert all the trouble and mess the Vice Bureau was in, trying to close up all those massage parlors.

"You don't look old enough to be a cop," Lambert informed him. "My God! So I go out, find a friendly bartender or something, I know the ropes, any city—and I run into this dame. Looks good—sounds good, she leads me out and next thing I know I'm coming to in a back alley some place, stripped clean—"

"Could you describe the woman, sir?" Conway's lips twitched.

"Damn right. Good-lookin' dame, medium-size, swell figure, one o' these little tiny skirts, good legs—she had black hair. By damn!" said Lambert thickly. "This is the damndest burg I ever struck, even the dames for sale shortchange a guy—"

After they'd called a cab to take him back to the hotel, they started to laugh. "General description, but could be that pair going around luring the marks," said Conway. "Little windfall for them. Did he say three hundred bucks and a diamond ring?"

"That's just what. We're in the wrong job," said Landers.

At Central Receiving Hospital, Schenke and Galeano met the two uniformed men in Emergency. "What's up?"

The older man shrugged. "She flagged us down along Eighth—screaming, hysterical, clothes all torn. Assault of some kind. She was pretty upset, we brought her right over here. The doctor's got her in there."

"O.K., you get back on tour. If we need any more from you we'll let you know." They waited five minutes before a doctor came out to them.

"You can see her now—she wants to talk to you. I've given her a sedative. She's calmed down now—just hysteria and shock, she's not hurt much."

"Raped?"

"Assaulted, I gather. No, she hasn't been raped. She said she got away from him before— She's a Mrs. Sidney."

She was sitting in a low plastic chair in one of the examining rooms, her head on one hand, moaning a little still as the doctor's sedative quieted her heart. "Mrs. Sidney?" said Galeano gently. "Can you tell us—"

"Oh, are you police? Please, are you— It's my husband!" she said urgently. "It's Ken—please find out what happened! I thought there was a shot—I tried to fight him, he dragged me into the car, I tried to scream and I couldn't— oh, please—"

"Where was this, Mrs. Sidney? Your husband was with you?"

"Yes, of course—oh, why won't you understand?" she burst out passionately. "Ken—we'd just come back to the car—in the parking lot behind the restaurant—when this terrible man—he had a gun, a big Negro man, and he robbed Ken and dragged me— Oh, please find out what's happened to Ken!" She began to sob, and the doctor came up efficiently.

They looked at each other. "Are you thinking what I'm thinking?" said Schenke.

"*Camerato*," said Galeano, "we all make mistakes. It looks as if Mrs. Macauley made one picking this Gosling. And he's running because he doesn't like our company, period.

It's not very likely, if he was the X on that one, he'd stop running to do it again." There was a public phone halfway down the hall; he fished out a dime and called the office, and got Landers. "Have you by any chance had a call to a new body?"

"Are you psychic? We're just rolling on it. Man, said to be shot."

"Where?"

"Parking lot of a restaurant on Wilshire—Il Trovatore. Why?"

"Oh, brother," said Galeano. "I can just hear what the lieutenant'll say tomorrow morning."

"What?" said Hackett and Higgins together. They were staring at Wanda Larsen.

"You mean, you're here to do our *reports? Type* our reports? I will be damned!" said Hackett. "We wondered why you were—well, I mean—"

"She thought we didn't like her," said Grace, grinning. "It's what she did for Goldberg's boys. A private secretary. Did you ever hear of such a thing?"

"Well, for God's sake," said Shogart, surprised. "You didn't know? I couldn't figure it—didn't like to stick my neck out and ask why you were giving Wanda the cold shoulder. We've all got our own ways of doing things, I said when Wanda asked me about it. Thought maybe you didn't trust her, or missed your own girl— You didn't know? You mean you didn't have a girl in your old office? Be damned."

"We're used to doing it the hard way," said Higgins.

"The lieutenant laughed like anything and said it was a comedy of errors," said Wanda. "Lieutenant Goldberg was always satisfied, and I'll try to do my best—you don't even have to dictate to me, just give me your notes—"

"Oh, Wanda's a whiz," said Shogart casually. "I haven't typed a report in four years, since she got assigned to us." Hackett and Higgins were dumb.

"Very truly sought after and wonderfully popular," said Mendoza sardonically from the doorway. "Same like Old

Man Kangaroo. We now have complications setting in. Whoever pulled the Macauley assault, it doesn't seem to have been Gosling. He did it again last night."

"You don't say," said Hackett.

"But the way he ran—" said Piggott. "And took a shot at us—" It was Glasser's day off, supposedly; in reality he'd be attending that board hearing up in I. A., because he'd fired the gun last night. Rules and regulations—

"All right, Gosling's got a rap sheet as long as my arm. Cops come after him, he runs. An involuntary reaction, if that's the term I want." They had followed him into his office: Hackett, Higgins, Shogart, Piggott and Grace. "We still want Gosling, to try to clear him out of the way. I doubt very strongly that, knowing we're on him, knowing we'll likely have the plate-number on his girlfriend's car, he'd succumb to temptation again last night. But it looks as if we start over again on that. *¡Condenación!*" Mendoza brushed his moustache back and forth. "And what the hell John's come across up there, on Lila—"

Sergeant Lake looked in. "A Dr. Locke at Central Receiving."

"*Bueno.*" Mendoza picked up the phone.

"You asked to be kept informed about Mr. Pound. He has regained consciousness—he's still very weak, but we think he'll pull through now. If you want to talk to him, very briefly, Lieutenant—"

"Thanks so much. Someone'll be over. . . . Pound. We can talk to him, very briefly, so says the doctor. Matt, you go and do that. Now we've got this new break-in, a Mr. Osney coming in to look at some mug shots—Jase, you can take him down—"

"What about Macauley, do we start all over?" Hackett looked annoyed, Higgins just resigned. The citizenry, however well-meaning, was frequently muddleheaded and mistaken.

Mendoza put out his cigarette and immediately got out another, turning it round in his fingers. "*Palabra suelta no tiene vuelta,*" he said. "Careless talk—she was upset, she'd just seen her husband killed, and photographs can be confusing. We can't blame her for an honest mistake. What we can deduce, she was right about the general type—'"

"Which is very damn general," said Grace.

"*De veras.* Feed the general description into the computer for some more names out of records. The long way round we usually go. And I do wonder what John's come up with. It was only on a vague hunch I sent him up there—"

"Your crystal ball," said Hackett sardonically.

"But," said Piggott, and was silent, and said, "Oh, well, they are spooky, the ones like Gosling—that's so. Even if he's clean, take off like a jackrabbit when he knows we're after him."

And Sergeant Lake was back. "New body," he said tersely. "Out at the Medical Center. One of the maintenance crew just called in."

"*¡Válgame Dios!* Come on, Art. We'll go see what that is. Talk about women's work!" But as Mendoza got up to follow Hackett out, Lake back at the switchboard put up a hand. "Here's John."

"You go on, I'll meet you there." Mendoza took the phone. "John? What have you turned up?"

"I don't know, could be nothing at all. I'm starting back in half an hour. I just thought I'd pass it on, so you can follow it up. This Gene Stover. He's supposed to be working for a brokerage—Stone, Fox and Meyer—on Spring."

"What's he got to do with Lila?"

"I don't know that he's anything to do with the murder. Just, you might ask him about it."

7

MENDOZA WAS DELAYED five minutes by the arrival of a
packet from the lab: Lila Askell's jewelry. He'd asked for
it, he remembered; he wondered why. There were four
modest items: a high-school class ring in ten-karat gold, a
necklace and a pair of earrings. Those were just costume
jewelry, but the necklace was rather unusual, large daisy-
faces, flat polished goldplate, strung together by a chain.

There was a note from Scarne: "We got two good latents
off the necklace. Not in our files, sent to Feds."

"Well, how gratifying," said Mendoza. But if they weren't
in the FBI's files either, not much help.

When he got out to the U.S.C. Medical Center, he spotted
Hackett's scarlet Barracuda parked in front of the first
building on Zonal Avenue, and turned up beside it. It was
a big four-story building, and over the tall front entrance
the graven letters read *U. S. C. School of Medicine.* There
were voices beyond the double doors.

In a large square lobby Hackett and Higgins were talking
to a little crowd of men, all in rough work-clothes, all looking shocked and shaken. "Luis," said Hackett, turning to
him, "another funny thing. It's upstairs—third floor. We left
it for the ambulance and lab men. There's a truck on the
way. One of the maintenance crew, a Joe Daly—"

"We aren't a maintenance crew," said one man. He stood
out from the other four nondescripts, two white, two Negro.
He was a stocky man about fifty with a shock of gray-

brown hair, and he said, "You another detective? We aren't nothing to do with the college. Superior Cleaners, office on Sunset Boulevard. We go all over, we got contracts, buildings, offices, public and private—houses too. But who in hell would want to hurt Joe?"

"Nobody had no call," said one of the colored men. "He was a good guy, never had no trouble with anybody. Just had their first grand-baby last week, and Joe was proud as punch. It don't seem possible, Joe up there all cut—"

"All right," said Hackett. "We haven't done much more than look at the body, Luis. Now, you'll be the foreman of this crew, Mr—"

"Hansen. Chris Hansen. Well, we just lay out the work like it falls. Listen, he musta never gone away last night. Jim—"

"Yeah, that just came to me now too. We see he's cold. But how in hell—"

"One at a time," said Hackett. "You were here last night? Cleaning?"

Hansen nodded. He got out a cigarette slowly and lit it: a methodical man, slow of thought. "I don't know what coulda happened or why. Or how. Joe! Joe's been working for Superior fifteen years, steady quiet guy. Never any trouble with anybody—a good worker. I don't know what coulda— Well, see, general speakin' we clean this place at night. Like a lot of public places. Once a week, floors and windows, it's one of the steady jobs. A contract on it. College's shut for vacation now, so it don't matter when we come in, but we was here last night, about five to eight I guess, doin' the first two floors. This is a big place, can't finish it all in one night." A little murmur from the other men. "So, we get the first two floors done, I'd thought maybe we could get to the third, but then I look at the time—"

"I and Dick was already startin' up there," spoke up one of the white men. "It comes to me, could be Joe'd already gone up, Chris. I don't recall seein' him after about then. You said leave it, on accounta that job that got wrote off for this mornin', we could finish up here today, and we all took off."

"That's right. I said as long as the college's shut, we finish off the top floors this mornin', we got a empty office building to do this afternoon. I didn't recall about Joe—I guess we all figgered he left when the rest of us did—"

"This was about eight o'clock?"

"A bit after. About. We come on about"—he looked at his watch—"forty minutes ago— I oughta say, I drive the truck with all the heavy cleanin' equipment, the other boys drive their own cars. And here's Joe's old Dodge right in the lot, he's early on the job I think, but he isn't nowhere, so we go looking—"

Scarne and Fisher came in with a couple of lab kits, and the ambulance attendants after them. Mendoza drifted up the stairs after them. The first couple of floors, open doors gave on obvious classrooms, blackboards and desks. Elsewhere would be autopsy rooms, laboratories—whatever they did have at a medical school. Their steps echoed in the emptiness of the big building.

At the top of the third flight of stairs he stopped and cocked his head. "Scarne."

"What's up?" Scarne turned, came to look. "Well, well. Hey, Pete." It was lying there on the second step down, almost against the outside wall. A pair of desk scissors, the blades about eight inches long, half-open, and dark-stained. Scarne squatted, opened his case, found a plastic bag and delicately edged the scissors into it.

They went down to the middle of the wide corridor. The rooms up here all seemed to be small offices: Mendoza glanced at the little plaques on the doors. Dr. William E. Danielson. Dr. Paul Friedman. Dr.—

"At a guess," said one of the ambulance men, "about twelve hours, Lieutenant."

"Mmh," said Mendoza. He pulled up his trousers and squatted over the body, which was sprawled face up just outside a half-open door. Joe Daly had been a middle-aged Negro, his skin curiously sallow-saffron in death, his scant tight-curled hair graying, and his face wore an odd serenity. He wore striped overalls and a blue shirt, and there were dark stains along his left side. The flaccid wrist was cold and limp. Mendoza stood up and looked at the open door. Dr. Frederick Loose. "*Extraño*," said Mendoza. Vacation, the college closed, who would have any reason to be here last night but the cleaning crew? "I want the works," he told the men from S.I.D. "Photographs and a careful look around here."

He left them starting to work and went back downstairs. The men were talking to each other, and Hackett and Higgins comparing notes. "Well, you heard the gist of it," said Hackett. "Short and sweet. They thought he'd left last night. He hadn't. What did he run into up there on the third floor? The two who started up didn't go all the way, but nobody heard a thing."

"What he ran into was a pair of desk scissors," said Mendoza. "Let's hope X left some prints. So that looks like the very impulsive thing."

"All they say about him, a very ordinary guy," said Higgins. "Respectable hard worker. Went to the Baptist church. Wife and family. Reliable, quiet, no arguments."

"Mmh," said Mendoza. "I think you can count out the crew, George. Those scissors came out of an office up there, very likely Dr. Frederick Loose's office. *¿Porqué?* Who knows?"

"So now we go break the news to the widow," said Higgins. "Wonder why she didn't miss him last night? Talk about shapeless things—"

"You might find out who Dr. Loose is, and who might have had occasion to be invading his office with him out of it," said Mendoza.

The hospital had released Mrs. Sidney; she hadn't been hurt much. It was a house on Milner Road in the hills above Hollywood, a section of older homes on narrow curving streets, not particularly fashionable. When she opened the door to him and looked at the badge, stood back to let him in, he saw she was alone.

"I know you've got to ask me things," she said. "I'll—I'll try to help you however—I haven't met you before. Lieutenant? They—they told me I couldn't make any—arrangements right away—"

"You haven't any family, Mrs. Sidney?"

She shook her head, a handkerchief to her eyes. "They said—the other man, he had an Italian name, I don't—he said something about identifying—K-Ken. That if there was some relative, or—but there isn't. We were both only children, and—"

"Where did your husband work?" Mendoza offered her a cigarette, and she blew her nose, sat up and took it.

"Thank you." She bent to his lighter. "He was a C.P.A. with a big firm on the boulevard—" She named it. One of the men there could probably make the formal identification. Mendoza let her take her time; this one, he suspected, was a little flighty, not as sensible as Mrs. Macauley, and he didn't want her fingering another wrong X. "Oh!" she said, and burst into tears and put down the cigarette in a big fancy ceramic ashtray on the coffee table. "But that just r-reminds me, it was all my fault! That we were *there* at all—last night! I tried, you know, I tried to keep expenses down and save and—but everything's so high now, he made good money but everything— And I'm not *used* to thinking about all that—and he was awfully patient but we did have sp-spats and—oh, oh, oh! We'd just m-made up and he said he was sorry and he'd take me out to dinner—"

Mendoza didn't press her. After a minute she sat up and said chokingly, "Oh, I'm sorry, I didn't mean to say all that —only you can see how I'd—I know you want to ask questions." She blew her nose again, forlornly, and looked at him.

"We won't press you too hard right now, Mrs. Sidney. Do you think you'd recognize the man who attacked you?"

"I don't know. I'm not sure. It all happened so fast—and of course it was dark. He was big, and a Negro, sort of medium dark I think, and—oh, it was awful! We'd just got back to the car—"

It was, she had told Galeano last night, a Dodge four-door, two years old. They had the plate-number from the D.M.V., and there was a call out on it.

"—When he just *lunged* out of the dark, I don't know where he came from, and we saw the gun, and he said, Give me your money or something like that, and Ken— And then he grabbed *me* and I tried to scream, but he got me in the car, I think he must have grabbed the keys from Ken—"

Definitely flighty, another proposition than the down-to-earth Mrs. Macauley. Mendoza wouldn't lay a dime on her chances of being right, picking a mug shot. She was a pretty woman, not looking her probably forty-plus years: a nice figure, her golden-brown hair exquisitely tinted and waved (or was it a wig, he wondered), and her fair complexion delicately made-up; her eyes were faded blue, a little sunken now. Her hostess robe was in excellent taste, dusty rose fleece. She had beautiful hands, small and long-fingered, and her engagement solitaire was a fair size; on the other hand she wore an oval opal set round with baguette emeralds.

"You can't describe him definitely? Height, clothes?"

She thought, "Well, he—he swore at us. Dreadfully. And Ken didn't try to put up a fight when he had that gun. I don't know anything about guns, I couldn't say what kind it was. But I heard the shot, and then he had hold of me and I tried to struggle with him, he tore my dress—in the car—and I think he must've thought he'd knocked me unconscious, because he let go of me and the car wasn't moving very fast then, we'd just turned a corner I think, and I managed to get the door open and I fell out—I hardly noticed that then, falling I mean—I just got up and *ran*— as fast as I could, toward the lights—and it was Wilshire and when I saw the police car—"

"Do you think you could identify him if you saw him again?"

"Why, have you arrested somebody?" she asked excitedly. "For Ken—oh, that other man too! I saw it in the paper. He did that before—and it didn't *say* he, you know, raped that woman but I thought probably— Well, I don't know," she said. "It was dark, and I was so frightened—"

The citizenry, thought Mendoza in the Ferrari. But they came all sorts, and you couldn't expect careful, sensible witnesses in every case. You could make allowances for Stella Sidney: she was rather a silly woman to start with. He started back to the office to see what else might have turned up.

The man in the hospital bed looked weak and gray; but the bright blue eyes were alert on Piggott. "You—p'lice?"

"That's right, sir." The nurse stood by watchfully. "Now don't tire yourself, but can you tell us anything about who did this to you? You were attacked and robbed, we—"

The head inclined slightly. Lieutenant Colonel Pound had been a handsome man in his prime and in old age might be called distinguished, dressed and upright. He had straight features, a strong mouth, his plentiful hair was curly and gray, and he had his own teeth. He said, "Damn—son o' bitch, con me—thought at first—"

"Just take it easy, sir."

"Got tell you," said Pound. "Must be—senile, old age. Said—officer back—Vietnam. Seemed—nice young fella. The men's store—new tie. 'Cross from—hotel. Fox. Fox, said. Carl—Fox. Lieutenant."

The nurse had her hand on his wrist. "Now don't strain yourself, sir," said Piggott. "I'm getting it."

" 'Vited—room for drink. But—not—so easy—fool ol' warhorse. *Not* officer—wrong—" He sank back with a long sigh.

"I think that's enough," said the nurse firmly. But the blue eyes opened again and glared at her.

"You—mind your business, bossy. I got tell—Goddamn common thief—call 'self Army Off'cer—son o' bitch," said Lieutenant Colonel Pound. "Fox. Carl—Fox."

"All right, sir, we'll try to pick him up." You had to admire the old boy, thought Piggott, chuckling to himself. Still plenty of fight left in him.

He went back to the office, automatically intending to write up the report on that interview, and it wasn't until he came past Wanda Larsen's desk that he remembered what she'd said. "You mean it? You can type up reports from notes?"

"Surely, Mr. Piggott." She extended her hand, "Oh, your writing's not nearly as bad as E.M.'s! So the old man gave you something. Good for him. I'll have this ready this afternoon, I've got one of E.M.'s to do and then one for Sergeant Hackett. *That's* a funny thing, that man stabbed to death at the medical college. No rhyme or reason, he said."

Piggott realized all of a sudden what a boon Wanda Larsen was going to be to Robbery-Homicide. Now he could go right back to the legwork, the tiresome typing off his mind. Doubtless the paperwork would pile up on occasion, but with Wanda doing all that (as long as the reports came along eventually, administration would be satisfied) it should make for a much more efficient use of the men's time.

"You," he said, "are going to save us a lot of work around here. Pity we didn't find out about it sooner."

Grace came in with, inevitably, a sheaf of Polaroid shots in one hand, just displayed to Sergeant Lake. "I've got Mr. Osney settled down looking at mug shots. Any new jobs?"

"You can come help me on a pretty wild goose chase," said Piggott. "Show me the snapshots first."

Grace laughed. "Bore you all to death, Matt. It's just, we've been married five years and Ginny so anxious—I suppose we're a little nuts over Celia."

"But she is a cute one, Jase."

There was a men's clothing store catercorner to the Biltmore Hotel on Olive Street, and another about a block up. They drew blank at the first one—none of the clerks or the manager reacted to a description of Lieutenant Colonel Pound. At the second one, a boyish-looking clerk very nattily outfitted in the latest mod style said, "I think I remember him. I noticed his West Point ring. Tall old fellow, about seventy maybe, but looked like somebody."

"That's the one. Do you remember him talking to anybody in here? He was only here once?" All of a sudden Piggott thought, but that couldn't have been Christmas Day when the old boy was assaulted, the store would have been closed. He'd taken it for granted that Pound had meant he'd asked this Fox up to his room right then, but—

"Yeah, that's right. It was the day before Christmas. Along in late afternoon. I couldn't say if he talked to anybody. We had a lot of customers all that day—women buying ties and belts and wallets, you know. He could have, I wouldn't notice. He'd been here, looking around like, awhile before I waited on him."

"Well, so where do we go from there?" asked Piggott in the street.

Grace scratched one ear. "I," he said, "have got a simple mind."

"We all know that, Jase."

"The old fellow said this Fox told him he was an ex-Army officer. Then for some reason—by implication, after Fox took up the invitation and came to see him—Pound spotted he wasn't."

"I took it that—"

"Well, it occurs to me," said Grace, "that the fellow must have known enough about the Army to fool the old boy even awhile. So let's ask Uncle Sam if the Army knows the name. I think the lab picked up some latents there."

"It's a good thing you've got a simple mind," said Piggott. "Let's."

Mendoza had just sat down at a single table at Federico's, for an early lunch, when Palliser came up and sat down across from him. "Head winds. And the flight was delayed. I only got into Burbank an hour ago. Jimmy said you were here. Has anybody found Gene Stover?"

"We've been a little busy. Elucidate. The small steak, Adam."

"Same for me. Well, it's the only link with L.A. that showed. She was a serious girl, not interested much in dating. Stover is a sort of pal of Monica's boyfriend, Ron Stettin—new teacher at the college. And—" Palliser filled him in on that. "It sounds like nothing, but the mention of L.A.—"

"*Pues sí.* Why a sort of pal?"

Palliser was silent; he'd cut himself shaving, and unconsciously fingered the nick in his long jaw. "Stettin," he said, "isn't going steady with Monica, who would pall on anybody—almost anybody. Nice enough girl, a little silly. He was out with somebody else last night, I don't know who. I got him on the phone about eleven. Introduced myself, and he said he'd be busy all day today. I pressed him, and he said oh, well, he was usually up early, I could come round about seven-thirty. He teaches political science—"

"*¡Ay de mí!*" said Mendoza.

"—And looks about as you might expect. Van Dyke beard —I suspect he dyes it, it's darker than his hair—and a bushy moustache. He said he and Stover went to college together down here—UCLA—and he hadn't seen him in at least three years until he ran into him up there about eight months ago, in a record shop. They both collect folk music." Mendoza uttered another groan. "Well, I can't help it. Anyway, Stettin says it was all very casual, those few dates with Lila, mostly Monica pressuring him to get her dates, and Stover obliged. It wasn't, he said, anything important. In fact, just what Monica told me, and it doesn't seem to have been. But Stover is said to be in L.A."

"And not interested in Lila or she in him. What was he doing up there?"

"Working in another brokerage. Stettin said he told him— Stover, that is—that he thought he might do better in a smaller town, but he didn't, and finally he came back here. To the brokerage he'd been with here before."

"And how would Stover have known—if he would have cared—that Lila'd be here for three hours only that day?"

"I don't know. It was the only link with L.A.," repeated Palliser. "But—"

"But?" said Mendoza. Palliser was not as diffident as he had been once, one of the youngest sergeants on the force; but he still had moments of self-doubt. "I've got the priority on hunches around here, John, but as I've told you before, never ignore your feelings."

"Yes," said Palliser uneasily. "He was nervous about something. Stettin. And he hadn't any reason to be. He told me about nine times what a lovely girl Lila was and how terrible it is she's murdered. And by everything Monica said, and everything else he said, as far as he was concerned she'd just been a dog he'd had to dredge up dates for."

"There's a saying about not speaking ill—"

"Oh, he could have been—just observing the amenities. Sure." said Paliser. "But he was nervous."

"Which might be interesting," said Mendoza.

Shogart had covered the Askell inquest: pure formality, the open verdict. The Macauley inquest this afternoon would be more of the same. This afternoon somebody had better chase up to that C.P.A. firm in Hollywood and ask one of Ken Sidney's coworkers to make the formal identification of his body.

As Mendoza and Palliser came into the office, a tallish gray-haired man was just coming out. He stopped. "Sergeant Palliser—nice to see you again."

"Oh—Mr. Osney. Don't tell me—"

"Yep, a break-in. Bet it was the same ones tried it that time. But I just made one of the bastards for you, out of your picture books." Osney smiled. "Guy named Biretta. I had 'em spotted as Mex, but turns out this one's Italiano. Well, people come all sorts. One thing, it convinced the district manager. I've been at him, like I told you."

"About what?"

"The dogs," said Osney. "A lot of our other stores have got hit too—crime-rate like it is. And he calls me last night, he'd been reckoning up how much it'd come to, got some estimates and all. Turns out it'd be cheaper to rent the trained guard dogs than put in a new burglar alarm system. He's got it set up, with one of these kennels hires 'em out."

"That's good."

"You bet. Dobermans, they are. Anybody think twice, try a break-in with something like that waiting the other side of the door," said Osney with satisfaction.

Hackett and Higgins had spent a tedious and largely unproductive morning. The reason Mrs. Daly hadn't missed her husband last night was that she was staying with her daughter helping with the new baby. They seemed to be a close family: everybody upset and crying and saying why did it happen to Joe. No trouble on the job, he never had fights with anybody—

They had got names of the faculty and where they could be reached. Hackett didn't think much of Luis' idea that this Dr. Loose had something to do with it, but sometimes Luis' ideas led somewhere; he'd see the man, anyway.

Belatedly he realized what a blessing their policewoman was going to be, handing over his notes to be transformed into a report. "You're going to make quite a difference around here, lady," he told Wanda.

He was still trying to skip lunch. The flu, going through the family, had been a virulent type: he'd been down to two-oh-six, and even with skipping lunch he was now up to two-ten. It was, he decided with dismal humor, a losing battle. George would be settled somewhere now consuming a steak sandwich or a hamburger with everything on it, and he never gained a pound. It wasn't fair, of course, but nothing said life had to be.

Thinking about hamburgers and french fries, he called the morgue. Bainbridge as usual said, "I've only just seen the damn body. Give me time."

"Well, you can say something, Doctor. We found a pair of scissors on the scene—desk type, about an eight-inch blade. Blood all over 'em."

"So what more do you want?" asked Bainbridge. "That's probably the weapon. It's the ragged kind of wound scissors would make, what I've seen so far. I can't do the autopsy until you've got a formal identification."

"Coming up," said Hackett. Daly's son-in-law had offered to do that.

He got up and started for Mendoza's office to bring him up to date on all that, but Lake stopped him at the switchboard. "Mr. Purdy. That latest burglary."

"Oh," said Hackett. That. The amateur burglar, and nowhere to go on it at all: no latents, no leads. He took the phone. "Sergeant Hackett."

"Now I tell you," said Dan Purdy. "I don't care which of you comes, but some detective just better come and ask this guy questions. See? Because there they are as big as life, I see 'em with my own eyes and the Lord knows both Millie and I ought to *know*. There they are, where this damn thief sold 'em—the man won't answer any of our questions, you he says he'll talk to, and you just better—"

"What, Mr. Purdy? What are you—"

"Why, Millie's garnet ring and pin that belonged to her ma! That's what I'm talking about! Plain as day in the window of this pawnshop on Grand Avenue, and it's only accident I noticed 'em. I happened to be up that way just now to a secondhand place, looking for a cheap radio—can't afford to buy another TV, even secondhand—and I come past, look all casual at the window, and there by God they were. Right in the window, for sale! So I come home and get Millie to look, see—I was on my lunch hour and I never thought to tell the boss, but what the hell—and she says they are too, so you better—"

"All right," said Hackett soothingly, his stomach rumbling. "I'll come right away. Where?" He jotted down the address. The burglar, taking the petty loot—if all the loot available: maybe now a lead of sorts. He went downstairs to the scarlet Barracuda in the lot and drove up to Grand Avenue.

Indubitably, there was a garnet ring and brooch, old-fashioned-looking, in the pawnshop window. He supposed the Purdys would know their own property.

"Damn right," grunted Purdy; they had been waiting for him. "So you just tell the sergeant where you came by them, huh?" He looked fiercely at the pawnbroker.

The pawnbroker looked at the badge uneasily. He was an undersized, scrawny man with a pug nose. "They weren't on the hot list, Sergeant. Are they stolen property? I couldn't know—when they weren't on the list. These people said—but how should I—"

"So, where'd you get them?" Hackett looked at the two

[113]

humble pieces as they were fetched out and laid on the counter.

"Well—he said he didn't want a ticket on them, wanted to sell. I gave him ten bucks apiece."

"*Ten—*" said Mrs. Purdy faintly. "Why, my mother set such store by—"

"Who?" asked Hackett.

"I never saw him before," said the pawnbroker. "I don't know. Describe—well, he was just a guy. A—an elderly guy. Ordinary. I got him to sign a receipt, of course." He started to scrabble through an ancient filing case behind the counter. "I always— Here it is." He handed it to Hackett gingerly.

Hackett took one look at it and began to laugh. He leaned on the counter laughing helplessly. They stared at him, indignant and surprised, and he bent double, guffawing.

In neat half-printing, across the bottom of the sleazy paper form, was the signature: *O. N. A. Fixedincome.*

It was too good a joke not to share; he took it back to Mendoza's office. "This burglar, Luis. I like him. I like him the hell of a lot. A sense of humor he's got. Purdy spotted some of the loot they—Luis?"

"*¿Qué?*" said Mendoza, looking up from a report. "But that's funny—an automatic— Some of the loot, yes?"

Hackett told him, produced the slip. Mendoza dropped his cigarette and laughed, began to cough, rescued the cigarette and gasped, "*¡Dineros son calidad!* More truth than poetry, Arturo. Oh, by God, that's priceless—" and they both dissolved in mirth at the word.

"If we ever catch him, I'll hate to arrest him," said Hackett.

Mendoza sat back and groped for a new cigarette; his dark eyes were alive and alight with laughter. "*¡Qué hombre!* And why the pawnbroker didn't spot— But that's another thing, of course. We see—what we expect to see," and he looked back at the papers on his desk without touching them.

"Meaning?"

"Well, I read it—Tom's report—and it was just another fact. Now—"

"What?"

"*No sé*. The wild ones can be—inconsistent. Traffic spotted Ruby Jewel's VW, by the way. Left down on Manchester. No smell of Gosling."

"Well, we're pretty sure he's out of the running now, aren't we?"

"*No sé*," said Mendoza again. "Let me see that thing again, I like it. More truth than poetry—" He laughed.

He sat, at seven-thirty, before the belated hostages to fortune, the twin monsters who, combining the unlikely genes of McCann, Weir and Mendoza, were unpredictable. Who were, of course, only three. And, speak of small mercies, hadn't inherited Alison's red hair. Two pairs of eyes regarded him solemnly—Johnny's his mother's hazel-green below his father's widow's peak, Terry's her father's dark-brown under his sharp-arched brows—and he said, "So, *hijítos*. More stories in the nice new book. About an emperor—"

"*No comprendo*," said Johnny uninterestedly. "*Mamacíta* say, maybe *el pájaro* come back, makes nice nest for *los niños*—"

"And this emperor was very fond of fine clothes—"

"Whooool!" contributed Terry. "*El pájaro* fly down an' bite Bast 'n' Sheba!"

Mendoza persisted, "And one day there were two very clever thieves—listen, *niños—dos ladrones muy hábiles*—came to the—" He stopped and looked at the twins resignedly. He had persisted with Andersen because he liked the stories—nobody had ever read Andersen's fairy stories to Mendoza, forty years back; but reluctantly he realized that Andersen's subtleties were a little sophisticated for the twins, just turned three. Alison would have to be convinced that Andersen could wait. It was a pity, but the emperor's new clothes were a bit beyond—

After the simple blood thirsty joys of Grimm.

Terry suddenly dissolved in tears. "Never no more 'bout *El rinoceronte*—or *El Jaguar*—"

And Johnny, suddenly reminded of past joys, shouted exuberantly, "*El Gato* all by himself! *Sí, El Gato*—"

Well, the Just-So Stories more suited to their age. Mendoza put Andersen down. And nobody ever any better than Mr. Kipling, at story-telling—but he rather liked Andersen.

The Emperor's New Clothes—

8

THE SIGNATURE on the pawnbroker's receipt had tickled the whole office. Wanda Larsen, arriving early on Saturday morning, thus had the privilege of telling Sergeant Farrell, who sat in for Lake on Lake's day off. Farrell was still chuckling when Mendoza came in, natty in silver gray, with the others straggling in within five minutes.

There were reports centered on Mendoza's desk; he scanned them rapidly. The Sidneys' Dodge had been spotted by Traffic just after the watch changed last night, parked on Leeward Avenue. It had been towed in for examination. A fairly quiet night, last night had been, for this office: a couple of accidents with D.O.A.'s, a mugging down on Fourth, another gas station held up.

"This Loose," began Hackett.

"About that Fox," said Grace. Mendoza lifted a hand as the phone buzzed at him.

"Scarne."

"Hold it a minute," said Mendoza, and asked, "Did anybody arrange for identification of Sidney's body?"

"I did, yesterday afternoon," said Piggott. "You said to try the place he'd worked. Fellow named Dombey said he'd be glad to oblige, he'll be in this morning. Shall I hang around to take him down?"

"I'll see him . . . Scarne? What have you got?"

"This and that. First of all, that hotel room. A lot of latents there, we covered the personal stuff first. And one of those glasses was wiped clean. But we picked up four pretty good prints off the other—"

"Belonging to Lieutenant Colonel Pound."

"Funnily enough, no. In fact, it looks as if in the heat of the moment your X wiped off the wrong glass. If they didn't make mistakes we wouldn't catch 'em. They're not in our records, I sent 'em to the FBI."

"All correct. That's a step on. Anything else?"

"Something," said Scarne, "I sweated blood over. That hijacked truck. I had to get the legit driver's prints for comparison, and he said something about the gear-lever being stiff. Truck was due in for an overhaul. Well, I just had a hunch—you know they haven't left even a smudge on any of those trucks, and we figured they were wearing gloves—but you can't get as good a grip with gloves on. I went over the whole damn gear lever practically with a magnifying glass, after I'd dusted it—it'd've been easier if I could have dismantled it first, but I didn't dare—and I picked up two pretty good prints, on the backside of the shaft. She was sticking, and he jerked off one glove to get a grip. I sent 'em to R. and I. before I left last night, and the answer was waiting when I got here just now."

"Don't tell me—"

"I do. In our records, one Kurt Kramer. I'll send up the details."

"*Por favor.* How very nice." Mendoza put the phone down and passed that on.

"Well, so maybe we catch up to Fox without the Army's help," said Grace. "I don't suppose we'll hear from them today. The FBI, possibly—they're on the ball."

"I've located Loose," said Hackett. "He's meeting George and me out at the college in twenty minutes. But what you've got in your head about Loose—there can't be any connection, Luis—"

"Go and find out. The computer, I see, ground out some new names to look for." Fed the general description which fitted Chester Gosling—but also a number of other men— the computer had obliged with a dozen other names out of their records. "No, I don't suppose anything on your fake

Army lieutenant will turn up today," and he handed over the list to Piggott.

"More legwork. And you know it'll stay up in the air," said Shogart phlegmatically. "Prove an alibi? Most of these fellows are drifters, sometimes drunks—couldn't say where they were yesterday afternoon, let alone five days ago."

"We've got a bullet," Mendoza reminded him. "That .22 slug can be matched to a gun, when and if we find—" he paused and added to himself, "¡Ca! There was that . . . Off you go. Rory, get me the lab."

This time he got Duke. "On the Sidney kill. Tom Landers sent down a shell-casing they found somewhere around the body in that parking lot. Anything on it?"

"In the way of prints, no. It's an ejected shell case out of some kind of automatic—domestic for a guess."

"Well, the pros can always get hold of any kind they want," said Mendoza. "Thanks. Rory, let me know when a Mr. Dombey shows up." He sat down at his desk and lit a cigarette, and for some reason he was thinking about the emperor's new clothes.

"I can't get over it, a murder here," said Dr. Frederick Loose. "One of the cleaning crew? I will be damned. I don't think any of us would know any of them—and I'm sometimes here when they're working, at night, but I don't think I ever exchanged a word—" They were climbing stairs in the big modern building. "But what do you want with me? Any way I can help you, as I said on the phone, but I haven't been here for a week—nobody's been here—we're closed for the Christmas vacation. Until Tuesday."

"Yes, sir, but the man was found, and probably killed, right outside your office. When were you here last?" asked Hackett.

"My office? Well, I'm damned. It was a week ago Friday. The last day of classes before vacation. I left, let me see, about five that afternoon—" They came to the third floor and started down the hall. "We were going out to dinner that evening and I—but, here!" He stopped, and then moved forward quickly. "What the hell is my office doing open? I locked my door then, it shouldn't be open now. Did you find it like this, when you—"

"That's right," said Higgins, a little surprised. "It was locked?" He and Hackett both looked at the door at once, examined the lock, without touching it. "No deadbolt. Easy enough to get in with a piece of stiff plastic. Doctor, you'd better check to see if anything is missing. Art, I wonder if it'd be any use to get a lab man out to dust the door."

"But I don't see— What about it, Doctor?"

Loose was already at the big desk, opening drawers, riffling through manila folders. He straightened up presently and looked at them perplexedly; he was a man in his sixties, but still erect and alert; with steady dark eyes in a clerkly face. "Well, there wouldn't be anything of value here, if you're thinking of a burglary. There's never any money or—" He got out a pack of cigarettes slowly and looked down at the stacks of folders neatly piled on the desk. "Dear me," he said. He lit a cigarette. "Dear me."

"What's struck you?" asked Higgins.

"Well, the fact is, when I say anything of value—why anyone might want to break into my office—there is just one thing here I can think of, which someone might have a—a motive to get at."

"And what's that?"

"The examinations," said Loose. "Dear me, I don't like to think that of any of the students. The end-of-semester examination questions for all my classes—exams get under way the second week of January, you see. Conceivably— though as I say I don't like the thought—some student might have wanted to get a look at those. Did you say this isn't a safe lock? I thought—"

"No deadbolt," said Higgins. "But, for God's sake, what's that got to do with Daly?"

"Nothing," said Hackett, "obviously. If that's what happened, which is the likeliest thing, it could have happened any time since a week ago yesterday afternoon."

"But Daly was killed right here, Art. Suppose he came up here and heard—"

"Oh, now, really," said Loose. "Really. Between snatching a look at examination questions and murder—"

"Farfetched," said Hackett.

"Is it? Don't drag your heels," said Higgins. "And trust your Uncle Luis' hunches. Here's two unusual things happened right here. I don't care how irrelevant they sound— to each other, as it were—doesn't the place sort of tie them up?"

Hackett passed a hand across his jaw. "Well, when you put it like that—but—"

"And what about the scissors? Dr. Loose, do you keep a pair of scissors on your desk? Are they there?"

It seemed they were missing.

"There you are," said Higgins. "You can read it. Purely an impulse kill. Whoever got into the doctor's office, for whatever reason—"

"When the building was filled with cleaners tramping around— But, by God! Of course—"

"When else could anybody get in the building? It was closed for vacation—and I'll bet that front door has a better lock on it than this one," said Higgins.

Ray Dombey showed up at headquarters at a quarter past nine, asking uncertainly if this was where he was supposed to come. He thawed quickly at Mendoza's overtures, accepted a cigarette and a cup of coffee from the machine down the hall— "Unless you're in a hurry, Mr. Dombey."

"Not to see Ken dead, I'm not," said Dombey. "Poor devil. Who'd have thought a quiet guy like Ken Sidney'd end up shot by a pro hood? Damndest thing. These days, I guess anything can happen to anybody, but you never think the— the violence can happen to you or anybody you know. How's his wife?"

"She wasn't as badly hurt as the other woman—she got away from him."

"That's good. I sort of gathered the first woman was raped. A terrible thing. Poor Ken. We've both been at Scott-Burnham a good many years—nearly twenty for me, getting on for twenty-five for Ken. It just shows you," said Dombey suddenly. He was a nondescript fellow in his late fifties, conventionally dressed, with a big Masonic ring on his right hand.

"Shows you?" Mendoza leaned back smoking lazily.

"How it's no use to worry. You know? Ken was a worrier. He worried about money—well, he made good money, but what I gathered, his wife could spend it as fast as he made it. He worried about her—she's a good deal younger, you know, they'd only been married about six years, he lost his first wife matter of ten years back—he worried about what'd happen to her if he had a heart attack or a stroke or something and couldn't work. Or if he dropped dead—he worried about keeping up his insurance. It just shows you, Lieutenant—like they say, the things we worry about never happen. Imagine him going like this—*shot*. Like the other one. It looks as if it was the same one killed Ken?"

"That's right. We've got a description of him," said Mendoza. "And we don't want to waste your time, Mr. Dombey. If you don't mind—"

"No, no, not that I'll enjoy it, but you can't ask his wife, I see that. Poor woman. He just doted on her, Ken—wanted her to have anything she wanted, and then worried because it cost money. Well—"

In the cold room at the morgue, he looked in silence at the body in the tray. Mendoza was a little surprised at the body, for no reason; Dombey had just told him that Sidney was older than his wife. And death wrought changes. But the body was that of an elderly man, sharp-nosed and sunken-eyed: a man in his sixties at least, possibly seventy. A thin old man with pinched cheeks, a few straggly gray hairs on his flat naked chest.

The bullet wound was in the right temple, and there was no exit wound. So they'd have another slug for comparison, unless it was damaged.

"Yes, that's Ken," said Dombey soberly. "I knew him twenty years. Do I have to sign something?"

Palliser was feeling annoyed. He was annoyed at Ron

Stettin for setting him off on what was probably a wild goose chase, and at himself because he knew logically he was wasting time but something he couldn't get hold of made him persist.

Yesterday afternoon, on the straightforward legwork, he had gone to the downtown office of Stone, Fox and Meyer and asked for Gene Stover. Nobody by that name was currently employed there. He asked for the office manager, who told him with circumlocutions that Mr. Stover had severed connections with the firm some time ago.

"Was he fired?" asked Palliser bluntly.

"Well, let us say we didn't suit each other," said the manager.

"Look, this is official business. Was he fired for dishonesty or office politics or what?"

The manager hedged. "Well, quite frankly, we suspected that he had been—er—making up to a couple of our more elderly—er—clients. Er—female clients. In a personal— You understand, he was merely a salesman and—" The manager looked unhappy. "He was working under Mr. Gordon, one of our top advisers—naturally a young fellow like Stover not a qualified expert on investments, but he had been—"

Passing himself off as, Palliser deduced, to the possibly gullible (and wealthy?) elderly clients. "Did he ever ask for a reference from you?" No, he hadn't.

Palliser had taken an hour to ask for Stover at seven other brokerages along Spring, and drew blank. So this morning he had got hold of Stettin on the phone, and again Stettin made him feel uneasy. For absolutely no reason.

"Well, I'm afraid I can't help you," said Stettin fretfully. "All I can say is, when he went back to L.A. he hoped to get taken back by that company."

"You don't know his home address here?"

"No, I'm afraid not. It was a very casual friendship, if you can call it that at all. He was just a fellow I'd known in college."

"Does he have any family here?"

"Really I couldn't say," said Stettin. "It never—ah—came

up. What we mostly discussed—that is, on the very few occasions when I saw him—was, ah, intellectual subjects. I don't know—"

"Such as."

"Oh, well—politics and the various protest groups on campus and—ah—I did tell you we're both interested in country western music—"

"You can't have talked exclusively about that."

"Well, no. But I really know very little about him and I—"

"You knew him well enough to have arranged dates for him."

"I won't be harassed like this," said Stettin. "That was Monica's doing, damn it. Must arrange a date for her roommate, and it wasn't the easiest thing to do. Gene was just—obliging, I don't see why—"

"You said Lila was a very nice girl."

"She was, she was! Don't get me wrong, Sergeant," and Stettin was placating. "But what *is* all this, anyway? It wasn't anything important, those couple of dates. And I expect Gene couldn't get another job down there and—ah—went on somewhere else. I wouldn't know. Really, I won't be—"

"Harassed," said Palliser. "Well, thank you, Mr. Stettin." He looked at the dead phone with dissatisfaction. It wasn't anything important, of course.

Coincidences—Mendoza's first answer was probably the right one. The other passenger on the bus, somebody who lived here. Who just happened to be on that bus heading home. Who got talking with Lila. Went with her to that Orange Julius bar—and having a car here, maybe offered to drive her around the city a little before her bus was due to leave. It had been broad daylight, people all around. She wouldn't have hesitated—

Damn Stettin and his political science classes and his beard; it was just nothing. He had wasted the morning on this. He had even taken the time to check all five phone books: Stover wasn't listed. Which didn't say he wasn't here, with or without a phone; some people had unlisted numbers. Or he might be sharing an apartment, the phone under another name.

Palliser decided that his imagination had been working overtime. He was still sitting there over a paper cup of coffee, wondering about Lila Askell, when Farrell had a call.

"Accident of some kind, Traffic unit's on it so it must be a D.O.A. when they route it to us. Public school playground on Ninth just past Hoover."

Palliser went out to see what it was.

Hackett, after some more argument, had called up a lab truck and ordered a thorough coverage of Loose's office, including the door. Loose said miserably that he couldn't be sure the papers had been disturbed, his examination questions for five classes. The door, of course, yielded a fine crop of smudges and partials, and the best pair of liftable latents turned out to belong to Loose.

The desk yielded a lot more; it would be a job to sort them out.

There were no dormitories here: the students all lived off campus. The college could produce a list, of course. There were about five hundred of them, but not all of those would be in Loose's classes.

"I still say it's up in the air," said Hackett.

"Well, I don't. I think we follow it up," said Higgins.

They got back to the office at noon, Hackett's stomach rumbling, and found Farrell sitting with a switchboard jack in his hand looking undecided. He brightened at sight of them. "Whatever you had in mind, forget it. Not another soul here, and I just had a call from one of our pigeons. Chester Gosling is sitting in a bar on the Row right now, so he says. The Aztec Room."

"Oh, for God's sake!" said Hackett, who had just decided to start having lunch again. "There's no reason—"

"He's been fingered and there's a warrant out for him," said Farrell.

"All right, all right. I suppose the boss is out to lunch?"

"I've got no idea where he is. He went out about ten, after that Dombey came in to make the identification on Sidney."

"Come on," said Higgins.

They took Higgins' Pontiac instead of the Barracuda, thinking of transporting the prisoner. Skid Row in broad daylight was old and tired-looking, the aged buildings, the dirty streets, the cheap little stores and noisy bars. The Aztec Room hardly lived up to its elegant name: it was a hole in the wall past a cracked narrow sidewalk, and the lettering on the one window was so old that it was illegible. Higgins parked the Pontiac in the red zone at the corner and they walked back. Neither of them was much looking forward to going into the place, not so much because it was dangerous—which it wasn't—as because it would be smelly and unpleasant and dirty; and as it turned out they didn't have to. As they came past the empty store next to the bar, the door opened and a man came out, a tallish, thinnish Negro in dark pants and blue shirt: Chester Gosling.

"All right, Gosling, hold it!" snapped Hackett, bringing out the gun. Gosling's head jerked round and then he ran, desperately, the other way down Main. They pounded after him and what with the crowds impeding all of them, didn't gain on him much down that block. But he made the strategic error of cutting across an empty lot at the corner of Third, and with no obstacles in the way picked up speed. Higgins, carrying twelve or fourteen less pounds than Hackett, caught up and tackled him from behind and brought him down, flailing wildly.

"Take it easy," he panted, and as Hackett caught up Gosling bucked under Higgins like a spooked steer, and there was a knife in his hand. "Goddamn!" said Higgins, and then Hackett had Gosling up, both arms behind him in a tight grip, and the knife dropped.

"Did he get you?"

"Scratch, I think," grunted Higgins, and twisted his head to look at his left arm. It was bleeding freely, and his jacket sleeve ripped six inches. "Goddamn it, this was nearly a new suit!"

"Come on, we'd better get you back to First Aid," said Hackett. His stomach was rumbling like Mount Vesuvius.

The package on Kurt Kramer, linked by two latent prints to the hijacking jobs, came up from R. and I. at eight-fifty. He had the expectable rap sheet, heists, muggings, break-ins. He was now off P.A. from the latest little stretch he'd done, but they could try that address first. Piggott and Glasser went out on that, and Grace and Shogart started out with a couple of the new possibles out of records on Ma-cauley-Sidney.

"This job can be a drag," said Shogart, yawning. "Sometimes you wonder why you picked it."

"It can get boring," agreed Grace. "But on the other hand, there are compensations. The things we run into—like that burglar."

"Oh, him," said Shogart, and began to laugh again.

They didn't find either of the first two on the list, so they went looking for the next.

Piggott and Glasser were disappointed too. At the address listed on Kramer's P.A. record, they found an ancient four-family apartment. Kramer's father still lived there. He was on Welfare; he didn't like the cops; and he told them they just liked to come bothering people who'd been in a little trouble. Kurt wasn't there any more, and he didn't know where he was living and if he did know he wasn't about to tell the cops.

"I suppose there'll be a warrant out on him sometime today," said Glasser. "We could probably get one to search the old man's place in case there's something to show where Kramer is."

"I suppose," agreed Piggott. "Let's go back and see if the boss wants to play it that way."

But Mendoza had already gone out.

Mendoza parked the Ferrari in a public lot on Van Ness up from Wilshire and walked back to Wilshire. He wasn't sure what was in his mind exactly—when what Hackett called his *daemon* was starting to operate, he frequently wasn't.

He knew this city like the lines on his hand. . . . That fortune-teller he'd once picked up for operating in city limits had told him he had the Mystic Cross in his palm, and pointed it out. The Cross of Intuition. He didn't know why he was here.

He walked across Wilshire with the light and on down Wilton Place. These side streets would be fairly dark at night. Wilton was more of a main drag than others, but still not as bright as Wilshire up there. He came to a cross street: Ingraham Avenue. Off the main drag here, humble single houses, small apartment buildings. It would be zoned for multiple residence.

Mrs. Macauley, escaping—after struggle and rape—had run to the nearest house for help.

He came to another cross street: Seventh Place.

It was, after how many years of very tough so-called gun-control laws in New York, very easy for any pro there to come by a gun. Any kind of gun. And the pros were not too particular, except of course for the droppers, the hirelings who would kill for money, and they preferred the big guns, the .45's and the big magnums.

Quite suddenly he remembered that hired dropper Pat had mentioned, Harry Singer. There was a warrant out on him. And Pat's reformed pusher ready to tell all sitting safe in protective custody.

He ought to call Goldberg, ask how he was coming on. Back to the new job next week, and he and Pat would grumble at each other and exchange insults and pull in harness just fine. But it was going to be, reflected Mendoza, a little shock to Saul to find that not every LAPD bureau was supplied with a smart policewoman to type reports for the men.

"*Una verdadera sorpresa,*" he said to himself. To be hoped Saul had appreciated what he'd had. And all the men from the old Robbery office screaming their heads off, having to type their own reports.

He came to another cross street: Leeward. He turned

down it at random. He didn't know why he was here. He walked down to Norton Avenue and turned up toward Wilshire again.

He felt, he decided, uneasy. No more. And about what he wasn't quite sure. The sure cold finger up his spine, the hunch that said, Look there, or Ask about that, was not present.

He knew this city—had ridden a squad car, not on this beat, but he'd had to know the city like a map memorized.

And he was wasting time, for no rhyme or reason. It was eleven o'clock. Always things to do—at the office, on the street, the routine coming along—

A faint lead to the hijackers. Anybody's guess how many in on that; the profits were high enough to stand splitting several ways.

The burglar . . . standing on the corner of Wilshire and Norton, he laughed. More truth than poetry; but they ought to put him out of business. Stash him where whatever income didn't matter.

And what the hell he was doing here—Mendoza pulled himself together. *Daemons* be damned. He collected the Ferrari, got stuck in a jam on the freeway where a head-on piled up traffic, and when he got back downtown it was twelve-thirty and he was starving. He went straight up to Federico's and consumed a shot of rye, four rolls, french fries and the luncheon steak.

When he got back to his office Hackett and Higgins had just come in. Hackett was savage with hunger, and Higgins bitter about his suit-jacket. In First Aid, the nurse had taken three stitches in his arm. "And what the hell *use* it is to pick up Gosling—I know there's a warrant on him, damn it, but we can have an educated guess now that Mrs. Macauley was wrong. It's a very damn general description." Higgins' arm hurt and he was querulous.

"Did he have a gun on him?" asked Mendoza.

"No. Just the knife," said Higgins bitterly.

"Mmh. We had a request in for a search warrant on the Gosling apartment and Ruby Jewel's. Are they in?"

"Why, for God's sake?" said Hackett.

Mendoza, replete, was shuffling the cards rapidly, a cigarette in one corner of his mouth; he dealt hands around, the deck neatly stacked, and surveyed the results with satisfaction. "The fixed income," he muttered. "Providing for the hostages to fortune—in case it all blows up— *Como sí.*"

"*Well?*" Hackett was exasperated.

Mendoza looked up at them vaguely. "There are all these new possibles to look for. We'd better question Gosling. You can have the jacket mended, George. Tailors. The Emperor's New Clothes—"

"For God's sake!" said Hackett. "He's no more use than a halfwit like this!"

"—And so we spent the rest of the day looking for the new names out of records," said Hackett disgustedly. "Gosling just clammed up and wouldn't tell us so much as his middle name. After he was reminded of his rights, of course. Talk about hamstringing us—inform him all polite he doesn't have to say a word, and then try questioning—"

"Yes, darling, very annoying," soothed Angel. "You sound hungry. Go round up Mark, will you? Dinner in five minutes—"

And it smelled very appetizing. Feeling somewhat mollified, Hackett went to find Mark watching a cartoon on TV, and Sheila for once patting the cat in civilized fashion. "How's my Sheila girl?"

"That sleeve's ruined," said Mary. "What a nuisance, George—"

"Does it hurt, George?" Laura's big gray eyes were sympathetic.

"But you got him," said Steve. "You mostly do. Say, George, I've got the new *Photography* magazine and there's a neat enlarger for only sixty-five bucks—"

"I suppose one of these invisible menders—" said Mary.

Feeling a little better for sympathy in the bosom of his family, Higgins grinned at Steve. "So let's look at it."

* * *

[130]

"—And when I mentioned taking the tree down," said Alison, "you should have heard the yells. Well, it's the first one they'll really remember much, the darlings. But once Christmas is over, it seems weeks ago—and the tree's dropping all over the carpet. I—"

Sheba leaped for Mendoza from behind and dug all claws into his shoulder. "*Monstruoso*," he said mechanically, and hauled her down to his arms.

His household was serene, Alison snug in one of the big armchairs, Bast coiled on her lap: Nefertite and El Señor curled together in the other chair: their hairy sheepdog Cedric snoring at Alison's feet. The twins had been settled down with Just-So stories and dinner had included Alison's special souffle and Mairí MacTaggart's scones.

Mendoza put Sheba down on top of El Señor and Nefertite. She spat at him amiably and began to wash El Señor's ears.

"You," said Alison amusedly, "are either experiencing a first-class hunch, or trying to. You haven't heard a word I've said since dinner."

"Yes," said Mendoza absently. "And tomorrow's New Year's Eve, and neither of us has even suggested going out on the town. I must be feeling my age—"

"When have we ever, *imbécil?* Neither of us enjoys that kind of thing—and besides, the one big night in the year to a Highland Scot is Hogmanay, and Mairí deserts us tomorrow for sister Janet. They may even hail in the New Year with a few wee drams of whiskey." Alison laughed. "We're stuck with the offspring . . . Luis? You don't really want to go out carousing?"

"Carousing. I think," he said, "I could do with a little dram, now you mention it." He wandered out to the kitchen, where Mrs. MacTaggart was just whisking open the oven on an appetizing smell.

"Your New Year's dinner, and all you've to do is hot it up," she informed him. "For I'll not be back till New Year's morn. A grand beef pie with dumplings. And there's a new bottle of rye if that's what you're after."

"*Bueno.*"

"I'll just set the oven to the automatic timing—Ach, that cat!"

El Señor had heard the bottle taken down, and arrived posthaste for his share. Mendoza laughed and poured him half an ounce in a saucer, filled a shot-glass.

"If I didn't know better," said Mrs. MacTaggart, "I'd say ye'd had more than enough as it is, man."

He carried the glass back to the living room. "I wish," said Alison, "it would dawn on you. Whatever it is. You're *muy difícil* in the throes, as it were. Would it be helpful if I asked questions? I don't know all the cases you're working, you've just mentioned that Mormon girl, and the hijackers, and of course Mrs. Macauley—and that burglar. That is really priceless, the pawnbroker's receipt—"

"*No sé,*" said Mendoza, swallowing rye. He turned and looked at her, and his gaze focused. She was smiling slightly, her one-sided provocative smile that took ten years from her age. His redheaded Alison, who had at long last domesticated—if halfway—Luis Mendoza: and given him the hostages to fortune.

"*Vaya, mi corazón,* don't be foolish," and he finished the rye. "I can think of other occupations—" And she squealed as his arms closed round her, lifting her from the chair.

9

It was Saturday night, and the last night but one of the old year: the night watch, sitting snug in the sergeants' office with the desk downstairs relaying calls, could only imagine what Traffic detail was handling on the streets: the drunk drivers, the accidents, the pile-ups on the freeways. It might be a busy night for them too, or not; they'd be finding out.

"Did you hear about that pawnbroker's receipt?" asked Galeano. They all had. "Sometimes I think Mendoza attracts the offbeat ones."

Conway opened a new pack of cigarettes. "I'll be just as glad to get off night tour. I've heard this and that about him, he should be interesting to work under."

"Too much so sometimes," said Landers. "Hackett says he jumps. No logical deduction from A to B to C, way we're trained. His mind jumps, like A to L. He says his poker game's ruined, but I don't know I'd like to sit in a hand with him. He's an artist with the cards."

"I heard he's a gambler. Also quite a chaser."

"Was," said Galeano sadly, "was. He got caught up to belatedly by a redhaired Irish girl. God, what a combination —I'll bet those twins are terrors."

They were called out around nine-thirty; there was a collision on the freeway with two D.O.A.'s, later a mugging up on Olive, but it was a quieter night than they might have expected. At eleven-fifty the desk relayed a phone call.

"H—Robbery-Homicide, Detective Galeano."

"I want Robbery-Homicide, the Robbery-Homicide office, he said that was—"

"Yes, sir, can I help you? Detective Galeano speaking."

"I want Sergeant Palliser—" It was an uncertain male voice.

"I'm sorry, Sergeant Palliser is on day watch, not here now. Can I—"

"When will he be there?"

"Any time after eight, sir. Who is this sp—" But the phone was dead at the other end. "That's funny," said Galeano.

Mendoza was supposed to be off Sundays; sometimes he was. When he drifted into the office that Sunday morning, he walked in on an argument between his two senior sergeants.

"Listen, it's wild," said Hackett. "There's no evidence at all—"

"I don't say there is, Art, I just say there might be. If we look. I know I don't usually get these spells, making like Luis, but on this one I just *saw* it—"

"Jumped," said Hackett. "As if Luis wasn't enough to cope with! And as for looking at it, my God, George, that doctor said somewhere between sixty and seventy students—and another thing that strikes me, they won't be an average lot. Medical students, solid academic records and older than the usual college kids, not very likely to be the type—"

"What is the type? I just saw—"

"Break it up," said Mendoza. They swung to face him, the pair of them looming over him.

"I'd just like your opinion," began Higgins, and Hackett swore.

"You just want him to back up your starting to have hunches. Look, Luis—"

"No," said Mendoza. "For the moment, forget about Dr. Loose and his students." He went into his office, sat down at his desk (polished and neat courtesy of their police-woman, who *was* off on Sunday) and lit a cigarette. "Over-night," he said, intently eyeing the desk-lighter, "my subconscious came through and revealed a hunch which has burgeoned out into beautiful flower. *Pues sí.* A very pretty thing indeed. Now what went down last night and what's on hand to work? I—"

"Oh, you're here," said Palliser, coming in. "Here's something funny. Somebody called asking for me about midnight. I was curious enough to put a tracer on it, and it was out of this area code. They're checking some more. What I'd like an opinion on is, where do we go on the Askell case now?"

"Askell," said Mendoza as if he'd never heard the name.

"Matt and Henry are starting to look for Kramer again," said Palliser, "and there's about ten more possibles on Macauley-Sidney to haul in. At least the burglar hasn't struck again. The woman who got mugged last night says she left her teeth-marks on his arm, so if we pick up anybody with—"

"And what are we supposed to do with Gosling?" demanded Hackett. "Now we've got him?"

"Find out if he had a gun," said Mendoza. "We had an application in for search warrants, his wife's apartment and Ruby Jewel's. Are they here?"

Lake had been listening, at the switchboard outside the open door. "I've got 'em, Lieutenant."

"*Bien.* John, you and these two—mmh—detectives go and execute them. Now. *¡Vamos!*"

"*What?*" said Hackett. "Search the—"

"That's right," said Mendoza. "Go, go, and have a good look. Jimmy, get me the lab . . . and close the door when you leave," he added to Palliser.

Temporarily speechless, they went out.

"Now what the hell is in his mind?" wondered Higgins. "I don't know why we kept Gosling at all."

Palliser was wondering about the phone call. From out of the area. Asking for him personally.

They took the Barracuda. They all thought this was a complete waste of time.

Mrs. Gosling was shrill and angry at cops invading her private place, but authority in the form of the warrant turned her sullen. They were trained to search thoroughly; they did. Beyond the fact that Mrs. Gosling was a very indifferent housekeeper they didn't turn up anything.

They went on to Ruby Jewel's place. They were unwelcome anywhere, this morning: she and an erstwhile boyfriend were just up and nursing hangovers; neither of them had the energy to cuss much, but they let the detectives know their feelings.

"Talk about silly," said Hackett. "What the hell he's got in his head now—and even if by some long chance we came across anything remotely incriminating, this isn't Gosling's place and there'd be no proof that he—"

"Well, I will be damned!" said Palliser. "I will be Goddamned!" He swung around from the old-fashioned chiffonier, and there was a gun in his hand. "Under her stockings." It was a .22 Colt.

They had left the bedroom door open, and Ruby came on uncertain legs to complain more about invading cops. "You got no call treat me like a— Hey!" she said. "Hey, you leave that alone! Chester give me that—for pertection, said isn't safe for a girl, I better—that's mine!"

"After it was Chester's?" said Higgins. He looked a little happier. "Any comments, Art?"

Hackett shook his head as if trying to clear it. "I still don't see what he's aiming at, George. All right, Gosling's got the right rap sheet for Macauley-Sidney, but it's way out of character, when he knew we were after him—"

"Give the lady a receipt, and let's go. I'm sort of curious," said Higgins, "to hear how the rest of the lyrics go."

They got back to the office at eleven-fifty and dropped the Colt at S.I.D. "He'll be on the phone to you," said Higgins, and Duke said he didn't doubt.

"He already has been. What the hell is he playing at now?"

"What did he want?" asked Palliser.

"I'll let him surprise you."

Upstairs, they found Mendoza on the phone. "You can send up a formal report when you get round to it, Doctor. Just the gist, please. What showed up? . . . Mmh. Slug in any condition for examination? *Bueno*. You sent it to the lab, I trust . . . That's interesting . . . Oh? . . . Now you don't tell me." Suddenly he laughed. *"Hoy por tí, mañana por mí.* Thanks, Doctor." He put the phone down, contemplated the extraneous object lying across the desk and picked it up.

"And what the hell do you want with that?" What he'd asked Duke for, they could deduce.

"The miracles of science do give us useful tools. . . . Mr. Kenneth Sidney," said Mendoza, "was killed dead by a slug in the right temple. The slug is in good condition and can probably be matched to a gun. But it was—mmh—a redundant kill. He wouldn't have had long to live. His heart was a good deal enlarged and he had started to grow a brain tumor. At a guess, says Bainbridge, he'd have been dead in three to six months."

"Not like the healthy Mr. Macauley, so what?" said Hackett.

"Did you come across anything?" Mendoza hefted the long length of metal and squinted down it absentmindedly.

"A Colt .22," said Palliser interestedly. "Ruby says Chester gave it to her for protection."

"Oh, I like that," said Mendoza. "I do like that, John. You left it at the lab." He picked up the phone and got Scarne. "Priority, please. That Colt .22 you were just handed. Test fire, please, and run a comparison with the slug out of Macauley."

"I was just going to lunch," said Scarne.

"How long will it take you, half an hour? Forget your stomach."

"While you go to lunch."

"No. While I study a map. *Por favor.*" He made a long arm and reached for the County Guide. "You can go snatch some lunch, but don't sit over it. We've got work to do." He opened the big book.

"You're skipping lunch now?" said Hackett.

"I'll get Jimmy to send in a sandwich. See you back here in forty minutes."

There was, as always, enough work for them to do. Piggott and Glasser had brought in two men to question on the hijacking, picked out of records as longtime pals of Kurt Kramer. Shogart was out looking for Kramer.

As Palliser passed the switchboard he asked, "Any calls for me, Jimmy?"

"Nope. Looks as if your midnight caller has changed his mind. Funny."

Funny wasn't the word.

Hackett, Higgins and Palliser went on out, and a moment later Mendoza came out of his office and said, "Have the canteen send down a sandwich, Jimmy. Doesn't matter what." He went into the sergeants' office and began to look into drawers in Wanda Larsen's desk.

When Hackett, Higgins and Palliser came back to the office, he was just putting the phone down, looking pleased with himself. Hackett looked at him shrewdly.

"A real kingsize hunch, huh, Luis?"

"The subconscious," said Mendoza, "is a peculiar thing, Arturo. Logic is all very well, but on this job what's even more important is human nature. In the end, damn the facts, it's human nature we're dealing with."

"Like I say, stupidity and cupidity," said Hackett.

"And quite often both. A thorough and cynical understanding of human nature is more valuable to a detective than every scientific tool down in S.I.D.," said Mendoza seriously. "Though—mmh—S.I.D. is useful to prove what we already knew."

"What do we already know?" asked Higgins.

"Yes, and that comes in too—seeing what we expect to see." Mendoza stood up, yanked down his cuffs where heavy gold links nestled, settled his Sulka tie, and reached for his hat with one hand and his requisition from the lab with the other.

Hackett looked at that. "Are we going treasure hunting? In the middle of L.A.?"

"That is just what," said Mendoza. "We'll take your car, John."

In the Rambler, they went up Wilshire Boulevard to Van

Ness, and left the car in a public lot. Mendoza led them across Wilshire down Wilton Place to Leeward three blocks down, and stopped, and looked up to the right.

"The black-and-white was just past Manhattan Place on Wilshire. So useful, the private secretary filing away precise facts. Mmh, yes. And it was dark. But without any doubt at all, there'd have been a dry run on it by daylight. *Como sí.* Because there wouldn't be much time at all." He looked up Leeward, and added, "A psychological strength there to bolster a rather weak point. Mmh, yes. Well, let's get on with our treasure hunt."

The others just exchanged exasperated glances. He led them down Leeward half a block, stopped, and said to himself, "Right here. But no possible place to be seen. No. And nothing on Wilton, so—" He went on to Norton and turned up that, toward Wilshire again. Up to Seventh. At the corner he paused. There was a small apartment building on one corner, single houses on the other three, small frame houses with cars parked in front of them. "No," said Mendoza. He went up Seventh, looking from side to side. Nearly at the corner where Wilton crossed, he stopped before an empty house. The blind windows were minus curtains and a sign was propped on the lawn: *For Rent by Owner.*

"*Es posible,*" said Mendoza, and went briskly up the front walk. "Now how the hell does this thing work? I read the directions, but—"

Hackett took the long metal-detector from him. "Where do we look?"

"Try the flower beds all round the front."

Fifteen minutes later, Higgins and Palliser showed him the collected loot: an old dog-collar with a rusty name plate, half a keychain, a blackened nickel, and several strands of wire.

"First cast," said Mendoza. He went on down to Wilton and turned up that; they almost saw his nose twitching, a hound casting for any wayward scent. Up Wilton to the next cross street, Ingraham, and he turned right on that. It was a block of old frame houses, mostly, with a couple of new apartment buildings, stark and square and ugly. Nearly up to the next corner, Mendoza stopped and looked across the narrow street, and his long nose did twitch once.

"The ideal place," he said. "But absolutely. What a beautiful place. Because just up there is Manhattan Place. And the foundation is already dug up, there might not be anybody digging around there for quite some time."

The house across the street had been readied for moving: its foundation had been cleared, and the house moved onto blocks all ready for the big dollies which would trundle it away to some new lot. It was a big stucco house painted dirty tan.

Mendoza crossed the street at a trot. "All right," he said to Hackett, "let's see what treasure we can turn up here."

Hackett trudged back and forth in front of the house several times, moving gradually toward it. The metal detector was silent. Presently it registered faintly and Higgins came resignedly to dig up a rusty bent spoon. "You should have had the foresight to borrow a spade too, Luis."

"All right, try over to the side," said Mendoza. "Along the hedge, Art." There was a scraggly juniper hedge between this lot and the next.

Three minutes later Hackett stopped. The detector was registering strongly. Higgins squatted and probed with the longest blade on his pocket knife. It touched hard metal; he dug the dirt away, and it came loose easily. They hadn't had rain in six weeks and normally the clay-heavy soil would be packed firm; but this had been loosened before, not long ago. Higgins grunted as he felt something heaved up under the blade. He dropped the knife and picked it up, getting slowly to his feet.

"And I knew it had to be there," said Mendoza with a long sigh. "Somewhere . . . Scarne called just before you got back. That .22 is the gun that killed Macauley."

They didn't exclaim. They were looking at the thing in Higgins' big hand.

Mendoza dropped his cigarette and stepped on it. "*Es hermoso sin pero.* That Hi-Standard Supermatic, brand sold by Sears Roebuck. It takes .22 long ammo. It hasn't been there long. And I would lay my current bank account, boys, that S.I.D. is going to tell us it is the automatic that killed Kenneth Sidney."

After a long mute moment Hackett said, "And haven't I said it before. A couple of hundred years back, *compadre*, you'd have burned for a warlock."

And Palliser said incredulously, "*Gosling—do you mean—*"

"That's just what I mean, John," said Mendoza pleasedly.

She opened the door to them, looking a little bewildered at four men on her doorstep, two of them looming. "Why, Lieutenant Mendoza—"

"And Sergeants Hackett, Higgins, Palliser. May we come in?"

She stepped back at once. She was dressed today, and well-dressed. Her good figure showed to advantage in a beige silk sheath, tastefully embellished with one large gold brooch where diamonds glistened; her golden brown hair was beautifully arranged. "They—they told me I can probably make arrangements—for the funeral—by Tuesday," she told Mendoza. "Have you arrested anyone yet? I'm sorry I couldn't be more helpful to you, but—"

"Mrs. Sidney," said Mendoza enjoyably, "Sergeant Palliser is about to tell you something, and I'd like you to listen to it very carefully. Give the lady her rights, John."

Palliser suppressed a grin at him as he stood there, hands in pockets, rocking slightly heel to toe, watching her. He said gravely, "Mrs. Sidney, you have the right to remain silent, and the right to the presence of an attorney before any questioning, and—" he recited the rest of the little ritual. "Do you understand these rights, Mrs. Sidney?"

"Why—" She stared at them uncertainly, and a first faint alarm showed in her blue eyes. "What do you m—"

"Do you understand your rights, Mrs. Sidney?" asked Mendoza. "As Sergeant Palliser just explained them to you?"

"Yes, I—understand what he said. But—"

Mendoza gave her a rather wolfish smile. He brought one hand out of his pocket and showed her the .22 automatic. Traces of dirt still clung to the grip.

She stared at it for a long moment, and then slowly she

began to back away from them. "Nobody," she said, "nobody could—"

"You read the story in the papers about the Macauleys," said Mendoza conversationally. "Last Monday. Christmas Day. The Macauleys accosted in the restaurant parking lot by a Negro, who robbed them and abducted and raped Mrs. Macauley after shooting her husband. We all know that violent crime is on the increase. You thought about it, didn't you? If a criminal did a thing like that once, nobody would be very surprised if he did it again, would they? And it would be a chance to take, but with luck and nerve you could bring it off."

"But nobody," she said, "could have—"

"You wanted to be rid of him, didn't you? Your elderly and perhaps difficult husband, always complaining about your extravagance—the husband you'd married only a few years ago, possibly thinking he had more money than he had. You knew he carried some sizable life insurance. And this gave you an idea how you might he rid of him, and nobody the wiser. Copy the Macauley crime and you'd be quite safe—another bereaved widow. I think you read the newspaper stories about the Macauleys very carefully."

She came up against the built-in bookshelves across the room. She was slowly shaking her head.

"But the papers don't always get all the details, you know. They told you that Macauley was shot, but not by what gun. They told you that Mrs. Macauley said it was a Negro, but not her description of him—you had to play that by ear, and it was a very nice act. The flighty female, too frightened to remember exactly what he looked like. And the papers told you that the Macauley car had been found abandoned, but not where, or that it had been wrecked. The car was a little problem, and I must say I admire the way you solved it."

"But how—did you—"

"You had to leave the car somewhere, and get rid of the gun, and you wouldn't have much time. It was rather strongly implied in the papers that Mrs. Macauley had been raped. And unless, presumably, you got away from your attacker rather shortly, he'd have raped you too, and that you couldn't fake, to a doctor. It took nerve," said Mendoza, regarding her with objective admiration. "You shot your husband, probably, as he was unlocking the driver's door. You got the keys from him, and you simply drove out of the lot. You knew where you were going—straight down Wilshire to Wilton Place, and down to Leeward. You parked the car and left the keys in it—and you'd remembered to wear gloves so your prints wouldn't show up as the latest driver. You had, of course, chosen the terrain by daylight. Spotted that house to be moved. That was a very convenient place to get rid of the gun. Because you really had very little time. And—mmh—talk about a double play," said Mendoza, "you could gamble that we wouldn't be too surprised at finding the car so near to where you turned up crying murder, robbery and abduction—when you'd got away from him, conceivably he'd be nervous about keeping the car, and abandon it at once. I like that."

Her eyes fixed on his, blind with desolate fury now. "Damn you," she said tiredly. "Damn you. You devil, *how did you know?*"

"Well, we had a suspect on the Macauleys, you see. And while a man of his type can acquire a gun very easily, it isn't often that he has the money or desire to acquire two. And your husband was shot with an automatic—we found the ejected shell-casing near his body. You don't know much about guns, do you? You intended, of course, after getting rid of it, to run up toward Wilshire all hysterical, stop someone on the street—the squad car was an unexpected bonus. Yes. The automatic belonged to your husband, didn't it?"

"Goddamn you to hell. Yes. He—showed me how to fire it—once. In case of burglars. That's funny. That's really funny."

"Oh, I can tell you something funnier than that," said Mendoza. His deep voice was sardonic, and genuinely amused. "He only had a few months to live. I just heard the results of the autopsy. You really needn't have gone to so much trouble."

"Oh—my—God," she whispered.

[143]

"He can be damned annoying," said Hackett to Higgins, "but I confess I always get a kick out of him like that— all lit up like a Christmas tree, one of his hunches working out just like a diagram. But what a hell of a thing—"

"And why anybody ever thought about it— She could have got away with it, you know. When we tied Gosling to Macauley by that Colt. The different guns looked a little funny, but the ones like Gosling, a pro hood—and he probably wouldn't have had any alibi to stand up."

Mendoza had booked Stella Sidney into jail himself, set up the machinery on the warrant. Palliser and Grace had Chester Gosling down the hall in an interrogation room trying for some admittal on the Macauleys. But in spite of the obstacles presented now by judges and courts, they thought they had Stella Sidney tied up tight for the D.A.'s office. And, with the lab evidence on the gun linked to Gosling, him too.

"So, Happy New Year," said Hackett.

And Joe Daly was waiting autopsy down in the cold room, and Higgins had had the unprecedented hunch on that, listening to Dr. Loose talk about examination questions. Hackett was still dragging his heels on that, but less reluctantly.

They would probably write tomorrow off as far as routine went. New Year's Day—even the citizens who wouldn't be celebrating its arrival with too deep libations would be watching the parade and the several big games, and resent interruption.

Dr. Loose had promised them a list of all the students in his classes by five this afternoon; Higgins started for the Looses' big house in West Hollywood to get that, and Hackett, reflecting on what a thing *that* would be to work —even if George's hunch was right, question every one of those bright medical students—wandered into Mendoza's office at four-fifty and found him swiveled around in his chair looking at the line of the Hollywood hills clear and cold against the horizon.

"What does the D.A. think about the case on Stella?"

"I haven't talked to him. He's not in his office. It's New Year's Eve," said Mendoza. "And Lila never got home for Christmas."

"You're back to that. I don't think we'll ever know what happened there."

"Dead grass," said Mendoza. "Cotoneaster leaves. *Caray.*"

"What?"

"The lab report on her clothes. I wonder. I'd like to know," said Mendoza. "By what John heard, I think she was rather a dull girl, Art. Serious and respectable and hardworking. No sense of humor and not much interest in the opposite sex. The earnest Christian, maybe looking down her nose a little at less puritanical females. But she wanted to go home for Christmas, and I'd like to know who stopped her."

"When you put it like that—"

"Without robbing or raping her."

"Yes, that is funny. But where to look—"

The phone buzzed and Mendoza picked it up. "Hom—Robbery-Homicide, Mendoza."

"Happy New Year, Luis," said Goldberg, and sneezed.

"Well, and to you, Saul. How are you doing?"

"Fine, just fine. Back on the job Tuesday. The new job. Say, I've been getting blasts from all my boys—"

Mendoza laughed. "Having to type all their own reports. No obliging private secretary attached to Narco. You never appreciated how good you had it, *hermano*. And thanks very much for Wanda. So well trained, and she's appreciating my nice polite boys after your roughhouse crew."

"Ah, you go to hell," said Goldberg. "I just hope you do appreciate her, Luis. A nice girl."

Mendoza put the phone down, laughing, and relayed that. "You know, Luis," said Hackett, "I've got a kind of suspicion that Glasser has his eye on that girl. Just a look about him—"

"Well, good luck to that—what am I saying? Get her married off and we'll lose our private secretary." Mendoza stood up. "I'm going home. Tomorrow will be wasted time. Nothing moving."

"Except maybe a couple of new ones to work."
"¡Dios me libre!"

Jason Grace took home a bottle of Cold Duck to chill. It was a very special New Year's Eve to the Graces. "Here's to us," he said, an arm around Virginia. Celia Ann was sound asleep in her new crib, under the padded coverlet embroidered with lambs and angels in pink for a little girl. "We made it, Ginny. We've got a family."

Virginia chuckled, sipping wine. "I didn't tell you what your father said. I mean, he should know—" Grace's father was chief of Gynecology at the General Hospital.

"What?"

"Well, he said it happens so often, right after the baby's adopted, the wife finally gets pregnant. Wouldn't it be funny, Jase—"

"The more the merrier," said Grace largely.

"Happy New Year, darling," said Angel, "and damn the calories for once." She'd had a bottle of champagne waiting. "Don't look so gloomy, you're only up to two hundred and fourteen."

"I was thinking," sighed Hackett, "about all those poor damned souls picked to police Pasadena. Happy New Year, my Angel."

"Don't be such a pessimist, Matt," said Prudence severely. Their first New Year's Eve in their own place, and her mother was there for dinner; Piggott liked Mrs. Russell. They were going to church after dinner, for the special service. "It *can be* a happy new year, however unlikely it looks. You got to have faith."

"Sodom and Gomorrah," said Piggott. But of course, a man in his job, dealing with human nature in the raw, was not conditioned to automatic optimism. "It does say, man He made a little lower than the angels."

Landers snatched five minutes to call Phil and wish her Happy New Year. "I can't tie up the phone. Listen, about

Tuesday night—you wear that blue thing, and the perfume like roses."

"Six dollars the bottle. Six-thirty, yes. That Castaways place, Tom. Because of the view."

"I told Rich. He's never been there. See you then, Phil. Oh-oh, there's a call on the other phone—"

There would be, on New Year's Eve, a lot of hard work for the LAPD, chiefly for Traffic.

Roberta had a bottle of champagne chilled. "To us, darling. And David Andrew—or Elizabeth Margaret—"

"Margaret Elizabeth," said Palliser. "Or what do you think about Martha? I like old-fashioned names—"

"Well, I'll think about that one," said Roberta, wrinkling her nose.

"I'll get her settled down," said Higgins. He patted Margaret Emily's small rump fondly.

"Well, if you can, George. I've got a bottle of champagne in the refrigerator—it *is* New Year's Eve—and you should have heard the wails when I said we ought to take the tree down—but Christmas seems years ago, and—"

"Oh, Mother! We don't have to take it down *yet*—"

"Can I have some champagne, George? I'm twelve now and— Just a sip, to see what it's like—"

It was Higgins' second New Year with a real live family of his own, and it was just as nice as he'd always thought it would be.

Alison offered him a glass of champagne. Mendoza was not a wine-drinker, but accepted the ritual resignedly, touching her glass with his.

The twins were settled down with Just-So Stories, and of course neither of the Mendozas was much given to carousing in nightclubs; they spent a domestic evening at home, Alison busy over letters and Mendoza uneasily prowling the living room; his mind was back on their other mystery now.

Later on, as he slid into the kingsize bed beside the familiar carnation scent that said *Alison,* he decided a little sleepily that he didn't mind being domesticated. Ten minutes ago, the whistles and rockets had signaled the official end of the old year; ten minutes later, as he was drifting to sleep, they died down.

Ten minutes after that, he suddenly sat up in bed.

Outside the bedroom windows, there sounded a Voice. A sleepy, low voice, but unmistakable. The crooning note of the mourning dove, *coroo-coroo, coroo-coroo.* A muffled *AWK. Tu-whoo.* And then, on a low note, but quite clear, *Yankee Doodle came to—*

"*¡Diez millónes de demonios desde el infierno!*" said Mendoza. That damned mockingbird was back.

10

"AT LEAST," said Alison sleepily, pouring his coffee, "it can't stay this warm, Luis—it's bound to turn cool again, and we're due more rain. The creature won't be nesting."

"I wouldn't put anything past *el pájaro*," said Mendoza darkly. The livestock was all out in the back yard, Cedric barking and the twins shouting. The mockingbird was up in the alder tree, cooing to himself.

"Have a good day," said Alison, yawning. As he backed the Ferrari down to the curve of the circular drive, with due care for cats, Mendoza reflected from experience that it would be either a feast or a famine. Holidays—

The streets, the freeways, were oddly empty, deserted. The Ferrari was the only vehicle to be seen on the Hollywood freeway for a mile, until he got closer in downtown. This one morning of the year, a large proportion of the citizens stayed home. And those who didn't—

Over in Pasadena, those specially-chosen ones (some of them with difficulty squeezed back into uniforms unworn since a few years and inches had been added) had seen the first of the coming crowds begin to straggle in at 3 A.M., finding parking places, finding their seats in the tiers of wooden seats that had lined Colorado Boulevard for a month, or just finding curbside spots to stake out folding chairs and blankets. Steadily, the crowds had been swelling ever since, to fill the street-sides. About five-thirty the television crews would have appeared, to set up cameras and platforms for their guest M.C.'s. The telecast would be getting under way about now—it was eight-fifteen—and for two hours the great gaudy parade, with its elaborate floats and marching bands headed by baton-tossing drum majorettes, and prancing equestrian groups, and local and national personalities on horses and in sports cars, would slowly stream in all its bright garishness down the long boulevard, watched by that tightly packed huge mob of people. This morning they wouldn't need the lap-robes and blankets and heavy coats, and the girls on the floats, mostly in diaphanous costumes, wouldn't be in danger of catching pneumonia. At last the great parade would turn off the boulevard, to disband a few blocks down, and the flower-covered floats would be trundled to Central Park to remain on public display the next few days. And the crowd—which would already have kept the uniformed men busy enough, with people fainting, being taken ill, losing children, losing mothers and fathers, losing dogs off leashes to get lost in the parade, quarreling with each other over curbside rights, and scattering food containers all over, and a hundred other difficulties—would begin to disperse, milling in the streets, losing more children, forgetting where cars were parked, raising rows over parking fees, filling every restaurant and coffee shop along Colorado and the side streets, and eventually most of it would be leaving Pasadena.

A lot of that crowd would be tourists from out of state, cramming every motel and hotel around and in Pasadena. The two roads leading away from the city would be one massive traffic jam to keep moving. And just about as it was all moved out, on its way home or to motels, the second crowd would be starting to arrive, again jamming the freeways and the roads into town: the great crowd bound for the Rose Bowl to watch the biggest football game of the year. Well, it was a nice day for football. . . . The game usually ended between four and four-fifteen, and then that second crowd would straggle out—having strewn the great stadium with litter, lost children, lost friends, forgotten where cars were parked—and make another traffic jam to be herded out of the city in an orderly manner.

Those special duty cops would be lucky to get home by the middle of the evening, after an eighteen-hour stretch. Mendoza returned devout thanks that with his rank and age he wasn't likely ever to get tagged again for New Year's duty in Pasadena. He had been caught twice in twenty-four years, and that was twice too much.

At the office, everybody else was in.

There was an FBI kickback from the query about those prints: the latents on Lila Askell's necklace. Mendoza looked at it hopefully, but it was N.G.—the Feds didn't know the prints.

Hackett and Higgins now had a list of Dr. Loose's students. "And you know what use it would be to start on that today," said Hackett. "Have you heard the details on this, Luis, and if so, is George going senile?"

"It's a fairly wild one, if he isn't," said Mendoza. "I don't know, there's a weird sort of logic in it. Two unusual things happening in the same place—it could say they're linked. Anyway, you've got a reason to go asking—Loose's office was broken into. But as you say, you won't find many of those home today, or if you did half of them will be nursing hangovers—"

"What, those hardworking medical students? More likely half of them are at the Bowl."

Sergeant Lake had brought a portable TV with him— "My oldest daughter's," he said—and was watching the parade, with Piggott, Glasser, Grace and Shogart looking over his shoulder.

A light flashed on the switchboard and Lake reached to turn the volume down, plugged in. After two weeks he had nearly trained himself; he said at once, "Robbery-Homicide, Lake."

"I want—Sergeant Palliser," said a hesitant voice sounding a distance off.

"I'm sorry, he's not here, can I—

"They said he'd be there—after eight."

"It's his day off," said Lake. "Can I help you, sir?"

After a little silence, "Can you give me his phone number?"

"I'm sorry, sir, against regulations. If you'd like to give me a number, I'll be glad to relay it to him."

Another silence. "Will he be there—tomorrow?"

"Yes, sir, but can't I—"

The phone clicked at the other end. "That's funny," said Lake. "I thought at first it was one of our pigeons, but they're not usually quite so shy as— My God, I wonder if it was John's midnight caller?" He retailed all that to Mendoza, who hadn't yet got as far as his office.

"*Extraño*. Put a tracer on the call, just for fun, Jimmy. And get hold of John."

Most of the population of L.A. and environs who didn't have hangovers and didn't have to go to work today were watching the parade on TV. Palliser had probably been among them. But he listened to Lake and said, "Now who the hell could it be? What did he sound like, Jimmy?"

Lake considered. "Male, high tenor, no special accent, and he hisses. His *s*'s."

"I'll be damned," said Palliser. "Who does that—that Stettin! Ron Stettin. Now what the hell—"

"I put a tracer on the call."

"Well, let me know if it was from Santa Barbara."

"Will do."

Just then a uniformed messenger came in from Communications; Mendoza took the manila envelope and a moment later said, "Oh, Jase—Matt. Here's your kickback on Fox. Only he isn't."

"Isn't what?" Grace took the teletype; he and Piggott read it interestedly.

It was from the Department of the Army. It identified the fingerprints sent from Scientific Investigation, LAPD, as belonging to one Carl William Fawkes, description appended, who was AWOL from Fort Ord. Fawkes was twenty-seven, five-eleven, a hundred and seventy, brown and blue, tattoo on right forearm of a hula dancer, a heavy drinker and a compulsive gambler. He was unmarried, had attained private first-class rank; he had been AWOL for three months.

"Well, it's nice to have him spotted," said Piggott. "I wonder if he's still here. I think I'll go and wish the lieutenant colonel Happy New Year."

Lieutenant Colonel Pound was sitting up in the hospital bed, looking a great deal better. "I remember you," he said to Piggott. "Police officer."

"That's right, sir. I'm glad to see you're looking better."

"I'm fine, just fine. Constitution of a horse—always had. But what a hell of a way to spend the holidays, eh? Hell of a thing. Have you caught that son of a bitch yet?"

"No, sir, but we know who he is. He left his prints on one of the glasses." Piggott showed him the information from the Army, and he growled over it.

"Stupid as well as crooked, eh? To think he fooled me for a minute! But he was pretty smooth. And he didn't claim to be a career man, y' know. Damn it, I *liked* the fellow— just talked to him a few minutes in that store, day before Christmas it was. Said I'd be here another couple of weeks, drop up to have a drink with me—fella all alone here, he said, and Christmas—" Pound snorted. "And when he did—"

"That was Christmas Day."

"'S right. About three in the afternoon. Well, talking with him, it didn't take me long to spot he was no officer. Let him see it. Here, I said, who d'you think you're kidding anyway—on account of this and that he'd said, y' know— and that's when he knocked me down. I gave him a fight," said Pound reminiscently, "but age does tell, I suppose. But I think I surprised him, fight I put up, or he wouldn't have grabbed my knife—it was on the table. But life in the old dog yet, eh? You think you'll catch him?"

"Have a look for him," said Piggott. That waiter at the hotel had just been mistaken about seeing Pound then. "There'll be a warrant out. Now we haven't any idea what he got from you, sir. Could you tell me roughly how much money? Do you carry any credit cards?"

"Fellow got my West Point class ring, damn him, and my watch. Aside from that, four dollars and seventy-eight cents cash, and I understand from Mr. Di Silva, who very kindly came to see me, my four best suits. Damned thief," said Pound. "I'm an old campaigner, Mr. Piggott, and my checkbook and travelers' checks were in the hotel safe. Credit cards? Don't use 'em. Don't like bein' in debt."

"And I wish there were more like you," said Piggott. "Well, I hope this hasn't soured you on California, sir."

"By God, no, sir. As soon as I'm out of here I'm looking for a nice little apartment in Santa Monica. Good luck on catching up to that son of a bitch."

"We'll have a look, but the devil," said Piggott, "is good at taking care of his own."

"And isn't that the truth," said Pound. "*I've* had some encounters with the devil in seventy years myself—"

Lake got Palliser again at nine-twenty. "That call was from Santa Barbara."

"Be damned," said Palliser. "You know, I think I'll come in. I'd like to hear what the boss thinks about this."

What Mendoza thought was not immediately apparent. He was shuffling the deck smoothly, and listened to Palliser absently.

"You think it was Stettin. Why?"

"That's what I'd like to know. Why the hell should Stettin be phoning me? What about? I don't know anybody in Santa Barbara, and from Jimmy's description it was Stettin's voice. But when I was there—and when I talked to him on the phone—he was very damned upstage. And all he and Monica gave me was Stover, and that's N.G. I said a link to L.A. but when I thought about it, it isn't, really. He just obliged Stettin—and Monica—and double dated with Lila a couple of times. She wasn't interested in him, and vice versa. How would he have known she'd be here, for just three hours that day?"

Mendoza squared the deck carefully and cut it once: to the ace of spades. "On the face of it—" He cut the remaining deck again and looked at the ace of diamonds. "No, he couldn't, could he?" He cut the remaining half of the deck, to the ace of clubs. *"Donde menos se piensa salta la liebre*—sometimes an answer shows up from way out in left field." He cut the deck again and looked at the ace of hearts. "And I get the feeling, John, that your Mr. Stettin—"

"He's not mine. I don't like him worth a damn."

"—Is blowing hot and cold. He calls you here at midnight on Saturday—but not again. Until today. Why?"

"That's what I'd like to know. I'll try to call him back—"

"No," said Mendoza. "From what you say of Mr. Stettin, and what we've just deduced, he's jittery about something. It's too easy to hang up a phone. I think"—he shuffled the deck together and put it down—"you'd better go see him again. Drop by headquarters and take a local officer along. Impress Mr. Stettin with your importance, and see what you get."

"Up there again?"

"It's only a hundred miles up the coast. And if by some incredible chance Mr. Stettin knows something to give us a lead on Lila, I'd like to know what it is."

"And this was supposed to be my day off."

"Well, you came in under your own steam."

For want of anything else to do, Hackett and Higgins went down to the jail on Alameda and pressured Chester Gosling some more. This time, they finally got it into his head that he was tied tight to the Macauley job by the scientific evidence on the gun. The actual lab work he didn't understand, but he knew that that was solid evidence. He glowered up at them and said, "I didden know what I was doin'. I wasn't in my right mind."

"Is that so?" said Hackett. "Were you drunk?" Mrs. Macauley hadn't reported any smell of liquor.

"I'd had a shot of the stuff. That afternoon."

"Heroin?"

"Yeah, yeah. The horse. I wasn't in my right mind."

"But you did hold up the Macauleys and then—"

"I don't remember nothin' else about that. I wasn't in my right mind."

That was something, of course. They went back to the office and handed notes to Wanda for a further report on that.

Palliser had got a flight up to Santa Barbara at eleven-fifteen.

The warrant came through on Stella Sidney. The D.A. would try for murder one on that. Gosling would be luckier: probably a charge of voluntary manslaughter.

Hackett had just got back from lunch—if you could, he thought, call cottage cheese and low-calorie peaches lunch —when Lake, plugged in to a call, started to laugh. "Oh, that's a good one. Just a minute, I'll get you— Oh, Art! Like to take this? It's Sergeant Barth up at Wilcox Street."

Hackett took the phone. "So what've you got for Central?"

"Maybe a nice solid lead to your hijackers," said Barth. He sounded amused. "There are a few honest men left among us, Sergeant, and one of this bunch made the tactical error of approaching him on a deal. The honest citizen grabbed him for us. I've got 'em both here. I didn't need to think twice to guess it probably ties in with your hijackings."

"Oh, isn't that nice," said Hackett. "I'm on my way!" He took Grace with him, and looked at last night's Polaroid shots on the way.

"But I'm beginning to think Higgins is right about that camera," said Grace thoughtfully.

At Wilcox Street in Hollywood, they found Sergeant Barth waiting for them. "You'd better hear the honest citizen first. He'll tie it in for you. You've got a warrant out on the other one."

"Who?"

"Kurt Kramer."

"Oh, very nice," said Hackett. Barth took them up to a little office on the second floor of this ancient precinct house and introduced them to Mr. Andrew Post. Mr. Post was a large, broad man in late middle age, dressed in very expensive sportswear. He had a bald head and bulging shoulders, and a diamond ring on his right hand. "You the men from headquarters like he said? Pleased to meet you. I wasn't born yesterday, see, and when this joker starts talkin' about—"

"From the beginning, please, Mr. Post," said Hackett. He sat down and offered cigarettes.

"O.K., O.K. I've got a restaurant out on La Cienega. The Blue Bull." They looked at him in surprise: it was a very well-known place, with a high-class reputation and prices to match. "I've been in the restaurant business all my life, and my father before me. And everything strictly aboveboard, see? So O.K., a liquor license costs in this state, the liquor costs too, but that's how things are. I make a good profit, I don't cheat anybody—my customers *or* the state, whatever I think about taxes. You get me."

"We get you."

"So my maitre d', he says there's this guy around asking to see me. Won't say what about. This was, oh, couple of days last week. I'm in and out, I got fingers in a few other pies, and my employees I can trust, run the place smooth. So am I interested in what this jerk might want? Anybody wants to see me can say what his business is plain out. But I happen to be there—this is about an hour ago—when he drops in again. And I'm curious enough, give him five minutes. And he's got the nerve, offer me a deal on the hot liquor for a cut price! No sweat, he says, all sealed and kosher—nobody'd know. And high-class brands. Do I need to be an Einstein to know it's this hijacked stuff? What else? And you don't need telling, all the stolen property, damn what it is, just ups the prices to you and me and Joe Doakes. So I grabbed him. I called up a couple of waiters to hold him and I yelled for the cops. I got him," and he nodded at Barth, "and he said it was your beat was on it."

"And thanks so much," said Hackett. "It's nice to meet an honest man, Mr. Post. We had this one tied to the hijackings, and there's a warrant on him."

"Say, is that so? Well, glad to do you a favor," said Post. "Hope you pick up the rest of the gang."

Kurt Kramer was about what they'd expected; and he wasn't saying anything at all. They took him back downtown and booked him.

"Now look, Mr. Stettin," said Palliser patiently, "we'll ask you to stop insulting our intelligence." He wondered if Ron Stettin, in acquiring his degree in political science, had ever been required to study logic, and decided it was unlikely.

Stettin looked at them with a curious blend of emotions passing over his expression: nervousness, fear, attempted dignity, incredulity, horror. "I mean," he said. "I mean—" and he stopped. He had, in the last half hour, got himself boxed in a corner, and he didn't know where to go from here. He wanted out, and there was only one way to get out and he didn't want to go that way.

He had been surprised to see Palliser and the local man Palliser had picked up: a big wide-shouldered sergeant named Delaney. Palliser had asked him why he'd been calling Robbery-Homicide and Stettin said, showing the whites of his eyes, he hadn't. Palliser said the calls had been traced. Stettin hesitated and then said he'd just wanted to know if they'd arrested anybody for Lila's murder yet. Monica had asked him to call, he added. Palliser asked him why he had wanted to talk to him and nobody else. Stettin said, well, he was the man he'd talked to before. Why had he called at midnight? Well, he'd just thought of it, didn't realize the hour—

Palliser asked him what he was afraid of and he said nothing. He shouldn't, he added hurriedly, have said anything about Gene Stover to them, or any of those dates. It wasn't important at all, and Stover had been just one of several men he'd known he'd got to date Lila. "So you said before," said Palliser, and asked him if he'd had any contact with Stover recently. No, no, said Stettin, he hadn't seen him for a couple of months. "I didn't ask you that. Have you been in contact with him?"

It was purely Palliser's instinct that kept him on the right line; that, and Stettin's essential stupidity. Palliser had been here before, on Mendoza's vague hunch, and he hadn't thought anything Stettin or Monica told him was important; the equally vague link to L.A. didn't, on examination, look like much of a link. But here was Stettin for some reason very jittery, and the mention of Stover's name seemed to make him more so, so naturally Palliser followed it up. "Well?"

"I—" said Stettin. He kept casting nervous glances between them. "I don't see what reason you have—it's no business of yours—"

"Why did you want to talk to me at midnight last Saturday?" And as he said it, sudden light dawned on Palliser and showed him a little way ahead. He'd been asking for Stover at that brokerage, and others, on Friday. Stover quite possibly had a pal or so still working there, who might have passed the word that a cop was asking for him. "He called you, didn't he?" said Palliser. "Some time on Saturday. You and Monica were the only ones who could have told us about his knowing Lila. He didn't like it, did he? You bringing cops down. What did he say?" A pang of doubt struck him even as he asked. It was so vague, so up in the air. Nobody could have known that it was the Askell case brought a cop asking for Stover there. And—

Stettin looked ready to cry. "That's an unwarranted assumption! I never knew the man very well, and it's quite absurd to think he could have had anything—anything to do with *that*. And I have a reputation to keep up as an instructor, I—"

"What's that got to do with it?" asked Delaney. Stettin opened and shut his mouth.

"I don't want anything to do with it," he said. "I'm not involved—in *that*. It's nothing to do with me. Monica asked me to call you—to see if anybody'd been arrested. That's all."

"What about Stover?"

"*Nothing* about Stover! I don't *know* anything about him —I shouldn't have—those dates weren't important. Not at all. Stover didn't care anything about that girl. She was a dead bore and a—a bundle of repressions and *nobody* could have cared a damn about her—"

"Did Stover call you? Write you? On Saturday? What about?"

"It doesn't matter," said Stettin. His hands were shaking and he gave up trying to fill the manly collegiate pipe. His little dark beard waggled as he talked, absurdly. "He wasn't —none of us was involved with *that*. People like us wouldn't—"

"Like who?" asked Delaney. "College people?"

"No, no, Gene's not attached—I mean, well, I mean *intellectual* people, Gene's very—"

"Did he contact you on Saturday, Mr. Stettin?"

"Who? He's—he's got nothing to do with it, he said so! I don't know why I thought for a minute—I haven't got anything else to say to you."

That was where Palliser told him to stop insulting their intelligence. "You seem very nervous, Mr. Stettin, and every time I mention Gene Stover's name you get a little more so. Why?" Why indeed, he wondered. What the hell this rigmarole was about—

"Just like Monica," gabbled Stettin rapidly, "a *bundle* of repressions—so unhealthy—these days, we are *aware* of the need for full expression of the natural emotional impulses— in time I'll make Monica understand that—but of course the other girl was hopeless—I said to—"

"Now what are you talking about?" asked Palliser.

Delaney shifted stance. "If I translate the double talk, Sergeant, they were both nice decent girls who had moral scruples about sleeping around."

"And what's that got to do with Stover?"

"I—I—" Stettin looked around wildly. "I *will not* be involved in this! Oh, my God—why did I ever—but he couldn't possibly have—a thing like *that*—and besides he said he didn't! He said he wasn't—and I hadn't any reason — Oh, my God, but if—"

"You'd better pull yourself together and tell us all about it," said Palliser. "Never mind who's involved. What are you talking about?"

Stettin shied like a spooked horse at the steel in his tone. "Oh, my God," he said wretchedly. "I—he was mad as hell about it, about the police—and about the other too—I thought it was funny—he's not *used* to a girl turning him down—and I—and I—it was a joke, damn it, she was such a dog, a nothing—I knew from Monica and I dropped him a note, she'd be there, L.A., so he could make another play for— It was a joke! And—then—he—phoned me—and said —and said—he hadn't seen her, didn't know anything about —but he sounded—but I—"

"My good God," said Palliser disgustedly.

"Of course he couldn't have—*that*. People like us— But I won't be involved," said Stettin desperately. "It wasn't anything to do with *me*—"

They'd towed in the car Kurt Kramer was driving: a beat-up Dodge. There wasn't anything significant in it.

Lake, Glasser and Shogart were watching the big game at the Rose Bowl.

Hackett and Grace thought it might be just worthwhile to take a look at the place where Kramer had been living. The address had been on a checkbook on him. When they got there they were gratified to find that it was a rooming house, not an apartment. Technically, no search warrant necessary if the owner granted them permission to search.

The owner of the old three-story house on Donaldson Street was a big spare old man, Hector MacFarlane. He was surprised about Kramer, stared at their badges curiously. "Said he was a salesman, dressed sharp enough, looked like a nice young fellow. He was never here much. But these days, you don't know t'other from which, good or bad. Can't judge a book by its cover, like they say. He was obligin'—polite. Got me a case of right good whiskey for wholesale cost, three weeks back."

"Is that so?" said Grace in his soft voice.

"I ran into him just comin' in that day—and not that I'm a man to tie one on, I like a little nip o' good whiskey now and then, and these days the price is just sinful. Sinful. I'd just bought a bottle, I said about prices, and he said—there was a fellow with him, friend of his I suppose—he said he could get me a good deal, if I'd take a case. I still got eleven bottles of it." That was interesting, and Mr. MacFarlane would be livid to have it impounded as evidence. "The fellow with him—Tiger, he called him, what kind of a name, but nicknames—he said, plenty more any time I— So he's a crook, hey? You got him in jail?"

"We'd like to look at his room, if you don't mind."

"Oh, I got no objection. Have to help the cops. Law 'n' order."

And Grace said, half an hour later, "How anybody can live like this—" The sordid single room, untidy and squalid: the flamboyant sports clothes in the cardboard wardrobe, the bottle in the dresser drawer. The ones like Kramer lived like this, uncaring about their private surroundings: he wouldn't have been here much. When the money was flowing in from some caper, it got spent elsewhere, on the cheap women and liquor and ephemeral entertainment. But they found, in the breast pocket of the one suit, a list of addresses. "So very stupid," sighed Hackett. A list of customers, could be—the less-than-honest men who were only too happy to make the under-the-counter deals for the cutrate liquor.

"Very helpful," said Mendoza, hearing that.

"Tiger," said Hackett thoughtfully to himself. "Tiger."

"Quoting William Blake?" asked Mendoza.

"It just seems to say something to me," said Hackett. "It's a funny kind of nickname. Not exactly like a nickname—"

"In this corner," said Grace lazily, "weighing in at." He lit a cigarette.

"My God, yes," said Hackett. "My God. I wonder—" He brought out his notebook, went into the sergeants' office.

It was a Hollywood west exchange. Truck drivers made money these days. "I hope I didn't disturb you, Mr. Donlevy."

"Just sittin' here watching the game, Sergeant. Can I do something for you?"

"Well, I just wondered," said Hackett. "You have been in the ring—if you keep up with it any these days?"

[162]

"Sure. I work out regular, help out some at Pete's Gym, my time off. Keep an eye on some of the young guys comin' along. Why?"

"Well. Fighters pick up names—nicknames, you know. Is there one around they call Tiger?"

Donlevy laughed. "Tiger Faley. Why're you interested in him? Tiger, my God. More like Canvasback, Sergeant."

11

"So there you have Stettin," said Palliser. "Did you say, blowing hot and cold? We took him back to the station and got a statement from him, here it is—but what it's worth is anybody's guess." He lit a cigarette moodily. He had had a rather busy day off. It was five-twenty and he'd just got back.

Mendoza regarded the typed statement without picking it up. "¿Quién sabe?" he said. "There's this and that, John. Stettin was nervous enough—at the notion that Stover could be X—to try calling you twice. That much of a—mmh—civic conscience. Getting cold feet each time, because it couldn't possibly be—and he didn't want to be mixed in. I wouldn't rely on Stettin's character reading, but—"

"Oh, I think we want to talk to Stover all right. The one hard fact that emerges is that Stover knew Lila would be here. Stettin gave me his address. I'll look him up to-morrow."

"Yes. It's the only excuse for a lead we've got—and those cotoneaster leaves, in the middle of town—*caray*." Mendoza looked up as Hackett and Higgins came in, and passed on the gist of that.

"You had a full day off," said Hackett to Palliser. "Look, Luis, have you any useful ideas about how to use this damn list of Loose's students? There are seventy-one in five classes, and while I dragged my heels on George's brain-wave I can just see there might be something there, but—"

"It'd take every man in the office and two weeks to question them separately," said Higgins. "And it's not worth the time—just *as* an idea."

"*De veras*," said Mendoza. He sat back in his desk chair and folded his long hands together, making a little steeple. "*Tomaremos otro rumbo*—more than one way to skin a cat, as they say." He looked at his two senior sergeants and grinned. "Make a good act out of it, boys—you both look so formidable and muscular. One of you, say, at Loose's first class, the other after lunch. The same act. It's often useful to let your quarry think you know the hell of a lot more than you do. Be sinister at them. Hint. Starting with the break-in of Loose's office—"

"He's worried enough about it, he's making up different exams."

"Very good. Mention that. It's obvious that that was the motive for the break-in. Let them think our miracle-producing scientific lab has turned up evidence—as budding young scientists they'll believe anything along that line. Experience convinces me that it's easier to con the intellectual scientific mind than any other kind."

"I believe you," said Palliser.

"And then what?"

"Stir up the animals," said Mendoza. "It's like any other school—there'll be talk. Gossip. And human nature always enters in. I'll take a bet that something will show up as a result."

"Well," said Hackett doubtfully, "it's a way to play it. George?"

"All right with me. Human nature—" He looked at Mendoza. "There's always a busybody somewhere, you mean. The rumors."

"*Exacto*. Wait for it." They shrugged at him, went out arguing amiably about ways and means.

Mendoza slid down in his chair and lit a cigarette. "You know, that burglar," he said meditatively. "We've dismissed him sort of airily, him and his fixed income—no lead on him. Art said, an amateur. *De veras*. So how is it he's so slick about getting in and out?"

"Most of the places in this area are old—useless locks," said Palliser.

"But how does he know it's safe to go sailing in? That the place is empty? Most people leave a light on when they'll be coming home after dark, even people without much money. It's not all that expensive, and a simple safeguard against burglars. I just suddenly wondered—"

Palliser yawned. "Those poor devils over in Pasadena will just about be shepherding the last of the traffic jam out. What a way to spend a holiday. Oh, well, I'm going home."

Mendoza went home, to find their Mairí MacTaggart back, supervising a ham baking in the oven and various pots and pans on the stove. Alison was mixing salad dressing. "You're early," she said as he bent to kiss her. "If you want to be helpful, you can settle the offspring—"

The offspring, audible in the distance as he came in, became more so by the moment. They were racing the course round the house, bedrooms to front hall to living room to kitchen, on the new tricycles, shouting at the tops of their voices. Alison dropped the spoon and raised her own voice as they appeared. "Johnny! Terry! ¡Bastante ya! Not the tricycles on the carpets! I told you—for heaven's sake, quiet down!"

They stopped, and abandoned the tricycles, only to plunge at Mendoza. "Daddy, read los cuentos! Read about el lobo again!"

"El Jaguar!" shrieked Terry. "El Jaguar in el bosque all painted!"

"Yes, yes, niños—I'll take them off your hands, amante— Did you have a good New Year, Mairí? Here, hijítos, don't strangle me—"

"Ach, good enough—not like at home. Just me and Janet together talkin' over the old years past. At home now, there'd be the visiting house to house, and the men going out first-footing—"

He took the offspring down to the nursery, nearly tripping over Cedric in the doorway. The cats would be napping elsewhere.

* * *

When Palliser got home, he found Roberta just finishing the task of dismantling the Christmas tree. "Now why didn't you wait till I could help you, idiot? Climbing that ladder—"

"I didn't mind. I only had to use it for the top branches and the star. And besides, if you helped me I wouldn't know where half the decorations had been put, the hall closet or wherever. But I'm glad we got an artificial one, John. They're so realistic looking, and don't drop—and I always simply hate to put a Christmas tree out for the refuse truck. It's almost sacrilegious."

"Sentimental!"

"Well, I am. You can take it all apart and put it back in the box for next year."

He kissed her again. "And next year we'll have a real honest-to-goodness family."

"Um-hum," said Roberta. "You know what occurs to me? You'd better get a camera and start practicing with it. To get back at Sergeant Higgins and Jason Grace."

"Well, now, that is a thought," said Palliser. "It is indeed."

Tom Landers' Corvair had just had a complete tune-up and was purring along smoothly. He wasn't thinking about the job, heading downtown at five-thirty; mostly he was thinking about the date with Phil tomorrow night. He got off the Hollywood freeway on the off-ramp which led him to Grand, and as he did so he clapped a hand to his jacket pocket and said, "Damn." He'd forgotten to get out a new pack of cigarettes, and the half-empty one was in the slacks he'd worn all day.

Well, he had time to stop. Instead of turning left on Grand, he went up right towards Sunset Boulevard, which had its unlikely beginning eight blocks away at the old Plaza. This wasn't exactly a classy section of L.A., and a holiday, with most places closed—but there ought to be a drugstore up on Sunset open, where he could get cigarettes.

He turned left on Sunset—in the other direction were the outskirts of Skid Row—and two blocks up spotted an open drugstore on the corner. There were other places open along that block, two bars and a dimly lit small restaurant labeled *La Cita*, which looked deserted but displayed an *Open* sign. Landers found a parking slot half a block away, and walked back to the drugstore, bought a couple of packs of cigarettes. Neatly stripping one open, he came out to the street and started back to the car. He'd been vaguely aware of a figure in the entrance of the second bar as he passed it—echoes of jukebox drifting out, mutter of voices —but now it moved out to the street, and a woman's voice accosted him. "Hullo, dear!"

One of these damned street girls, Vice ought to do something about it, thought Landers, and shook off the hand on his arm.

"Ah, don't be like that, dear. You look like a nice guy, and my place's just up the block—I show you a real good time, honey—"

Landers lengthened his stride, and she stepped around in front of him, almost directly under a street light. "Five bucks," she said in a seductive voice; and Landers stopped. About twenty-five, a mop of black hair to her shoulders, good figure in a very miniskirted outfit, not at all bad-looking, if the makeup was a little heavy. That con pair, he thought. Could it be?

"That's right, lover," she said, and linked her arm in his. "You just come home with me, we have a real good time—"

He was going to feel like a damn fool if she wasn't that girl, thought Landers; but a minute later he was sure. She led him up past the Corvair to where a narrow alley cut through between buildings. "Shortcut to my pad, lover— you just—"

She had him, luckily, by the left arm. Landers peered ahead cautiously—the man would be somewhere ahead ready to jump him. Faint light drifted into the alley from the street lights at either end, and he made out, about twenty feet ahead, a pile of crates of some sort stacked man-high. He hoped that was where the man waited.

"Come on, cat got your tongue, dear? My name's Sue, what's—"

He judged it as best he could in the semi-dark. They came alongside the crates, he sensed a movement there, and felt her arm slacken in his. He jerked out the gun and snapped, "All right, come out with your hands up! You, you stay where you—"

"Jesus, it's a heist!" she yelled, and started to run. Landers lunged and grabbed her with his left hand. A man came plunging from behind the crates, took one look, and bolted.

"Stop! There's a gun on you—" the girl was screaming, and apparently that was what stopped the man. He halted in his tracks.

"Don't hurt Sue, mister—we ain't got much, but you can have—but don't hurt—" Landers got hold of him then, one arm behind him, and headed him back for the street. He only had two hands; he'd had to let go of the girl, but she was yelling now not to hurt Barney, and circling him like a gadfly.

"March!" he said. And just how the hell he was going to take them both in—there must be a call-box somewhere around. He could see himself going into either of those bars and telling the bartender to call cops—but the clerk at the drugstore had looked respectable enough. Take them up there and—

The girl suddenly said, "My God, Barney, it's a cop! My God—" and she started banging Landers with her handbag. "We didn't do anything! You let him go!" She kicked him and connected painfully with his shin.

"Aw, Sue, he's got a gun—"

She hit Landers in the face with the handbag, which was large and heavy. He staggered back, hanging onto Barney desperately. They were at the mouth of the alley, nearly under the street light. He shoved Barney onto the sidewalk, and the girl ran around and hit him in the face again, screaming. In the confusion of the moment, he thought, if the customers in that bar came out—likely none of them liked cops very much—

"Damn it, shut up," he said, dodging her and wishing he had a pair of cuffs on him; better, two pairs.

"You let him go—we didn't do anything!" This time she

remembered one of the oldest tricks—she snatched off one spike-heeled pump and aimed it at his eyes. He jerked his head to the side and it connected with his left cheekbone. He renewed his grip on Barney, and then quite suddenly a blinding searchlight caught them all in its glare and a re-assuringly hard young voice said, "All right, break it up—"

Like Mrs. Sidney, Landers was pleased to see the black-and-white, even when one of the Traffic men in it pulled him away from Barney and tried to take his gun. He said, "Well, the Marines to the rescue. Thanks very much." The other man had Sue and Barney up against the wall.

"So what's going on here? Have you got a permit to carry—"

"I don't need one." Landers reached for the badge. "Rob-bery-Homicide. I'm on my way to work, I'm on night watch. It was just a fluke I spotted the girl, we've been hearing stories about this pair—" And about then he realized that the Traffic man was Bill Moss. "Say, you brought in one of the—"

"My God, Landers—I didn't recognize you in the tangle —you're bleeding, you know? We'll take 'em in, and you'd better stop at First Aid—"

Landers finally got up to the office at seven-fifteen. When he walked into the sergeants' office three voices enquired sarcastically, "And where have *you*—" before they took him in. "My God," said Conway, "what did you tangle with, a she wildcat?"

"Reasonable facsimile thereof," said Landers. It was the shoe had done most of the damage, though the handbag hadn't done much less. In the handbag had been, among other things, a pint flask full of cheap gin, a large compact, and a goodsized switchblade knife nine inches long even when closed. Whichever of those it had been, Landers had the beginning of what would be a fine black eye, and a couple of savage three-inch cuts on his left cheek from the shoe-heel. He told them about it, feeling the cuts: the nurse at First Aid had painted them and put a bandage on.

"It was just a fluke she picked me—I suppose, looking back, she hadn't found any likely marks in that bar and was about to move on, when I showed up—"

"Looking a little more prosperous than any other pedestrian she'd seen down there," said Galeano. "You took a chance, Tom."

"Well, nobody had said he was going armed. It didn't turn out just exactly the way I thought—but anyway, we've got them. I wonder if any of the marks will identify them— that Dakin— Oh, and Barney had that Lambert's diamond ring on him, by the description. Hadn't got round to fencing it yet."

"And you are going to scare both our girls by tomorrow night," said Conway. "That eye's going to be all colors of the rainbow."

Landers laughed. "Good thing they're both LAPD officers too, isn't it? They won't scare so easy, Rich."

Mendoza read the condensed report on that at eight o'clock Tuesday morning, and passed it on with a grin to Lake and the early arrivals—Glasser, Piggott, Shogart. It was Grace's day off. Hackett or Higgins would be at the U.S.C. College of Medicine play-acting at Dr. Loose's first class. Off the top of his mind, that one—Mendoza didn't know that it would produce any results, at that. First cast, he thought.

It was Higgins who had done that; Hackett came in and said he was going out to look for Tiger Faley. "If he isn't one of the gang, he knows about the hijackings. And if he's the bumbling lamebrain Donlevy says, he may come apart when we look at him."

"So go and look. John—" Palliser had just come in. "You're hot on Stover, I suppose."

"You're damn right. It's still all up in the air, but I'd like to hear what he has to say."

"So would I. If you find him, bring him in and we'll listen together."

Palliser cocked his head at him. "You've had a hunch?"

"*Pues no*. I'd just like to—mmh—size him up for myself," said Mendoza.

"And there's an A.P.B. out on Fawkes," said Piggott. "It's a dead one for us, unless he turns up, but I'd like to get him if he's still here."

"You might," suggested Mendoza, "go and ask Perce Andrews about gambling dens."

"Vice? What—"

"The official description of Private Fawkes tells us he's a compulsive gambler. If he's still here, he'll be hunting games to sit in. Of course he might be down in Gardena gambling all legal— ¡Dios! I'm going senile, why didn't I think of that before? Jimmy—"

"What?" asked Piggott.

"You upright moral Christians with no vices," said Mendoza. "I think it's a handicap to a law officer, Matt. Your minds just don't work the same way as the felons—"

"Well, I should hope not," said Piggott.

"Jimmy, get me somebody on the Gardena force, *por favor*." He was handed around, finally got a Captain Fordyce. "I'll send the Army flyer on him down—" Fordyce said he'd seen the A.P.B. "Well, the Army wants him too, naturally, but we've got priority—robbery and assault with intent. He's said to be a compulsive gambler. It doesn't say what his preferences are, draw or dice or parchesi, but I just thought—"

"Sure," said Fordyce. "We try to keep an eye on the gambling houses anyway." It wasn't always too careful an eye, thought Mendoza cynically, thinking back to that peculiar case when he'd been hanging around down there himself, playing the pro sharp. "We'll have a look around."

"Thanks very much."

And the first call of the day came in. An accident down at the Stack, one D.O.A. Shogart went out on that.

Palliser was due to have another frustrating day. Stettin had given him an address on Romaine in Hollywood for Stover; it turned out to be one of the new, square, ugly eight-unit apartments going up everywhere in mid-Hollywood these days. But apartment four was not responsive to its bell. There was a sign in front of the place, Apartment for rent, 2-bedrm., $195. The hell of a lot of money to pay out every four weeks, thought Palliser, shoving the bell marked *manageress*. "Mr. Stover," he said when the door opened. "I'm looking for—"

"Oh, Mr. Kemp got married," said the woman in the doorway. She wasn't very old, in her forties possibly, but she was thin and gray and anxious-looking, without makeup. The word *dreep* slid into Palliser's mind.

"I'm looking for Mr. Gene Stover—"

"Yes, that's what I said. Mr. Kemp got married," she said. "Last month. The rent was paid to the end of December. Mr. Stover moved because it was too high for him alone and I guess he couldn't find somebody else to share with."

"Oh." Palliser was annoyed. "Did he leave a forwarding address?"

"Oh, yes, sir. He moved to La Crescenta. They're buying a house there. It's so nice to see young people starting out, and I'm sure she's a very nice girl, he introduced me to her once, her name's Doreen."

"Mr. *Stover*," said Palliser. "Did he leave a forwarding—"

"Oh, him. No, he didn't. They never got much mail anyway."

"He didn't mention to you where he was moving?"

"No, he never. He wasn't as friendly as Mr. Kemp, and in and out a lot."

Well, thought Palliser, if Kemp and Stover had shared an apartment, Kemp ought to know Stover's present address. "May I have Mr. Kemp's new address, please?"

She took some time to find it, and apologized. "I made sure I put it right by the phone, but then I recalled I'd just started a new phone-book and I was still copying numbers in—"

Palliser thanked her, walked back to the Rambler down the block and started for La Crescenta.

It was a very new house, frame-stucco-redwood, on one of the newest curving streets up there. It was L-shaped, and sat above a steep terrace very newly seeded with variegated ivy, and there was a wide paved apron beyond a very steep driveway. Palliser was absently thankful, trudging up it, that they hadn't bought a house in the hills.

The new Mrs. Kemp was a pretty girl, brown-haired and brown-eyed, in a neat housedress. She looked at the badge in surprise and curiosity. "For heaven's sake," she said. "What do the police want with us?"

"LAPD," said Palliser, "not local. I'm trying to find a man named Gene Stover. I understand your husband once shared an apartment with him."

"That's right," she said. "Until Walter and I were married. What do you want Gene for? Don't tell me he's—"

"Just a few questions," said Palliser vaguely. "He's moved from the apartment."

"Yes, I know." She looked him over again, and said, "You'd better come in."

Everything in the living room looked spanking new, all early American. "So, do you know Stover's new address?" Palliser sat down on the couch.

Her eyes were still curious. "Well, Walter will be interested in this. Police asking for Gene. And I know you won't tell me why, but I'm dying to know what it's all about. Gene—well, no, we don't. That was the— Well, I suppose you'll have to hear about it. Or you'd think it was funny we didn't know, when Walter shared an apartment—" She sighed. "There was a row."

"A row?"

"A fight. And I don't flatter myself it was any compliment to me. Gene Stover thinks he's God's gift to all females. If you see what I mean. It's a—a kind of automatic reaction with him, make the pass at any girl who comes in ten feet of him."

"I see," said Palliser.

"He knew Walter and I were engaged. I don't think he *meant* anything by it, exactly, it's just how he is. But neither of us liked it. And—well, we were getting married in just a few days anyway, Walter'd be moving out, so it just— ended. When I said a fight, well, Walter told him off and"— she smiled faintly—"I told him off, and that was that."

"When was this?"

"About a week before we were married—call it five weeks ago. Walter said Gene wasn't there an awful lot anyway, mostly just to sleep, and he hardly saw him again. And you can see why we weren't interested in his new address. Walter had been getting pretty fed up with him anyway, he said, for a while before that. The way Gene was always boasting about—well, you can guess, I suppose. Girls."

"Where did they meet each other, do you know? Has your husband known him long?"

"Oh, when Walter was at the brokerage downtown—Stone, Fox and Meyer. Only a couple of years. He's transferred to a better firm now. I'm just dying to know why the police are interested in Gene. I'll tell you—you might try his sister. I expect she'd know where he is."

"Do you know her address?"

"No, but she uses the name Rena Rowe. She's trying to break into TV, she's had just a few small bits."

Hackett, entering Pete's Gym out on Vermont, had met the expert eye of a beefy man in sweatshirt and shorts, who looked him up and down and said, "Haven't seen you here before. Want to work off some of that lard, hey?"

Annoyed, Hackett brought out the badge. He'd been up to two-sixteen this morning, but that was less than before he'd started the perennial diet. "I'm looking for a Daniel Faley."

"A cop," said the man, presumably Pete. "What the hell the cops want with Tiger? He's right over there working out with the weights."

Surveying Faley, Hackett thought that Mike Donlevy had summed him up to a T. He looked the prototype of the dimwitted third-rate pro fighter; and, confronted by the badge, he acted that way, saying all the usual things.

Economically, Hackett told him, "We picked up Kurt Kramer yesterday, Faley. For these hijacking jobs. What do you know about it? Who else is in on it?"

"What?" said Faley. "What? You got Kurt in jail—"

"That's right. I wonder," said Hackett, "if you were the strongarm that waited for the drivers. How about it?" Faley blinked at him. "And how long did it take Kurt to drive it into your head exactly what you were supposed to do?"

At this hour, Pete and Faley were the only men here, no crowd of physical-fitness nuts to interrupt and exclaim. Pete was listening open-mouthed. Faley looked around wildly.

"I—how'd you pick up Kurt? I don't know nothin' about what you're talkin' about—" He wasn't quite as tall as Hackett, but carried as much weight or more; he had a forehead practically nonexistent, dull blue eyes, and a Prussian-cropped head. He looked about twenty-five.

"He left us some nice fingerprints on one of the trucks," said Hackett. He wondered, on second thought, if Faley had been the strongarm; if so, why had Kramer been driving that truck?

"So he thinks he's a brain," said Faley, astonished. "He did? He was allus tellin' me to be careful about that, an' then he goes an'—" he stopped.

"I thought you were in on it," said Hackett.

Faley swallowed. "I didn't do nothin' except hit them. When they come back to the truck."

"Is that so? You didn't drive the trucks?" asked Hackett gently.

"Oh, hell, I couldn't get the hang o' those things," said Faley. "Them air brakes an' the handle thing—"

"I see," said Hackett. "Was anybody in the deal besides you and Kurt?"

"It was Kurt's idea. He made the deals, sell all the stuff. He paid me fifty bucks every time I hit one of those guys."

"Yipes!" said Pete behind Hackett. "I knew he was dumb but I didn't think he was *that* dumb. This is the hijackings with all the liquor stole? Jee-sus Christ! The other guy conned this poor dumb Mick into—and what he musta took in profits— Yipes!"

Feeling a little tired of human nature, Hackett took Tiger Faley down to jail. He hadn't made any notes on it; he gave the gist to Wanda, who said she'd type it up. "You certainly make a difference around here, lady." Now to apply for a warrant on Tiger, and some time today talk to Kramer again, try for some kind of statement. And all those probable customers would have to be questioned, though it wasn't likely the D.A. could make any charges stick on them. "Where's the boss?"

He did his play-acting at the college at one o'clock, having conferred with Higgins. "How did it go?" Higgins had said, "I don't know, Art. I said a lot without saying anything. The sinister implications, just like Luis said. That we know more than we're telling. But the kids—I shouldn't call them that, they'll all be in the mid-twenties—they're poker-faced. I don't know. I talked about the break-in, told them about the exams being changed, and the murder—I'm not an actor, damn it," said Higgins plaintively. "It's making bricks without straw. I can say I jumped to the conclusion, the two things connected, but there's no evidence at all, and anybody can see that."

"Not everybody," said Hackett, "even the ones with the scientific minds, have to know as much about what constitutes legal evidence as we do, George." But now, having done his play-acting at that classroom of poker-faced young people, he was wondering. He sat over a late lunch (lunch: Rye Krisp and cottage cheese) and wondered.

"Sometimes Luis' ideas pay off," he said, finishing his black coffee. "It's a tricky one, George—even if there's anything in the connection at all. Wait and see."

"And the sister is out of town on location for a TV part," said Palliser. "I found her agent. She'll be back on Thursday, he thought."

"Frustrating," agreed Mendoza. "Yes, I'd like to talk to Mr. Stover too. These things are sent to try us, so they say." He glanced at his watch: four-thirty. The routine getting cleared up; as usual, a couple of cases dragging on; and all too likely, new ones coming along.

12

HACKETT HAD SPENT a little while hunting for Al Dakin; when he finally located him, Dakin agreed amiably to take a look at Sue Carter. It had turned out that Sue and Barney were *bona fide* man and wife. It wouldn't be much of a charge but what evidence there was they wanted to get. No need to arrange a show-up; Hackett had her brought out to an interrogation room and Dakin identified her.

"That's her all right. The man I couldn't say about—I never saw him. Damn little cheapskate cheat," said Dakin. "I'm glad you got 'em."

Hackett went home to find that Angel had dismantled the Christmas tree. Mark was too engrossed with a new coloring set, and Sheila too young, to notice. "Don't tell me he's going to be an artist," said Hackett with misgivings.

"Heaven forbid, let's hope it's just a phase. I found a new low-calorie salad dressing for you," said Angel.

Hackett, thinking of Pete, scowled.

Mendoza, wandering into the living room after dinner, vaguely missed something and discovered that the tall Christmas tree had disappeared. The holidays were officially over; and up to five years back he hadn't gone in for the decorations and festivities, but—being domesticated—he thought they were nice to have. A lot of work, he supposed —"I could have helped you with that," he said to Alison, nodding to where it had stood.

"*¡Qué disparate!* Mairí and I managed fine—and you should have heard the wails of protest over it. Thank heaven it was warm enough to chase them out in the back yard, and *el pájaro* distracted their attention."

"That creature. This early—"

"Well, at least he's still alone," said Alison. "No sign of the Missus yet. And if it turns cooler—and heaven knows we're due more rain before the end of the season—"

Bast floated up into Mendoza's lap and he stroked her sleek Abyssinian head. "All your fault, *niña*—you brought him here to begin with," he reminded her.

"I think it was more Mairí's," said Alison thoughtfully, "dosing *el pájaro* with your whiskey until he recovered."

The waiter at The Castaways looked at Landers doubtfully and went away for menus. "You really are a sight," said Phil. "That eye is just like an Italian sunset."

Landers felt it gingerly. "I noticed it."

"I'll say one thing. It makes you look five years older." Landers, who was always being told he didn't look old enough to be a cop, grinned reluctantly.

"I think," said Margot Swain, "the cuts are quite distinguished—if she'd only alternated sides, you'd look like a Prussian officer."

"That's why he did it," said Conway, "to get all the attention. Intrepid they call him—venture down a dark alley with a beautiful brunette—the female of the species being, as we all know, more deadly—"

"All right, all right," said Landers. He looked at the girls. It was all right; they were going to like each other. Margot was a brunette, not much bigger than Phil, and she had an infectious chuckle and bright brown eyes.

She said now to Phil, "I never realized—"

"Just what I was thinking. It's one of the standard techniques we get told about in unarmed defense," said Phil, "but I never realized how much damage an innocent shoe could—"

"Look," said Landers, "there's a lot prettier view out the window, girls."

Schenke and Galeano had sat alone on night watch quite awhile together, and unless it turned out to be a busy night they wouldn't miss Conway and Landers. No calls came in the first hour, and then the desk relayed one from Central Receiving that sent Galeano over there in a hurry, to Emergency and Dr. Emmanuel in charge of that wing.

"So what's the story, Doctor?"

Emmanuel took off his glasses, pinched the bridge of his nose; he was half-sitting on the corner of his desk. "These things," he said. "We never do quite get used to it, do we? The woman brought the child in about half an hour ago— little girl about three. Interns called me, but it was too late. Woman says she's the mother, says the child fell downstairs. Well, the child was beaten, of course—actual cause of death a fractured skull, I think."

"That's definite?"

"Absolutely. Mrs. Sardo is in the waiting room out there."

Galeano talked to her; she was sullen and tearful at once, and went on denying that anybody had done anything to Rosa. Galeano took her home and talked to her husband, a hulk of a man who smelled of stale wine and sweat, and refused to talk to any cop. It was a thing they saw, and the beat didn't matter: it happened in Beverly Hills too. Galeano went back to the office and filed a report on it for the day watch. They'd check with Welfare, Social Services, for any back record on the Sardos; apply for a warrant if the D.A. thought a charge would stick.

The next call came in at ten-forty, and it was—"He was about due," said Schenke—another burglary. Another old apartment with useless locks, and again the burglar had pried open a back window. Mr. and Mrs. Clifford were alternately bewailing losses and blaming the landlord for not installing decent locks and bolts.

"I know they cost something, but damn it, we pay a good rent—"

"And my mother's opal ring—and my pearl earrings—"

"Damn it, we were just out to the movies! You'd think—"

It wouldn't be much use to get the lab men up tomorrow,

dust the place; he hadn't left any latents yet. It was a funny mixture of amateurishness—he wasn't getting much in the way of loot—and cunning. They got a list of what was missing, and left the day watch to do any follow-up.

They were sitting there talking desultorily at eleven-forty when a new call came in, reported routinely by a Traffic unit. Attempted suicide. Galeano went out on that. In legal terms, suicide was a felony, but an attempt was as a rule only prosecuted in theory: as a rule the probation would be tied to psychiatric examination. It wasn't anything much for their office, but as always the paperwork had to be done.

The address was Mariposa Avenue, toward Hollywood. When Galeano pulled up in front, in a red zone, the ambulance was just pulling away. A little gathering of people stood just inside the open front door, and Galeano went up and produced the badge. "Can anyone tell me what happened here?"

Most of them were in night clothes, dressing gowns: a thin gray-haired woman just outside the door labeled *manageress*, a man behind her, another couple hovering outside the open door across the hall. The exception was a very smartly dressed young woman who looked extremely shaken, white-faced and trembling. She had neat dark hair cut short, a triangular kitten face, and big brown eyes, and she was wearing an ankle-length royal blue evening dress, a little velvet cape, one long white glove, and high-heeled gold slippers. She kept clutching the long fashionable rope of fake pearls that hung to her waist. "Miss? Could you tell me—"

"But it isn't anything that *happens*," she said. Suddenly she began to sag, and Galeano got hold of her and guided her to sit on the first step of the stairs, got her head down between her knees. The other women rushed to support her. "You poor dear—" "But that nice Miss Baker, it doesn't seem possible—"

"I'm all right," she said after a minute, and sat up. "Really I am. And they—they have to ask questions. I k-kept my head all right—until just now. I'm sorry. Are you from the hospital?"

"No, miss, police." He showed the badge. "Can you tell me what happened?"

She nodded. "It's my—roommate. Pat Baker. I can't understand it, and oh, my God, I've got to call her mother and father—"

"Take it easy now, Miss—"

"Cerny. Evelyn Cerny. I just got home—from a date with Bill—we're engaged. And of course I thought Pat'd be asleep—I was quiet, but I turned on one lamp—in the bedroom—and she didn't look right, she was—like snoring and she doesn't—and there was the empty bottle marked morph— I don't believe it, it just couldn't—*Pat!* I c-called an ambulance, and the police— But why? Pat? There's no reason—"

"Her parents live here in town?"

She nodded. "I'll call them. I—Pat and I've been all through school together—"

"Was there a note?"

"I don't know. I didn't notice . . . Yes, you can look. Apartment six."

It was a small one-bedroom place, nicely furnished, neat and clean. In the bedroom was a pair of twin beds, one on the window side unmade and much rumpled. Nothing on the bedside table but the lamp and the empty bottle, with the label on it: Morphine all right. No note. Galeano looked around: there was a female handbag on the chest on that side of the room. It was a large pouch bag, gaping open. He looked, and reached in. On top of everything else there, an envelope. He took it out and lifted its flap.

No suicide note emerged, but four long brown cigarettes, looking home-made. "Well, well," said Galeano. He wondered if the Cerny girl knew that her roommate had been using the Mary Jane.

Mendoza was scanning the list of the night's happenings, as related to Robbery-Homicide, as the men drifted in. He frowned over the attempted suicide: a tiresome piece of routine, all the paperwork to bog down their private secretary. He tossed the report to Higgins, who made a little grunting sound, reading it.

"What?" said Hackett, peering over his shoulder.

"I—well, I don't know, the name rang a little bell. Baker —I don't know why, it doesn't—"

"And our burglar has struck again," said Mendoza. "Him and his fixed income . . . *¡Diez millones de demonios!* Here's one we follow up hard, boys." He gave them Galeano's report on the Sardo child. "Neanderthal—a thing you never quite believe. George, you'd better run a check on the Sardos—if they're on Welfare, see what Social Services knows about them. See if he's got a rap sheet of any kind. Bring him in and we'll lean on him—I don't suppose he's any brain."

"God, no," said Higgins. "I'd better check with the hospital on the suicide try first."

Private Fawkes hadn't turned up yet. There were inquests scheduled today and tomorrow, on the bodies piled up the last week or so, the accidents on the freeways. Police evidence would be taken at all of them. The Askell thing—that was bothering Mendoza by its very shapelessness, and the frustrating fact that there was nowhere to look on it. Until Palliser located this Stover—and that very small lead could collapse when he did.

"Where's John?" he asked Lake.

"Oh, he came in early and got a call right off. I don't know where."

"Don't tell me, something new. I—Art? Now what has struck you?" Hackett was standing gazing into space, a forgotten cigarette in one hand. "*¿Qué ocurre, hermano?*"

"I just," said Hackett, his eyes slowly focusing, "I just remembered—or seemed to remember—they were out at the movies. The Purdys. And—I wasn't on all of them, of course, but I think Matt said—and it just occurs to me, I wonder—because it'd be very funny—"

"Pull yourself together and make sense, Arturo. What are you talking about?"

"Well, I suppose it'd be in the reports." Hackett turned

[183]

and went into the inner office, to Wanda Larsen. She was already busy at the typewriter. "Our copies of all the first reports on the burglar, lady. Got 'em handy?"

"Oh, certainly." She and Shogart were weeding out dead wood from the old Robbery files in their spare time, but she had started a new set of filing cases for the new bureau. She produced ten reports all filed together, and Hackett started to go through them.

"Just what is the brainwave?" asked Mendoza.

"Well, I will be damned," said Hackett two minutes later. "I will be— And what the hell can it say? They were all at the movies, Luis. The burglar's victims. Every single one of them. When the burglary occurred."

Mendoza reached for the reports, making for his office. Then he looked over the reports, sat back and lit a cigarette. "Is it a little funny, or just coincidence? I didn't think the silver screen was all that popular these days. And most of these people are middle-aged—not the audience producers aim for now, ¿cómo no? It does seem—mmh—a little too coincidental. But on the other hand—"

"On the other hand be damned," said Hackett. He was taking down phone numbers from the reports. "Let's ask. Just for fun." He took up the outside phone and at random called the Purdys.

"Now what do you want?" asked Purdy ungraciously. "You caught that thief yet?"

"Well, no, I'm afraid not. You were out at the movies the night of the burglary, you said—"

"And what about it? Entitled to a night out once in a while, not that we can afford much, prices so high even for movies now."

"Er—which one had you gone to?"

"Now what in the name of goodness you want to know that for? I don't recall the name of the picture, it wasn't very good, but it was the Bijou up on Broadway. We hadn't been to a movie in a year or better, but when the tickets came—"

"The tickets?"

"Yeah, yeah, complimentary from the manager, the note said. Advertising stunt of some kind, I—"

"Thanks very much." Hackett put the phone down and dialed again. This time he talked to Mr. Jarvis, who told him that they hadn't been to a movie in a couple of years, just bad luck they'd been out that night when the burglar— but of course when they were sent the complimentary tickets by the manager—

"I will be *damned!*" he said at the end of the fourth call. "Do we need to check it further, Luis? They were all sent tickets through the mail! They all—"

"But it's beautiful," said Mendoza, fascinated. "So simple and so human, Art. I like this fellow. That's very psychologically sound, you know. You get sent free tickets to something, the chances are you'll use them. Especially— mmh, yes—especially people like these, without much money to squander for entertainment. It's a beautiful piece of logic. The tickets sent for a certain evening, so he could be practically certain they were out, he could walk right in at his leisure. For the price of a pair of movie tickets."

"But how the hell can we follow it up? Would the girl in the ticket-booth notice if somebody bought a couple of tickets and then didn't—but wait a minute, that's wrong, because if there was a date on them—"

"Yes," said Mendoza. "And another thing—he's kept to that general area. Of the four couples you called, three were sent tickets to the Bijou, the other to a theatre not far off. ¡Vaya! I don't know about this, but if there are dates on the tickets, I should think it'd be fairly unusual— Let's see what we can turn on this, Arturo." Fired with sudden interest, he put out his cigarette and got up, reaching for his hat.

Palliser had noted the address of the urgent first call with surprise. It was the third time he'd been here: that chain market out on Third.

When he got there, the Traffic unit was just pulling off. In the big parking lot, empty except for two cars and a tall van, Raymond Osney was talking with angry gestures to two other men. Palliser parked beside the van and went up to them.

"Well, Mr. Osney—don't tell me you've had any more trouble here? I thought you said the district manager—"

"Me," said the shorter of the other two sadly. "Ames. Bill Ames."

"—That you were going to have the guard dogs here at—"

"That's right," said the third man gloomily. "Protection Service, Incorporated. Rent guaranteed protection day or night."

"But if—"

Osney looked ready to burst into tears. "Now they've stolen the dog!" he said.

Before he could stop himself Palliser began to laugh. "I'm sorry," he said, "but it just— How in hell could anybody steal a trained guard dog? A—what did you say—"

"Dobie," said the third man. "*My* Dobie. Eric von Rothenburg, Ricky for short. I ask you. I just ask you—" he raised eyebrows at Palliser.

"Sergeant Palliser."

"I just ask you. They got you coming and going. So you train guard dogs, for protection. I was with the K-nine corps, Army. There's a call for more guard dogs every day, and you want to breed from the best to get the best, no? So how can you spay and neuter all your best dogs? It isn't feasible. You also want 'em to breed more good guard dogs." He spat aside.

"But what—"

"Well, that's how they did it, of course. Ricky's three years old and a good stud. As well as a good guard. If somebody fetched a bitch in heat and broke in a door—it was the back stockroom door, matter of fact—any idea of bein' on guard'd fly right out of his mind, and you can't blame the dog for that. It's nature."

"Yes, I see—" Palliser nearly dissolved in mirth again, but saved himself.

"A mess—just a mess," said Osney. "All the liquor and cigarettes again—we'd just got new stock in—"

"*And* my dog," said the third man.

"Excuse me, I don't think I heard your name—"

"Katz. Al Katz."

This time Palliser managed to turn the laugh into a cough. "Well, we'll get the lab up here and see if they can find any evidence—" He didn't suppose it would be much use, but you never knew. "What about the dog, Mr. Katz? Would they have—er—hurt him, or—"

"Where's the need? Let the bitch lead him off, he won't remember he was on guard for quite a spell. God knows where he might've got to, down here. Running the streets, and worth five hundred at least—not that it's all the money. He's a damn good dog. I'll take the van and tool around awhile—he'll come to a silent whistle, and it carries quite a way." Katz swung over to the van in the lot. They watched it out.

Palliser called up a lab truck and they looked at the mess and clutter in the stockroom. The lab men didn't look hopeful, but got out their kits and started to work.

Just as Palliser was starting back for his car, a dog came loping up the side street and turned hesitantly into the parking lot. He was a goodsized dog, long and lean, black and tan, with ears laid despondently against his head. His long tongue drooled out of his mouth, and he was covered with dust and wild-mustard blossoms from some empty lot. His chain collar chinked.

"Ricky?" said Palliser doubtfully. "Come here, boy." The dog came over to him and plopped down, panting. He looked tired. "Well, at least you're all right," said Palliser. Thinking of Osney's expression, he began to laugh again.

Higgins had checked Central Receiving on the suicide attempt. The girl had been pulled through, the family was there; she could probably be talked to this afternoon. Higgins put the phone down, wondering why the ordinary name had rung a little bell in his mind; if it was important it would come to him. He went on to start the follow-up routine on the Sardo child.

And for once he was inclined to agree with Matt about the devil. If not an active force for evil driving a man, how could there be a thing like this, the tiny corpse with the bruises and cuts—the child hardly in the world before she was brutally sent out of it by her begetter? Inevitably Higgins thought of Margaret Emily at home, his new darling—and Mary was just teasing him, saying he'd spoil her. . . . The Sardos were on Welfare; according to Social Services, she had twice accused him of beating her, beating the children, and then refused to sign a complaint. And God knew that in a democratic republic the Sardos had rights like everybody else, but Higgins wondered if Bruno Sardo understood the recited ritual.

Shogart sat in on the questioning. They didn't get anywhere. "The baby, she fell downstairs," was all they got out of Sardo. But the medical evidence was firm.

They talked to the mother alone, and she finally broke down and admitted that Bruno had done it. "She's crying, he don't like it, he tell her stop, but she don't, an' he—" And she might retract that later, but they had it on record. They applied for the warrant.

"And only manslaughter," said Shogart. "Have they got any other kids?"

"Three, according to Nick."

"People," said Shogart. "That's a thing I guess a normal man couldn't ever understand, any more than suicide."

And a little bell rang again in Higgins' mind. Suicide, he thought. Now why—

Hackett sometimes felt a little superstitious about Mendoza. He'd seen the thing happen before, and wondered if among the unknown ancestors that had gone to produce Luis Rodolfo Vicente Mendoza there had been any warlocks. Mendoza would sit there at his desk, covering the routine like the well-trained detective he was, and occasionally watch his boys sweating out the offbeat tough one, throwing out suggestions that might or might not be helpful.

But let him get really interested in a thing, go out on the legwork himself, and all of a sudden—as if his guardian angel was leading the way—something would turn up.

He had ruminated about the burglar, but now with the simplistic little cunning of the movie tickets turned up, he was fascinated. He took Hackett out Broadway to the Bijou Theatre, which of course was closed, but the required sign on the door gave him an emergency number. By ten o'clock they were sitting in the living room of the theatre's manager, Mr. Edward Rea, in a modest house in Hollywood. Mr. Rea was looking rather bewildered at this invasion of the law, but answered questions docilely. He was a little man with a bald head and horn-rimmed glasses.

"Dates?" he said. "Dates on the tickets? Why, yes, of course. To give us some check on attendance. And the prices —if any loges are— But really I don't understand why you're asking all this—"

Mendoza smiled at him. "Each day's tickets are in the ticket booth just that one day? But you do have—mmh— tickets ahead, as it were? That is, I could come and ask to buy a ticket for next Friday?"

"Well, you *could*," said Rea.

"But that'd be sort of unusual, wouldn't it?" asked Hackett. "The girl in the booth couldn't—the tickets wouldn't be there yet, if I understand you." He felt a little confused about it. "Where would they be?"

"I beg your pardon, where would what be?"

"The tickets ahead. For the next week, say."

"Oh, in my office, of course. At the theatre. They come in rolls, for the machine—"

"So," said Mendoza, "if I wanted a ticket for next Friday, I'd have to come to you?"

"Well, or the ticket girl would ask me— As a matter of fact," and Rea emitted a shrill tenor laugh, "we have one faithful patron who does buy tickets ahead, and heaven forgive me for laughing at the poor soul. She—"

"Who's that?" asked Hackett interestedly.

"Mrs. Devlin. Dora Devlin. She never misses a change of feature. She's on Social Security, and she always buys her tickets a month ahead because otherwise it'd all go for cheap *vino*. Poor soul."

"Oh," said Hackett. "But you'd know, that is there'd be a way of checking, on tickets sold for a showing several days later?"

"Certainly. But what is this all about?" asked Rea. "Really, I'd like to help the police, but I don't see what you're driving at—"

"He took the chance," said Mendoza softly to himself. "That we wouldn't notice. Yes. Movies—do you get much of an audience, on the average, any more?" It was an absent question; it opened the floodgates.

Rea deplored the films being made today, the unrealistic ratings. "It's all but killed the medium. People simply don't go to movies any more—except the young people, and not too many of them. And what with union wages, and inflation, prices have gone up so— Why, I don't know why the owners keep the theatres open afternoons! If we have twenty people in between one and six— But I mustn't bore you with all that. Twenty years ago, when I took over the Bijou, it was a great deal different, I can tell you that. A lovely theatre, it was, and the crowds—I tell you, gentlemen, to those of us who can remember when there were films that were genuine artistic productions—some of the great pictures and great stars, you know—the stuff turned out today is—is—" He had no words for it; he gestured angrily. "It's a crying shame! I tell you, I've been sorry to see the Bijou run down the way it has—but at the same time, I'm just as happy that we don't often get the first-run stuff any more. Once in a while we'll get one of the great old ones, from the forties—but even the ones ten years old are better than the stuff they're turning out now. To think how they've cheapened the medium—I was saying to Mr. Pollock only the other day—"

"Yes, yes," said Hackett. "But these tickets—can you tell us who did buy any ahead"—he reckoned the days—"for last night? It'd have been on Saturday, probably—" Because he'd have had to have time to get them sent by mail.

"—And of course he agreed. Mr. Pollock is a real connoisseur of films. I suppose he's seen every film ever made—a projectionist for nearly fifty years, a remarkable record when you stop to think. Of course these days even that is getting automated," said Rea mournfully. "And he's retired now, of course, he must be seventy-five or so. But he still appreciates the good old ones. As I say, we sometimes get the great ones to run, and always, or mostly, the older ones, and the old man— Well, that's a case in point, just what you were asking, gentlemen. I always give him a discount, of course. You could say he served the industry long and faithfully. He does occasionally like to send out tickets to friends—and I'm glad to oblige him, of course. Such a fine old fellow—"

"Now you don't tell me," said Mendoza gently.

"Oh, now, Luis," said Hackett. "It can't fall into our laps from heaven like that."

"Where," said Mendoza, "does old Mr. Pollock live, do you know?"

"Why, he's only got a small pension, he has a couple of rooms over a store near the theatre—but really I don't understand what this is all about," said Rea. "The address? Mr. Pollock? Really I can't make out why the *police*—"

Higgins had given the gist of the Sardo case to Wanda to put in a formal report. Piggott and Glasser were out seeing those supposed customers of Kramer's. That would be a dead-end: no charge.

Grace had some more snapshots. "But you're right about that camera, you know. The film pack—it mounts up. Jimmy said Hackett had a brainstorm, and he and the boss went out on it. Something about that burglar."

"Burglars," said Higgins morosely. "Set us hunting for small-time burglars yet. Damn it. Damn it, I can't—it's something to do with— No, it's gone."

"You having a brainstorm now?"

"It's something right on the tip of my mind, sort of," said Higgins, "and I can't put a finger on it."

"If it's important it'll come to you."

"Yes, I keep telling myself."

There were always the routine things to do. He could help out Piggott and Glasser on that thankless job, or—Higgins lit another cigarette, sitting at his desk, and thought coldly about the Sardo baby and fondly of Margaret Emily, who would be four months old on the fifteenth of this month. The new year officially under way—and probably it would bring all the same things with it that the old year had. Nothing new or different or unexpectable about human nature.

"You seem to be the only one in," said Sergeant Lake. "Teletype from Communications. Just the routine thing."

"What?" Higgins started and looked up.

Lake repeated that. "Fellow committed suicide—this is from the chief down in New Orleans. A William Howerton —the suicide, I mean—and his father lives here, address up in Monterey Park. Will we please notify and ask about disposition of body, etcetera. The routine."

"Break the bad news," said Higgins with a sigh. And then he said, "By God! By God, but that was why— By God!"

"Something hit you?" said Lake.

"By God—Pat Baker," said Higgins. "Patricia Baker. Out of seventy-one names—but I swear she was on that list of Loose's— Where's Art? By God—"

13

ALONG THIS BLOCK of Second Street the buildings were old, two- and three-storied, of dirty dark brick. There were small shops on the ground floor, and windows above gave vague clues as to what lay behind them: dirty white curtains, plain windowshades, nothing at all. Mendoza had parked the Ferrari down the block; they walked up past a dingy men's clothing store, a shop displaying Mexican silver jewelry, a shop advertising *Sandals made to measure*, a pawnshop. "How the hell do you get upstairs?" asked Hackett.

At the corner, there was a somewhat larger place: a doll factory. Hackett averted his eyes from the collection of torsos, arms, and heads in the window, and Mendoza said, "*Aquí está.*" Almost hidden in a recess between this door and the corner of the building was a single narrow door. A small sign on it read, *Rooms By Week or Month, call Mr. Adams,* and a phone number.

They climbed rickety old stairs. At the top was a narrow hall, unlighted, leading left and right. Mendoza flicked his lighter at the nearest door, which bore the single numeral nine. "*Sí,*" he said, and knocked on it loudly. There was a step inside and the door opened. "Mr. Pollock? Mr. Roger Pollock?"

"That's who I am. And you, sir?" Light streamed out from the room; as he stepped back in tacit invitation, and they went in, they saw that this was one very large room, the three windows to their right looking out on Second. It was a tired old room, here and there plaster cracked, but very neat and clean. It was arranged in sections: up near the windows was a daybed, neatly made up, with a screen beside it. Farther down, against the inner wall, was a built-in sink with a table beside it holding stacked dishes. Out from that was a kitchen table with a chair, an electric hot plate on its own metal stand. Opposite the door was a tall bookshelf full of what looked like either photographic albums or scrapbooks, and nicely arranged before it an old leather armchair with a table beside it holding one dime-store glass ashtray, and an old standing lamp.

Mendoza had the badge out. "Lieutenant Mendoza—Sergeant Hackett. You took the chance that nobody would connect the complimentary theatre tickets. I'm afraid we're a little smarter than that."

"Well, you didn't do so for some time," said Pollock in a mild voice. He was a tall spare old man with thin white hair carefully plastered over a pink scalp. "I'm not sure of the etiquette involved—do I ask you to sit down?"

"Certainly." Mendoza sat down in the old leather armchair and lit a cigarette. "You know, Mr. Pollock, you shouldn't have done it. Taken to burglary at your time of life."

"Ah, it wouldn't have been my choice," said Pollock. He pulled the kitchen chair around and sat on it. "But I do not believe in forcing my fellow citizens to support me, which is what public welfare amounts to. I have supported myself since I was twelve years old, Lieutenant, and it would have been very distasteful to me to take money I had not earned."

"But the welfare—" began Hackett, and was quelled by a look.

"Money forcibly extorted from honest citizens by compulsory taxes is not true charity. I wanted no part of it. When I found, what with the increasing inflation, I simply had not enough for necessities, I said to myself, I would rather steal. For by doing that, you must admit, I was at least expending some labor for the—ah—return."

Mendoza laughed. "Well, it's a way to look at it."

"Life," said Pollock, and sighed, "plays tricks on us,

gentlemen. I was a saving man, and I always earned steady money. I had quite a nice little nest egg—in a savings and loan company. But my wife's last illness—we hadn't any family, only ourselves to rely on—Parkinson's disease, and then cancer—when she died I hadn't much left at all. All the doctors' bills, the hospital—I have only the Social Security now. And what with the rising inflation—" He shrugged. "I've lived here twenty years, I know this part of town very well. And the people. The idea—er—came to me in a flash, you could say. Of course it was natural in a way, my having been connected with the industry, in a sense, nearly all my working life. I suppose you have a warrant for my arrest?"

"Not yet. We just heard of you a short while ago. But you'll come back to headquarters now and I'll apply for one."

"Yes, I see. Dear me, I suppose I won't be allowed to take all my scrapbooks—" Pollock looked anxious. "Am I allowed to telephone a friend?"

"Certainly. And an attorney—"

"Oh, I don't think that's necessary. But I must ask Mr. Rea if he will kindly take care of all my scrapbooks. They go back a long way—really a miniature history of the industry. And Mr. Rea properly understands—I have left them to him in my will, of course." He blinked at the bookshelves lovingly. "One thing I can be grateful for, you know—I've lived through a great era of entertainment. I'm afraid the industry is committing suicide these days, the completely valueless material it's turning out—but ah, in the early and middle years, we had some great talents with us—really great! I do believe, one or two of them, the greatest ever among us. It's sad to compare what is offered today—you know, gentlemen, I find one can live a little too long." He stood up. "I suppose you could say," he added reflectively, "about the burglaries, that I was only acting by my lifelong conviction in the superiority of the free-enterprise system. Up to a *point*." And he laughed, a genuinely mirthful chuckle. "I am also aware that such a comparison of—ah—theft with capitalism is entirely fallacious, as these muddleheaded youngsters may one day find out, let's hope. But at least I—I paid my own way for a little time after—there simply wasn't enough to do that any more."

"Mr. Pollock," said Hackett, "your pawnbroker's receipt made our day. We appreciated it."

Pollock chuckled again. "A—ah—small commentary on this end of the twentieth century, Sergeant. And yet—in the middle years there was such promise, such fun, such talent, such memories in the making! Well, the memories one can keep. What will I be allowed to take, Lieutenant?"

Mendoza smiled at him. "We'll see that Mr. Rea looks after your things here. Not much, I'm afraid. Cigarettes—a book—you won't need clothes."

"I just wondered—" Pollock glanced at the wall beside the bookshelves, and went over there. Mendoza shrugged and nodded. They could argue about it at the jail.

Two framed photographs hung there: the only two pictures in the room. They were autographed black and white photographs, in cheap gold frames. Pollock took them down. The first showed a slim young man very dapper in the white flannels and navy blazer of the early thirties, smiling broadly into the camera. It was autographed in a scrawl at the right bottom edge. *Stan Laurel.*

"The very greatest," said Pollock, touching it. "Infinitely a superior pantomimist to Chaplin."

The other was a photograph of John Wayne which must have been taken twenty-five years ago.

"Well—" said Pollock, and looked around his home, "I'm quite ready. . . . And it did take you quite some time to find me, didn't it?"

Palliser, having shared the joke about the dog with Lake and Grace, was about to share it with Wanda, just back from a coffee break, when a new call came in: a head-on down at the Stack with one D.O.A. He went out on it, annoyed.

Even the out-of-state tourists these days mostly came from places where there were also freeways, and should be used to them. The L.A. Traffic Bureau prided itself on the placing, clarity and convenience of its freeway markings, and—always barring the drunks, of course—it was hard to see how drivers could get confused, try to enter on off-ramps and vice versa, causing the accidents. But while the signs were nearly infallible, the people were not.

When he got to it—traffic tied up on the inbound Santa Monica freeway, two squad cars, an ambulance, and a crowd of ghouls—it was, of course, a mess. The D.O.A., by what the Traffic men had sorted out, was the guilty party; he'd managed to get an old beat-up Dodge going west on the eastbound side, and rammed into a brand new Impala with Arizona plates. There had been a woman alone in the Impala, and the ambulance men had her on a stretcher. She was moaning, "No, no, no, where's Azzie? Azzie—please, is he all right? You can't take me anywhere until—please where's—"

Palliser squatted over the stretcher and one of the ambulance men said kindly, "You're not bad, ma'am, you've got a broken leg and probably some ribs, but you'll be O.K., don't worry—"

"No, no—" she moaned. She was a nice-looking woman about forty, with dark hair and a good complexion. "My dog —please find him, is he all right? Please—"

"Oh," said Palliser. He stood up. "Any sign of a dog around?"

"I got it," called a voice from the little crowd. "Big savage dog, I can't hardly hold—" And the dog came through the crowd, towing a citizen, tugging at a braided leather leash. He flashed up to the stretcher, tongue out frantically.

"Oh, Azzie! Oh, thank God you're all right— Please," and her gaze fastened on Palliser, "please will you see he's taken—some good boarding place, where he'll—I don't know anybody here, I can pay—please—"

"I'll see to it," said Palliser soothingly.

"I'm Madge Borman—the address is in the car—now, Azzie, you go with him. Go with the man here—it's all right, darling." The stretcher went into the ambulance, and it purred off quickly; Traffic wanted to get the freeway unjammed. Palliser stood there with the dog's leash in his hand. The dog was the biggest black German Shepherd he'd ever seen. He went to look in the Impala, and rescued Miss Borman's handbag from the front seat, together with a wooden box bearing a printed label: *Borman's Dark Angel of Langley.* Inside the box were several brushes, a hard rubber ball covered with teeth marks, and a box of Dog Yummies. "I guess this belongs to you," he said to the dog, and the dog moved his tail politely. He had strained after the ambulance, but seemed to understand that he was in Palliser's charge. He was a very handsome dog. Palliser put him in the Rambler, and after getting the names of the D.O.A. and a couple of witnesses, drove off the freeway and stopped along Venice Boulevard, wondering what to do with the dog. He didn't know anything about boarding kennels at all.

Mendoza, however, would. Palliser found a public phone and called in, explained his predicament to Sergeant Lake. "Well, this and that's been happening, John. They got the burglar—nicest old chap you'd want to meet—the warrant's applied for—and then Higgins— Well, just a minute. I'll see—"

There was silence, and then Mendoza's voice. "John? I understand you've acquired a dog. Why?"

Palliser told him. "A Miss Borman, from Arizona. She doesn't know anybody here. By the tag on his collar, the dog is Borman's Dark Angel, but she called him—"

"What is it?"

"What—oh, a great big black German Shepherd."

"Not that it matters. Evidently a show dog. Well, you take the dog up to the Los Feliz Small Animal Hospital on Los Feliz, and tell Dr. Douthit—"

"Dr. who?"

"Douthit. Tell him the circumstances, and that I'll guarantee the bill. And then you'd better come in."

"Yes, thanks," said Palliser. He drove across town to the hospital and left the dog; a brisk Dr. Douthit said he was a fine specimen. The dog licked Palliser's hand politely, and

Palliser thought about what Roberta had said. That was quite a dog. And with the crime rate up—

But it bothered him a little, all the way back downtown, as to why she called the dog Azzie.

Higgins had got sidetracked. The routine was there to be done. And the LAPD liked to do it right. The LAPD did not call people on the telephone to tell them about sudden death to family members. Higgins drove out to Monterey Park to break the bad news, as requested by New Orleans, and gave the elder Mr. Howerton the addresses and phone numbers to use, making the arrangements. He then came back to the office hunting for Hackett, and Lake told him about Roger Pollock.

"Funny, the things we run into," he said. "The nicest old fellow—"

But Hackett and Mendoza had gone to see Pollock into jail. They'd be back shortly.

He was still thinking about that girl, Pat Baker. He'd been a little surprised to find several young women in Loose's first class; he shouldn't have been, girls went in for a lot of professions these days. Attempted suicide—and Galeano had said, the marijuana cigarettes. Higgins wondered more about that. A *medical* student—you'd think if anybody should know the truth about that, it would be—

He was surprised to find it was ten past twelve. He didn't know where the morning had gone. He went on out North Broadway to Federico's, and found Mendoza, Hackett, Grace and Glasser just sitting down at the big table.

"And wait until you hear about the burglar," said Grace. "Art had the hunch this time."

"Not a hunch. I just remembered about the movies."

Higgins listened impatiently. "A very funny little thing, yes. Listen—it just came to me awhile ago—that attempted suicide last night. Girl named Pat Baker. I'm pretty sure she was on that list, in Loose's classes."

"What?" said Hackett. "It's an ordinary name, George." Palliser wandered up and sat down beside him.

[199]

"Yes, I know, but I'm sure. We can check. I think we'd better check. I called the hospital on it this morning, and we can talk to her this afternoon."

"Coincidence—"

"Once, not twice," said Mendoza. "*¿Cuánto apuestas?*—how much do you bet? Stir up the animals, I said, didn't I? I wonder—I do wonder—if you stirred that up, boys, or if she was already thinking about it."

"Talk about reaching—oh, we'd better see her," agreed Hackett.

"I hear you got the burglar," said Palliser, and heard about that. "Very funny. *I* can't make out about that dog. His name is Dark Angel of Langley, and she called him Azzie. A funny sort of name—"

"Most show dogs have names for short," said Mendoza.

"Yes, and others too—like Ricky. Did I tell you about Ricky?" He did so. "And you should have seen Osney's face—"

"That old devil sex," grinned Mendoza. "*De veras.*" He put out his cigarette as the waiter came up with a tray, "And after lunch, I think we go and ask Miss Baker why she tried to take the hard way out."

All three of them had been cops a long time, Mendoza and his two senior sergeants, and they had for their sins seen a lot of people like Dr. and Mrs. James Baker. The kind of people, happy, successful, with the good life, suddenly seeing their world fall apart as Fate—or whatever it was decided such things—took a hand.

He was in general practice in Hollywood, distinguished looking, upright; she was the typical well-groomed efficient housewife. And they were saying to the police officers what they had been saying, probably to hospital staff and to each other, all night and day.

"But all of a sudden—there wasn't any hint of anything wrong—" "—Living with Evelyn, old friends and good experience for her—" "—Never any trouble with Pat, a good quiet girl—" "And she won't talk, she won't tell us what—just thank God they pulled her through, but—"

Mendoza listened to that a little while: the background. The girl had her own money; a grandmother had left her a trust fund. She hadn't been pressured to study for an M.D. degree, it was her own ambition. She was twenty-three, in her second year as a med student. She hadn't any steady boyfriend, dated sometimes. She'd always been a responsible girl, affectionate, steady, and she was home for dinner at least once a week, there hadn't been any hint of worry—

"Yes, well, it could be she'll talk to us," said Mendoza. They looked at him doubtfully; but he had the doctors' permission.

When they went into the little single hospital room she was lying flat in the high bed, her face turned toward the window. She turned slowly to look at them. She might be a middling pretty girl, made up and happy; she had a round face, very fine white skin, blue eyes and dark hair, uncombed and tousled now. Her voice was thin and listless. She looked at the dapper slim Mendoza between the two bigger men looming, and she said, "You're the police. I knew you'd come."

"That's right, Miss Baker," said Mendoza.

"They kept—asking and asking. About why, you know. Mother and Daddy and the doctor, and they got Evelyn to come and try to—and it was all just too long to explain, to make them understand—because it was all just one thing leading—I just thought I'd wait till you came, because you —already know—some of it."

"Miss Baker," said Hackett, exchanging a glance with Mendoza, "before you tell us anything we have to inform you about all your rights." He recited that.

She waited patiently, and nodded. "Yes—I know about that. You see, I never *meant*—any of it. I didn't know— things could happen like that—without your meaning it. But they do. And it was—all—just too much. Too *much*. All at once." She stopped there, turning her head restlessly.

Mendoza waited and then said quietly, "You broke into Dr. Loose's office?"

"Yes. I'd been worried—I suppose I ought to start from there—I'd been worried about grades. My—papers. I got

A's and B's mostly all last year, but it was—harder, this year—and then—and then Donny gave me some of those cigarettes—" She swallowed and said, "But everybody knows—he said, everybody knows—marijuana isn't dangerous—like the other things. It'll be legal pretty soon, everybody says—just like ordinary cigarettes. And it seemed to help, sort of. I felt—"

None of them looked at each other, but Higgins gave an expressive sigh. As law-men they had to keep up with all sorts of things; some of what they knew wasn't general knowledge, but that recent story had been carried by the wire services to most newspapers: the painstaking research turning up the interesting fact that prolonged use of marijuana had the effect of physically shrinking the brain. And a medical student—but maybe the operative word was *student*. She was twenty-three, and on almost any campus these days, the silly, sordid, and dangerous talk was loud.

"—Felt better about it, as if I was doing fine—but then I went on getting bad marks, and I—was worried. Daddy—so proud—all last year, and I wanted— But along in November, I got to thinking—about the end-of-year exams—I tried to study, but then there was Christmas coming—presents to think about, things to—Mother's party, I had to—pretend there wasn't anything wrong—and it got harder and harder—"

"Miss Baker. How often were you using marijuana then?"

She looked up vaguely. "I don't know, when I tried to study—sometimes. I haven't now for about a month. I got —scared. I got scared one night about it. It was—way before Christmas. Evelyn was going out on a date. I was trying—memorize—for Anatomy class. And I—she'd just left, I *thought*, and then all of a sudden she came home and it was—one in the morning and I didn't know what had happened, what I'd been doing—all that time. I got scared. I haven't—had any since."

That was one effect it had, of course.

"And Daddy *would*—all through Christmas, people coming in—boasting about me—and I wasn't any good! I couldn't do the work— And there were exams coming up— You know about that. *That* was why. You know."

"We'd like to hear it from you, Miss Baker."

After silence, she said, "It's so long. Telling about it. I— I don't want—to see them when you tell them. You'll—tell them, won't you? Mother and Daddy. I never *meant* anything—it just happened. The exams—I got to thinking, if I just knew what *some* of the questions—it'd be a help. Dr. Loose's office—" She moved restlessly. "I read detective stories sometimes, I knew about deadbolts and all, and I looked at the door one day when I'd been up there—you could get in *there* easy enough. The building—and then— I thought—about the cleaning men. You see? It was just getting *in*. You could get out—easy enough—after they'd gone, the front doors open from inside with one of those bars even if the lock's thrown—I was there late one day— and—Dr. Loose showed me—"

"Go on, Miss Baker."

"I—got there just after they did. The cleaning men. That night. They were all—working down the hall, in the class-rooms—I got upstairs right away, they never saw me. It was all right to turn on a light up there, if anybody saw it they'd just think—Dr. Loose—working late. And I found the exam questions—and—I was going to wait till the men left. And then one of them—came up to that floor, I heard him on the stairs and I was—so terribly scared—all I could see, all of a sudden, was them finding me and an awful scandal about the exams and me expelled and Daddy so ashamed, after— and I wanted to get *away!* I just wanted to get *away!* I— I grabbed up something from the desk, I thought a ruler or—just any way, I wanted to get *out* of there— But I didn't know he was so close! I ran out the door, I thought —the back stairs, before—but the man was right *there!* A man—I hit out at him, I didn't know what I did, I just— and I ran. I just threw that thing away—and I ran. Down the back stairs—and out the side door. And—"

They waited. "I didn't know—until I heard—people talking about it. I don't see a newspaper much. But Donny said—and everybody—about that man there. That poor man—dead. Murdered, they said. And some scissors—" Her voice dropped to a near whisper. "I don't *remember* any scissors. I turned the light off—when I heard him on the stairs—and I grabbed up a ruler or something—I thought. But when I knew—I knew that was *me*. Had done that. Not meaning anything—I was—just scared. I've been scared —ever since." She looked up at Higgins' craggy tough-looking face, and closed her eyes. "You came—yesterday morning—and I thought—I thought you knew, looking right at me. And it just seemed better not to—have it all open and in the papers and Mother and Daddy so—" And after a long silence she said, "I got the morphine from Daddy's bag. The office is closed till next week, he wouldn't find out right away. They were going to a party last night, and I've got a key to the house, of course."

"I see," said Mendoza quietly.

"And—that's—all. You can go and tell them now. And— and do whatever you have to do to me. But I'm so tired. I just wish Evelyn hadn't—found me so soon."

"Maybe you'll feel different about that some day," said Mendoza.

They went out, first to tell the story to the parents. Who asked numb questions, and said all the inevitable things. And the D.A. might call it manslaughter or murder two; she might get three-to-five, she might get a suspended sentence and probation; it was anybody's guess. It would probably drag on in the courts for some time; and by the time a judge and/or a jury decided Pat Baker's immediate fate, everybody would have forgotten who Joe Daly was, except the family that mourned him.

"Just the random chance really," said Higgins on the way back to the office. He sounded uneasy. "I'd hate to think it was my ugly puss scared her enough to push her over the edge."

Hackett laughed sharply. "Say it was cumulative, George."

"And I'm the one who told you to try to scare them," Mendoza reminded them. "I wonder if anything new's gone down. Woman's work—we get one cleared up, we get something else coming in."

Palliser, at loose ends, told Wanda and Shogart about the dog. "That's the funniest name for a dog I ever heard," said Wanda.

"We had a dog once named Dog," said Shogart.

Grace came back from a session with a couple of the supposed customers of Kramer's. "All up in the air," said Grace. "We'll never prove it."

Palliser told him about the dog. "Well, that is a funny name," said Grace. "I've heard some peculiar names for dogs, but that takes the cake."

Hackett and Higgins came in, looking rather glum, and told them about Pat Baker. "My successful play-acting," said Higgins. "Scaring the girl into—my God, if I'd had any inkling—"

"I did some of it too," said Hackett.

"And do we say," said Grace, "there but for the grace of God?"

"No," said Higgins, "because most people with any grain of common sense know better than to experiment with the Mary Jane."

"Most people," said Grace. "Who aren't twenty-three and hearing all the fool talk from—"

"Oh, Art," said Sergeant Lake from the anteroom. "Call for you."

Hackett picked up the phone on his desk and punched the outside button. "Robbery-Homicide, Sergeant Hackett."

"Are you *telling* me," said an outraged voice, "are you telling me—I just saw it in the *Herald*—arrested for complicity in those hijackings— Are you *telling* me it was *Tiger Faley* knocked me out cold? Me? *Me!*—that—that tanglefooted lout who hasn't got a punch to lick a bantam with any science—that it was *Faley*—"

"I'm afraid so, Mr. Donlevy," said Hackett, choking back a laugh.

The silence at the other end was eloquent. Then Donlevy said hollowly. "My God. My God. Faley—that damn punch-drunk— My God, I'll never live it down. Me! Basher Don-levy—"

"Well, you weren't expecting it," said Hackett.

"Expecting be damned. I'll never live it down. *Faley!*" said Donlevy, as if it was the worst cussword he knew, and the line went dead. Hackett sat back and laughed.

Piggott and Glasser came back at four-thirty and Glasser went to hand Wanda a couple of pages of notes.

"The devil," said Piggott, "is busy these days. Going up and down. All those customers of Kramer's, and absolutely no proof. We may as well forget it."

"Waste of time, I said so," said Grace. He was leafing fondly through the batch of snapshots. "And I should have listened to you," he added to Higgins. "You did warn me. The film pack for this camera—even if it is convenient, getting the picture right away—"

"And you haven't heard," said Higgins moodily, "about my ugly mug scaring that girl—" He started to tell them about that.

"If the head doctors are right," said Hackett, "he'll be growing a trauma about his looks."

"Oh, don't be a damn fool," said Higgins. "Though I will say, I hope Margaret takes after Mary instead of me. But—"

"I," said Palliser to Piggott, "seem to have got mixed up with dogs today. You didn't hear about Ricky—speaking of cameras, if I could have a shot of Osney's expression! And—"

Glasser was laughing over something with Wanda.

"And the thing on the freeway," said Palliser. "It beats me, with all the signs posted, how anybody with common sense could—but there was this dog. A show dog I suppose. With another name for short, but such a funny name. Azzie, she called him."

"Azzie," said Piggott, yawning.

"The tag on his collar said Dark Angel of Langley. A great big dog," said Palliser. A good watchdog, a German Shepherd would be. And he'd been a smart dog, understanding he should cooperate with a strange man. A good watchdog for the baby, a dog like that would be.

"Oh," said Piggott. "Oh, well, that explains it."

"What?"

"The Dark Angel," said Piggott. "Didn't you ever read the Bible? Azrael, the Dark Angel. Probably—"

"Well, I will be damned," said Palliser. "I never heard—" And Lake broke in urgently.

"Heist at the Federal Savings and Loan, Wilshire and Rampart—"

Mendoza came out to join them as they all got up. A bank job—the Feds would be alerted and on the way too.

And irrelevantly Palliser thought, not a bank job. The banks were all closed by now, it was long after three. But the savings and loan associations would be open till six.

There was always something new coming along to make work for the law-men.

14

THE FEDS WERE of the opinion, after listening to what the tellers and patrons at the savings and loan branch had to say, that the three heist-men were the same gang that had done a job on a bank in Pasadena last month and Stockton the month before that. "All we need," said Mendoza. It had been a professional job: ski-masks, a lookout at the door, very businesslike. The first estimate was that they'd got away with about eleven grand. There wasn't even a close make on the car; several people had seen them get away, but their descriptions varied from a tan Dodge to a white Ford, and nobody had seen any part of the plate-number.

"It's what we usually get, isn't it?" said Bright of the local FBI. "Bricks without straw."

"Fortunately there aren't too many bright ones," said Mendoza.

They were all late getting away, and met the night watch coming on. Landers' eye was still colorful, but fading. Grace stopped to pass a few snapshots around. "How you doing with that blonde, Tom?"

"I think I'm making an impression, but she's a damn level-headed girl," said Landers.

As Palliser sat over the warmed-up and savory beef stew, he told Roberta he supposed he ought to go and tell Miss Borman where her dog was. Roberta had heard all about the dog, and said he certainly had. "She'll be worried to death. Of course they're nice dogs, but too big for the city. And you needn't help with the dishes—you'll just about make visiting-hour at the hospital." Roberta smiled at him. She was looking—his normally svelte and slim Robin—fairly rotund these days, with David Andrew (or possibly Margaret).

He found Madge Borman in a four-bed room, propped up against the pillow. Her face cleared when he told her about the dog, and Lieutenant Mendoza knowing about the boarding place, and Dr. Douthit; she thanked him warmly. "I don't know a soul here, I don't know what would have happened—we were on our way to the Pasadena show. I'll never forget how kind you've been—"

"Well, the LAPD tries to do its best for everybody, Miss Borman. He's a fine dog. My wife's been saying we ought to get a dog after the baby—but of course not—"

"You shall have one of Azzie's pups, Sergeant. No, I insist! I'm breeding Marla to him next month, just say which you'd like and you shall—of course the bitches are better watchdogs if that's what you were thinking of—"

"Well, but they're—" *Too big for the city* was lost in the volume of her gratitude.

"You shall have one of the girls. I just don't know what I'd have done if you hadn't been so kind."

Miss Borman had a strong personality. Uneasily Palliser wondered how to tell Robin, and decided to put it off. Possibly Miss Borman would forget all about it once she was back in Arizona.

Hackett, Higgins and Shogart were off on Thursday.

The night watch had left them a legacy: a break-in at a big pharmacy on Beverly Boulevard. The pharmacist and his employees would be taking stock this morning, to reckon what was missing, but not until the lab men had been there; Mendoza chased them out on that early. There had also been a mugging near MacArthur Park, and a new body reported by Traffic about midnight. The body, found in the street on Temple, was described as male, Caucasian, late twenties, probable overdose. Mendoza knew how that would go. If they didn't identify it from prints, sooner or later some relative would come in—or maybe not. Once in a long while they got a body they never could put a name to.

Piggott and Glasser went out to talk to the pharmacist. Mendoza wandered out of his office and said to Palliser, "You said something about that Gene Stover—his sister, who ought to know where he is—"

"Yes, I'm going to do something about it right now," said Palliser, picking up the phone. "I told you I found her agent. These boys so damned upstage—all they can think of—"

"I don't," said Mendoza, "like the ones like Lila Askell. No handle. No shape. *No sirve—es difícil.* Witnesses—too many witnesses, John."

"What?" Palliser was dialing.

"Down there. Broadway and Seventh, the day before Christmas. How many people saw Lila and the strange young man?—but never saw them at all. To notice. Only Louise Chaffee—and she couldn't say at all where they went after they had that—mm—peculiar lunch. An Orange Julius bar, *Dios.* And the cotoneaster leaves— Who are you calling?"

"The damn agent. Rena Rowe's. There's no—"

"At this hour? Show biz people don't keep our hours, John. He won't be in his office until eleven at least."

"But he was so damn worried about publicity, he wouldn't give me the address—"

"Who is she? . . . bit parts, on the make for the big time and all the odds against her if she hasn't strings to pull. Mmh," said Mendoza "*¡Ca! Esto me da en que pensar.*" He started back for his office with Palliser trailing him. At the desk, he flipped over the pages of the phone-list rapidly. "Maybe we'll pull some strings ourselves. It's always helpful to have friends in exalted places."

"I didn't know you had," said Palliser.

"Oh, that was before you made rank and joined us, now I think. I had—mmh—occasion to oblige that well-known producer Mr. Toby Pickering in a rather delicate personal matter—" He had dialed rapidly and now said, "Lieutenant Mendoza, if Mr. Pickering has a moment, please . . ." Within three minutes he was apologizing for disturbing the great man. "I'm trying to get in touch with a would-be starlet, she's had bits and pieces I understand—one Rena Rowe. Would you have any idea how to locate her? . . . Oh. Well, I would appreciate it. Thanks very much." He put the phone down, circled thumb and forefinger at Palliser. "He can demand the head powers at Central Casting and bully an address out of them. A mere LAPD officer, not a hope in hell."

"It's nice to have friends in high places," said Palliser.

Grace came back from a routine check at nine-fifty. Five minutes later R. and I. called in the crisp voice of Police-woman Phil O'Neill. "That new body of yours," she said. "S.I.D. sent its prints up, and the computer made them. In our records. William Francis Jay, little record of posses-sion. Do you want his package?"

"Well," said Lake, "if there's any relative listed—"

"Wife. St. Andrews Place, but this is two years back."

"Give it to me," said Lake resignedly. "We'd better check."

He handed the address to Grace, who went back down-stairs. The job could get boring. But as he drove he thought fondly of their very own family—now all the red tape had got cut—plump brown Celia Ann, such a good baby. Only, of course, that camera—he wondered what it might cost him to turn it in on the same kind Higgins had.

At the old brick apartment house on St. Andrews Place, he found Linda Jay still listed on a mailbox. When she finally opened the door to him, she looked blearily at him around it—slim brown Grace nearly as dapper as Mendoza —and peered at the badge. "For God's sake," she said. "Come around at *this* hour—cops! What you want with me? I haven't even had a traffic ticket lately." She wasn't bad-looking, blonde by request, clutching a terry bathrobe around her tightly.

"It's your husband, Mrs. Jay. I'm sorry to have to tell you he's dead. He was found last night—"

"Dead?" she said. "Bill? Well, goody-goody! I've been saving up for a divorce, and now I can blow it. Is that for real, it's really Bill? In your morgue?"

"By his fingerprints, yes—"

"Thank *you*, mister! This really makes my day!" she said, and banged the door in his face.

People, people, thought Grace. They did come all sorts forever.

Within five minutes Pickering got back to Mendoza on the phone. "It's Sweetzer Avenue off the Strip," he said tersely. "Never heard of the girl myself, but Central Casting had her down all right. Not at all, glad to oblige. Any time."

Mendoza put out his cigarette and looked at Palliser thoughtfully. "How do you feel about this Stover?"

"Any hunches, you mean? No. But he's the only thing, and the last thing that showed at all on Lila, and I just want to see him," said Palliser, "To—round it out, do I mean? To—feel as if we'd done everything we damn well could on it, if it has to wind up in Pending."

"Yes. I don't like shoving cases into Pending, but once in a while there's just no handle. So, good luck on finding him. If it was anybody else," said Mendoza, "I might come along for the ride in case you do find him. But if so, I'll trust you to size him up."

"Well, a compliment from the maestro himself." Palliser went out past the switchboard.

On the way to Sweetzer Avenue, which was out in county territory in west Hollywood, Palliser thought again about that dog. Or rather pup. He had the feeling that Robin might go straight up in the air. Well, nice dogs, but in town—they'd been talking about a chain-link fence, or some kind of fence round the yard, on account of the baby. If Madge Borman remembered about that pup, and Palliser thought she wasn't a woman to forget promises, there'd have to be some kind of fence. Well, there was time—the baby due in April. Just about, he reckoned up hastily, the time those pups would be due, by what she said. . . .

The address was one of the stark square new apartments. The rent would be median out here, near fashionable areas but not of them; exactly the sort of address a girl like this would have. He wondered as he climbed the front steps what delicate service Mendoza had performed for the exalted Mr. Pickering.

Eight mailboxes. Rena Rowe was listed at apartment six upstairs. They were uncarpeted cement stairs; above, a narrow hall with four doors. Six was at the left rear. He pushed the bell.

When the door opened he had the badge out. She was a tall girl, perhaps five-seven, a natural blonde, leggy and very much a Hollywood type, almost oozing synthetic glamor. "Who the hell are you?" she said in a throaty voice. "Where'd you get my address? I'm not listed—what's that?" She looked at the badge. "A cop? Where'd you get my—"

Palliser was tempted to tell her; the mention of Pickering's name would doubtless earn him instant welcome. "We're trying to locate your brother, Miss Rowe—Gene Stover. It's nothing to do with you. Do you know where he's living?"

"What's it about? Is Gene in some kind of cop trouble?"

"We just want to ask him some questions," said Palliser.

"Oh." She thought that over. "Oh, well, if it gets in the papers, any publicity's good. Sure. Come on in. He always runs to big sister, he's broke. But you aren't going to get any willing answers to your questions at this hour, before he's had some coffee."

"He's here?"

"Sure. The other bedroom." She gestured, uncaring that the nylon peignoir over very little underwear slid open revealingly. She walked over to the coffee table, bent to light a cigarette. It was an ugly square room, painted stark white, furnished in violent modern, with two surrealist prints on the walls.

Palliser knocked on the indicated door. "Mr. Stover! Police! I'd like to talk to you, please."

"You won't get anywhere that way," she said. She went past him, opening the door. "Gene? You up yet? Come and see the nice handsome cop, dear. I don't know if it's a traffic ticket or what, but he wants to talk to you."

"What the hell?" It was a high tenor, sounding boyish. He came out to the living room slowly, with her prodding him behind. Gene Stover would be at least Stettin's age, twenty-five or so, but he looked younger. He was also too good-looking for a man. Only his sister's height, he was a little stocky, very blond. He had regular cameo features, the fair skin that showed blood easily, very white teeth, a mouth slightly too small. He was wrapping a white terry robe around him, and he looked at Palliser with dislike and a curious fury in his pale blue eyes.

"A cop!" he said. "What—do you want with me?"

And Palliser knew. In that split second, he knew and was sure. Whether it was a thing akin to Mendoza's *daemon* he didn't know, nor could he say exactly what told him. Little things: things not evidence, except to whatever it was in him which on occasion read between the lines about human nature. The hand clenched on the belt of the robe: the eyes: the mouth too taut.

"About Lila Askell, Mr. Stover," he said, and the warm satisfaction spread through him like light. "I think you can tell us something about Lila Askell."

"I can't. I don't know a damn thing about that," he said roughly. "That damned Ron Stettin! He said you'd come nosing around up there, and he had the nerve, tell you about that—just a joke, the note to tell me she— Well, like I told him, I never got it, so I never knew—and if you ask me it was slander, him even suggesting—"

"Hey, don't get worked up," said Rena. "You got some girl in trouble, Gene?"

Palliser eyed him interestedly, thinking. There were the two latents from Lila's necklace, not known to any records. Unfortunately, without much more legal cause than they had, they couldn't ask Gene Stover to let himself be printed. There wasn't any other solid evidence at all, so far. If Stover stuck to that story, and they couldn't prove he'd had Stettin's note—if Louise Chaffee couldn't identify him positively—there was nothing to tie him in.

"So what have you got to say to that, cop? Slander—try to make out—I want some coffee," he said querulously. He started for the kitchen at the other side of the apartment.

Palliser thought, this was January fourth. A week ago

last Sunday, Lila Askell had been on her way home for Christmas, with a three-hour wait for her bus in Los Angeles. And she'd never made it home. Ten days. But the lab sometimes made miracles; and the average citizen didn't realize just what evidence the lab could turn up, when they went really looking. And then, of course, when it came to fingerprints, they *had* the two latents from the necklace, and if—

"Mr. Stover," he asked, "do you have a car?" Stover had just come back with a cup of well-creamed coffee.

"Well, of course I've got a car. Why?"

"Where is it?"

Stover looked at him narrowly. "Why?"

"Where?"

"It's in the alley at the back," said the girl. "There's only one carport, mine's in that. What's this all about?" It had penetrated her mind that this was about something more than a traffic ticket. "It's a Corvair. What's—"

"I'm afraid," said Palliser, "I'll have to ask you to get dressed, Mr. Stover. I'd like you to come back to headquarters to answer some questions. We'd also like to examine your car."

"But I *told* you! I don't know anything about that! I—I don't think I was even in town that day—"

"What day?"

"I don't *remember* what day it was! You can't make me—you can't—"

"Well, I'm afraid we can, Mr. Stover, when we have reason to think you might be able to help us. We'd prefer you to cooperate voluntarily, but—"

"I can't—all I can do is go on saying—I don't know anything about it," he said too breathlessly. "I—oh, damn it, that bastard Ron—"

Palliser asked to use the phone, got the Traffic garage, and asked that the Corvair be towed in at once for examination. "Priority," he added. "Tell Duke. . . . You'd better get dressed, Mr. Stover."

A new call came in at ten-thirty, just as Palliser came

back with a blond fellow in tow. Grace and Piggott were in. "You'd better both roll on it," said Lake. "It sounds like a thing, what the uniformed branch had to say. It's Carroll Avenue—" He added the address.

It was a thing. It was going to be quite a thing to work, and was probably the next offbeat little mystery—sometimes they got the little mysteries—to occupy them for a while.

This street of modest old houses, a few apartments, close in to Echo Park Avenue, was rental-zoned, and most of the houses had smaller houses on the back of the lot. The address was one of those. The squad car was still there, and the two uniformed men were in the yard between the houses with a fat woman in a bright pink dress. The house was on a corner, and there was a chain-link fence round the yard with a gate open on the side. Grace and Piggott went through it.

"I didn't see her all yesterday, I told you that, I just saw she hadn't gone to work today, her car still there, I wondered was she sick, and when she didn't answer the door I just looked in the wind—" she'd have been saying it over and over; and was crying a little, more in excitement and shock than sorrow.

"You'll want the lab boys on this pronto," said one of the patrolmen. "All we got so far is, she was a divorcée, Mrs. Ellen Reynolds, worked in an office somewhere. Lived here alone. The back door was forced—"

They went around the little house, which would contain about three rooms. There was a single step, to a narrow rear door; a screen hung half off its hinges, and there were savage pry-marks on the open inner door. It led to a tiny kitchen. In there was a body, and a good deal of blood.

In the middle of the floor, which wasn't more than six feet square, she was spread-eagled. By the dark hair, the slim figure, she was probably young; her face and upper body were so covered with long-dried dark blood, it was hard to say. She was naked except for a white lace brassiere tangled around one arm, stockings crumpled about her ankles. Things lay on the floor: a couple of broken dishes, in the opposite doorway a green ceramic vase, broken. Mutely they followed the trail to a tiny living room, where a chair was overturned, a love-seat pulled away from the wall, a scatter-rug wadded up. The telephone lay on the floor, its wire pulled out and broken. One high-heeled shoe lay upside down near another door.

"She put up a fight," said Grace. "It started in here." The tinier bedroom was a shambles—bedclothes on the floor, a straight chair broken in two parts, the big mirror over a vanity table shattered, half of it in shards on the table. There was probably, they could hope, a welter of scientific evidence here to be picked up.

They went, avoiding possible pieces of evidence, back to the kitchen.

"Did you see the note?" asked one of the patrolmen through the back door.

"Note?" said Piggott.

"On top of her handbag in the living room. We didn't touch it, there might be prints—"

They went to look. The handbag was a workaday affair, brown leather much worn. It was on the coffee table, neatly closed with the clasp fastened, as if it had been put there to be noticed. On top of it was an empty used envelope, with something scrawled on the wrong side.

"My God," said Grace. "My God, Matt."

It was a nearly illiterate scrawl: but it seemed to shout a certain lunatic arrogance into the silence. Crookedly across the back of the envelope it ran—*god bles th parol bord.*

"Satan," said Piggott, "getting around these days, Jase. And how the lieutenant is going to love this."

Palliser came into Mendoza's office alone and said tersely, "The long way round, but we do get there. Let's hope there'll be the lab evidence to prove it. I want to call Duke."

"*¡Parece mentira!*" said Mendoza. "Don't tell me—"

"Oh, you'll have the feeling about him too, I don't doubt. The trouble is, he's saying loud and clear, don't know nothing about it, and unless we do turn up the solid evidence—

Jimmy, get me the lab," said Palliser. "Duke? That car just fetched in to the garage—blue Corvair—give it everything you've got. Now. I've got our man here, but we can't hold him, we haven't even got enough to warrant holding him overnight—and I have the definite feeling that if he slides out from under us now, he'll run. If there's any evidence we want it in the next hour."

"Fun and games," said Duke. "What are we looking for?"

"Some people," said Palliser, "always drive in gloves. Let's hope he's not one of them. Those latents you picked up from the Askell girl's necklace—if you get any liftable ones from the driver's side of the Corvair, run a comparison. I don't think it'd be much use to look for any of her prints, it's ten days back. And anything else interesting about the car—"

"O.K.," said Duke. "We're on it."

"So, elucidate," said Mendoza.

Palliser shook his head. "How do you know these things? You can't explain it. He's too handsome. His voice is too high. His clothes are a little too fancy."

Mendoza laughed. "*Como sí.* The little cold finger down the spine, saying the fellow across the table really does hold a full house. Well—where is he?"

"Interrogation room down the hall. But we can't stall him too long, he's already yelling about citizens' rights."

"Sometimes," said Mendoza, "they can yell too loud. And talk themselves into trouble. Let's let him sit for half an hour and then see."

And, in the interrogation room, he looked at Gene Stover and felt as Palliser had felt about him. "Who're you?" asked Stover angrily. "You can't keep me here for no reason —I *said* I didn't know anything about it and nobody can prove—"

Mendoza introduced himself. "What are you afraid of, Mr. Stover?" he asked blandly.

"I'm not afraid of anything, damn it! I don't know anything about all this," he said doggedly. "I told you I never got that crazy damn note Ron said—I told him—so I didn't know about her—I wasn't interested—"

He said it all over again, several different ways, to a few leading questions. He began to sweat, and Mendoza leaned on the wall smoking and watching him. Stover moved restlessly, sitting at the small table; he wasn't a smoker, and was unsure what to do with his hands. He folded them, unfolded them, scratched his cheek, and his pale eyes moved too. When at last a silence had held to tension, he sprang up and shouted, "Damn you, stop *looking* at me! Who the hell do you think you are, standing there *looking* at me—I told you I don't know anything—"

"About Lila Askell," said Mendoza gently, "who wanted to go home for Christmas." And he had wondered about the motive on Lila; they didn't have to show motive, legally, and often motive was very slight in any case. But when the girl hadn't been raped, he had wondered. Now, looking at Gene Stover, it came to him what the motive must have been, the very little, sordid, silly motive. Matt talking about the devil . . . "It rankled with you, didn't it, that she didn't fall for your masculine charms? That doesn't often happen to you, does it? If the girls don't fall for your pretty-boy looks, they'll feel motherly about you." That was the type. "And Lila annoyed you, didn't she? So obviously uninterested. Turning you down."

"I never— She was a nothing," he said. "Strictly from Boresville—why the hell should I—"

"But you called and asked her for dates, several times—after the double dates with Monica and Stettin," said Mendoza. "And she turned you down. The only reason you did ask her was to prove you could get to her, wasn't it? You were annoyed because she hadn't any use for Pretty Boy, weren't you?"

"You go to hell," said Stover furiously. "I never—and you can't make me say I did! I don't know anything about it!" But his hands were shaking.

It went on like that another ten minutes. A weak character can be very stubborn, and he had pinned his faith on the magic reiteration. The last time he said it, it was pure automatic reflex.

There was a gentle tap on the closed door. Palliser opened

it and went out to the corridor, shutting it behind him. "So?" he said to Duke.

"Bingo. He doesn't," said Duke, "drive in gloves. Quite a few good prints on the steering wheel, dash, and rear view mirror. They match the prints off the necklace. But also—"

"We sometimes get lucky. Thanks, Duke."

"But also," said Duke, "people trying to wipe off fingerprints forget the most obvious places. You thought that was the car the Askell girl rode in. None of her prints on the dash, passenger's door. But he forgot the seat. Where it curves under at the front. It's vinyl upholstery, takes prints medium well. You watch a woman in a car, if she's not driving, she'll take hold there round a curve, keeping her balance, you know? We got two dandy prints off that spot, on the passenger's side. They're Lila Askell's."

"Bingo," said Palliser. He went back into the interrogation room and nodded at Mendoza, smiling. Mendoza came away from the wall, upright.

"So let's stop hearing the broken record, Stover, and get the truth. It had rankled with you—Lila so uninterested, turning you down. A girl like that too," said Mendoza softly. "Not bad-looking, but in the slang a dog—a boring girl, a very normal and respectable girl, a girl all wrapped up in her dull little job, helping the hospital patients. A stupid girl like that, turning *you* down. Good-looking Gene, all the girls falling for him—"

"Damn you! No—I never saw that girl here—"

"Then how," asked Palliser, "did her fingerprints get inside your car? And how did yours get on that necklace she was wearing? That's nice solid physical evidence, Stover, and it's going to send you up on murder one."

Stover went muddy gray. He said wildly, "But I wiped all the places she—her *necklace*—" And then he put his head on his arms across the table and moaned, "No. No. I didn't mean to *hurt* her. Like that." After a long silence he sat up a little, huddled miserably in the straight chair. "Yes, I was mad about it—damn her—that stupid boring small-town *thing*—going to church and talking about her silly job—and turning me down as if I was—as if I wasn't —And Ron's note. Damn it, damn it, it was all Ron's fault— like a joke, saying she'd be here then, I should make another try at her—and she didn't want to go with me, but I—and after we had lunch, I thought about Echo Park— nobody there then and there's shrubbery—but she got mad again when I tried to kiss her, she *hit* me, and I was so damn mad—treating me as if I smelled bad or—me! And I—all of a sudden she just—" He shook his head. "I don't know how it happened." But it was a very easy way to kill somebody without meaning to. "I didn't know what—I nearly left her there, but I was afraid, I thought some place even—emptier, and I got her back in the car— She might have been *nice* to me!" he said. "She might have been— but that stupid, stupid girl—"

"Stupid is a word for it," said Mendoza. Palliser had just come back from booking him in. The warrant was applied for. "Human nature is damned monotonous, John." He was shuffling the deck dexterously.

The inside phone burred at him and he picked it up. "Mendoza. Oh, Saul. How're you doing, boy?"

"My sins are finding me out," said Goldberg. "This big Mick ordering me around. And no girls attached to Narco. Damn it, I haven't typed a report in years—" He sneezed.

Mendoza laughed. "So you're doing some work for a change. We appreciate the legacy, Saul. Very much."

"You'd better appreciate her. I just wondered if you ever caught up to the burglar."

"Oh, yes. We're just as efficient as ever. And it's my office now, *hermano*." He put the phone down, smiling.

And Piggott and Grace came in, with the details so far on the new one, Ellen Reynolds. "We got a lab truck up," said Grace, brushing his moustache in unconscious imitation of Mendoza. "But the queerest damn thing—and you're going to cuss—is the note." He produced it. "It's been printed. Nothing."

Mendoza looked at it and said loudly, "*¡Diez millones de demonios negros desde el infierno—Por el amor de Dios!* Why in hell's name I stay in this thankless job—"

Hackett and Higgins, and their new faithful plodder, Shogart, would hear about the new one tomorrow—the little offbeat one to give them the most work for a while.

Hackett was up to two-eighteen and feeling what-the-hell about it. Angel tried to stop him, but he had a piece of her latest devil's food cake.

Higgins was feeling adventurous, but only so far. "I tell you, Steve," he said, "suppose we try developing our own negatives first, see how that goes, and think about the enlarger later."

"O.K.," said Steve. Laura was at the piano again. Mary, scooping up Margaret Emily from the blanket on the floor, for bath and bed, smiled at her menfolk indulgently.

Glasser, unlocking the door of his apartment, thought dimly that it might be kind of nice to have somebody to come home to. Somebody there, when he came home. He hadn't any family but a couple of cousins back east.

Grace stopped on the way home and got a new film-pack for the camera. Higgins was right about that camera, but it was nice to get the prints right off. And very nice, at long last, to have their very own family—

When Piggott let himself into the apartment, thinking pessimistically about the new case (it did say that Satan should be loosed for a little time), Prudence was in the kitchen, her good contralto voice raised lustily on "Rock of Ages." He felt a little better, going out to kiss her. It was good to have a place of his own, and Prudence. And God would not be mocked; eventually the truth would prevail.

Palliser, thinking uneasily about Madge Borman, the chain-link fence, and that German Shepherd pup sometime around May, reflected suddenly that Robin shouldn't be upset. The baby due in April—David Andrew or possibly Margaret—and Robin shouldn't be annoyed. His conscience cleared slightly.

It would be time enough, after the baby was here, to tell her about Madge Borman's notions of gratitude.

It had, the last twenty-four hours, turned cool and gray: more like what January was supposed to be, even in southern California. Alison reported that the mockingbird had disappeared. "*¡Gracias a Dios!*" said Mendoza.

For a man who had walked alone so long, he had gone in for the domesticities with a vengeance. The Just-So Stories had been duly read to the twins, pink from their baths—*El Gato* who walked by himself, *El Rinoceronte* with his skin full of cake-crumbs—and Mairí MacTaggart would be lulling them to sleep with Jacobite fervor on "We're no awa' to bide awa'," the current demanded favorite.

Bast was coiled on the credenza, ruddy and plump; Nefertite was washing El Señor's ears on the sectional. Sheba was poised on top of the bookcase, and Alison said, "*¡Cuidado!*" too late. Sheba launched herself for his shoulder and Mendoza caught her and hauled her down to his arms. "*Monstruoso* . . . If I had a kind and generous nature, I should call Art and George, warn them about this new damned thing we've got . . . Mystery be damned. The parole board!" said Mendoza as if it was a new oath. "*¡Dios!* Letting the wild ones loose—" He put Sheba down on top of Nefertite, who spat amiably and started to wash her.

Cedric the hairy sheepdog marched in, jowls dripping from his water-bowl, and Mendoza said, "I need a drink. The damned thankless job—why I stay on at it, the dirt at the bottom—"

"*Amador*, you wouldn't know what to do with yourself," said Alison amusedly.

And El Señor understood English. He galloped after Mendoza and floated up to the drainboard for his half-ounce of rye.

"The parole board," said Mendoza balefully, pacing back

to the living room with his drink. He had stripped off jacket and tie; he looked keyed-up and dangerous. "And God knows what else turning up—"

"Don't bring the office home, *amador*," said Alison. He looked at her, his lovely copper-haired girl who after too long had domesticated him, and he laughed, finished the drink and went to put his arms around her.

"You know me too well, *mi corazón*. *Y mañana es otro día*—tomorrow is also a day."